FEISTY OLD LADIES

Cynthia Weitz

ISBN-10: 149746207X
ISBN-13: 9781497462076
Library of Congress Control Number: 2014906172
CreateSpace Independent Publishing Platform
North Charleston, South Carolina

DEDICATION

To my son Marc whose help and encouragement made this book possible.

"You don't stop laughing when you grow old,
    you grow old when you stop laughing."
— George Bernard Shaw

DISCLAIMER

This book is a work of fiction, but businesses, locations, and organizations, while real are, used in a way that is purely fictional.

CHAPTER ONE

O n the day of the accident, Margot Manning stood near the entrance of the LA Art museum, checking her watch. For weeks, she had anticipated the new exhibit by her favorite artist, British painter, David Hockney. If Mirabelle didn't come soon, they'd be late. And Margot didn't want to miss a word of the tour.

That morning, Margot had eyed her shoe collection debating between a pair of sensible, but boring, walking shoes or her new five-inch Jimmy Choos—ridiculous for a woman, age sixty-five—and especially for museum going. A hard-core shopper with a flair for style, the strappy stilettos were her special weakness. So which to choose? Now, while waiting, she smiled down at the precious designer heels adorning her feet.

Margot quit her post and walked to the long set of stairs leading up to the museum plaza. Spying her friend at the bottom, she waved, and in motioning frantically for Mirabelle to hurry, she lost her balance. Tumbling forward and ricocheting off the wrought iron railing, she landed face down on the cement with a broken ankle, a fractured vertebra, a bruised shoulder, and worst of all—to Margot—facial lacerations.

At Cedars-Sinai Medical Center in LA, Margot underwent surgery to repair her fractures. Knowing how much Margot prized her appearance, her friends sought out a top plastic surgeon to repair the damage to her face. Two weeks later, in mid-April, she transferred to a skilled nursing facility at Shady Palms, a sprawling Life Care Center close to her home in Laguna Hills.

The center had three levels of care. The main residence offered large apartments for Independent Living or for Assisted Care. Behind the building, a separate structure housed the skilled nursing center where Margot continued her recuperation and took part in a physical therapy program.

Being in a convalescent home did not equate with Margot's image of herself as a glamorous, still-vital woman, but the doctors assured her that if she made good progress she could go home in a few weeks.

Soon she made friends with two nurses, Sharon and Ginger, who helped her adjust, and one day, as both women sat working at the nurses' station, they heard a shriek.

"What was that?" Ginger said.

Sharon shrugged. "She's at it again."

They rushed off to Margot's room where they found her, a hand on each side of her face and rocking back and forth.

Sharon wagged her finger. "I told you to stop looking." A tall woman in her early fifties, with unremarkable features, she took a no-nonsense approach to life and cared for the patients with a kind but firm and steady hand.

"But my face, my poor face!"

"Healing takes time, sweetie," Ginger said. Your face is already light years better than when you were admitted."

"Better? You call this better?" Margot wailed. "Even my black and blue marks have black and blue marks."

Sharon patted her shoulder. "Take it easy, Margot."

"And my nose—it's so swollen, I look like Jimmy Durante.

"Who's Jimmy Durante?" Ginger asked.

"Never mind. I had the perfect nose—straight, slender—the perfect size, not one of those little pugs or a big proboscis."

"You got me," Ginger said. "What's a proboscis?"

"Never mind that either," Margot said. "Photographers would tell me I was photogenic, even in profile. I didn't have a bad side."

A head-turning beauty, even at this age, Margot's looks were arresting. Black curls, which fell below her neck, were pulled back from her heart-shaped face to emphasize her smooth porcelain complexion. Her large almond-shaped baby-blue eyes, fringed in long dark lashes, gave her an exotic, dreamy appearance. Suitors often said she had "bedroom eyes." Following current fashion, she outlined her bow-shaped lips, using dark blue-red lipstick and filled the center with coordinating lip-gloss.

Margot continued her tirade. "I used to be five-foot nine, but even before the accident, I knew I'd shrunk; I had to bring my clothes to the tailor's for shortening. I hope I haven't lost more inches since the surgery. I like being tall."

When the phone rang, Ginger answered. She put the receiver down and grinned. "The desk says there's a hunky guy with a sexy continental accent asking for you. I should tell them to send him along, right?"

"I can't possibly see him—not with this face." She reached up to feel her hair. "And this mop is a dry, matted mess, begging for a dye job at Luigi's."

Ginger, a red head with a spicy personality to match, refused to listen. Hands on hips, she swayed from side to side. "Don't be ridiculous. The guy's been here every day. He knows what you look like, and he keeps on coming back; that's loyalty for you."

A weak, "I guess I'll see him" escaped from Margot's lips.

Soon, there stood Hans, a tall, lanky man, grinning down at her. He bent to kiss her hand and sat on the bed, wrapping her in a tight embrace. "How's my lady today?"

"Oh Hans, I've missed you. I guess my face is pretty horrible?"

He studied her, gently moving her face from side to side. "Much better than two weeks ago—you're healing nicely. I spoke with your plastic surgeon at Cedars; he doesn't expect any permanent scarring."

"Thank heavens for that."

"You're a lucky woman. You could have broken your neck."

Feeling reassured, she reached up to tousle his light brown hair. "I love your hair; it's nice and thick, though the front *is* getting a wee bit thin."

"Stop that."

She rubbed the bald patch at the back of his head. "What's this?"

He pulled her hand away.

"I see more sprinkles of grey there too."

"That's your fault for making me worry. I should march over to your place and toss those lethal stilettos before you injure yourself again."

"Don't you want me glamorous for you?"

He kissed her forehead. "You know we're not kids anymore."

"Don't say that; you're making me feel terrible. Anyway, I'm younger than you."

By a whole three months. She chuckled to herself.

Flashing him a smile, she tapped his nose. "You're lucky I'm into older men."

"Older by. . .?"

"I didn't hear that question."

Whenever the subject of age intruded, Margot would act offended and ask, "Could you trust a woman who confesses something as important as her age?"

The retort always stopped the questioner dead. Her late husband, Ted, had loved telling her age. She complained, but he defended the practice, saying, "I do it because I enjoy the disbelief on their faces. You're still a youthful temptress."

Margot would laugh at the compliment, but she hated when he told. Even so, Margot had been happy to meet the age qualification for government health insurance; otherwise, the medical bills from the accident would have been ruinous.

As Margot and Hans took turns teasing each other, loud knocking interrupted their happy interlude. The Relatives had arrived.

Margot often wondered how she had been born into the same family as her nephew, Rudy, and his younger sister, Clarissa. They were *nothing* like her. Rudy, a domineering and stridently aggressive man, had a hawkish face that made him look ready to peck and attack. Clarissa, a quiet and reserved woman, obeyed Rudy's every wish. Both were almost six feet tall and obese; in Margot's eyes, they resembled Tweedledum and Tweedledee.

After the entrance of the two beefy relatives, the room appeared to shrink. With insufficient space for all four bodies and their conflicting personalities, tension arose immediately.

Margot noted the sharp contrast between Hans and Rudy. For an ordinary hospital visit, Rudy wore an immaculately tailored 4XL navy blue, double-breasted blazer, and grey flannel pants; he sported gold monogrammed cufflinks and a diamond pinky ring. Even his tie coordinated with his breast pocket handkerchief. Hans, on the other hand, had shed his European formality, adopting the Southern California dress code—slacks and short-sleeve shirts for casual wear.

After introductions all around, Rudy immediately began quizzing Hans, "You sound foreign. Where you from?"

"Denmark."

"Where in Denmark?"

"Aero; it's a small island."

Rudy let loose a rat-a-tat of questions. "Where did you attend college? What did you study? What do you do now?"

"I attended the University of Denmark." Hans rolled his eyes sideways at Margot.

"You mean you didn't graduate?"

"I raced sports cars, and I left college, when I turned Pro. Now I ...."

Waving his hand dismissively, Rudy said, "Enough about you, we're here for Margot."

Hans and Rudy exchanged baleful looks until Hans bid everyone a hurried goodbye and escaped.

Throughout Rudy's performance, Clarissa had remained silent. A plain woman, she could be pretty, if, according to Margot, she would color her grey hair and find a more stylish hairdo, instead of pulling her hair straight back with tortoise shell barrettes. But her appearance suffered most from her off-putting habit of blinking her eyes, as though trying to focus. She hung her head as Rudy scowled at Margot.

Without waiting to ensure Hans had disappeared from earshot, Rudy asked, "What's a woman your age doing hanging around with a race-car driver?"

"He raced cars a very long time ago."

Rudy persisted. "And a college-drop-out no less."

"I'll have you know Hans owns an extremely successful business, distributing classic car parts."

"Who cares about classic cars?"

"Plenty of people, from all over the world; enthusiasts willingly pay top dollar for old model Chevys and Cadillacs, then spend a fortune to fix them up."

"Little boys, tinkering with their toys. I say, dump him."

"Face facts, Rudy; you both have objected to any man I've ever dated."

"That's understandable, considering your choices—your late husband, for example."

Margot bristled. "Don't you dare say a word about Ted."

He gave her a long, withering look, and, like air from a deflated balloon, Margot felt the fight go out of her. She always had trouble making explanations—especially to Rudy.

Biting her lip, Margot mustered all the civility she could. "Thanks for coming, but it's my nap time."

Long after The Relatives left, Rudy's angry command, "Dump him," reverberated in her head, keeping her awake.

There had been bad blood between her late husband and Rudy. Early in their marriage, Ted had reluctantly agreed to invest in Real Estate with Rudy, but when Ted caught him manipulating transactions behind his back, their business relationship deteriorated into a series of arguments, and Ted moved to dissolve their association.

After studying the financial documents and signing the papers, Rudy had stormed off shouting, "I'm not sure how, but I know that your accountants cheated me out of my rightful share."

Ted had shaken his head wordlessly. "We're lucky to be rid of the guy."

Only after Ted's death had she agreed to see Rudy and Clarissa again. That day at the hospital, Margot vowed not to let them come between her and Hans.

⊨⊨ ⊨⊨

A few mornings later, as Margot lay dozing in her room, a voice startled her awake.

"I take a vacation, and while I'm gone, you go and mess yourself up. Do I need to watch you every minute?'

Margot looked up to see her best friend Rachel's lovely face, an oval framed by blonde curls; the remaining childhood freckles sprinkled across her delicate features gifted her with a still youthful appearance. The two women hugged, and Margot said, "I'm thrilled you're here. How did you find out where they stuck me?"

"I have my ways." Rachel pulled up a chair and sat down. "Tell me all the gory details."

Margot described the accident, her surgeries, and her treatment at Cedars. She pointed to her left ankle. "Wanna sign my cast?"

"You pulled a good one this time; at least it's not your driving ankle."

"I'm not worried about driving; it's my face. What do you think?"

"Let me get my glasses." Rachel smiled mischievously.

"No you don't; just tell me."

Rachel leaned in close. "Not bad for an old lady."

"Wanna get hit? My arm's not broken."

"Hm. There's some discoloration and maybe a little swelling, but pret-ty good—yes, pret-ty good."

Margot rolled her eyes and sighed.

"Nice place you've got here; looks brand new," Rachel said.

"Built a few years ago—around '09."

"How many patient rooms?"

"Twenty-four or thirty, I guess."

"All one-bedded like yours?"

"Affirmative, but why the questions—thinking of moving in?"

"I'm curious. On my way in, I passed a comfy-looking reception room—with sofas and high-back chairs and a big fireplace."

"Never been there."

"How about I take you for a spin—check out the joint."

"And pick out a nice room for you."

Rachel helped Margot slide into a wheel chair. "Hey, you lost weight. You're a mere slip of your former self."

"You're not lying to me, are you?"

"I swear to Zeus."

At the front desk, Loretta, the plump and cheerful receptionist greeted Margot. "It's nice to see you up and about."

"I'm showing my friend Rachel around." She paused. "Actually, I'm the one taking a tour. I don't even remember checking in."

Loretta laughed. "New patients are pretty much out of it the first day."

"Well it's good to finally meet you."

They continued past a small waiting room, the reception room Rachel mentioned, and a conference room. The name plate on a private office read, Norman Norwood, Director of Skilled Nursing; another said, Helga Hasse, Head Nurse.

Rachel said, "Helga Hasse? That's a scary name."

"Haven't seen her yet; she's on personal leave."

Past the nurses' station, Margot saw Sharon and Ginger drinking coffee in a small kitchen. She waved, and they stepped out to say hello.

Sharon extended her hand to Rachel. "I'm Sharon and this is Ginger. We're having fun with Margot."

Rachel introduced herself and said, "Margot *is* fun, but watch out, she loves being in charge."

"You're such a friend," Margot said.

The two nurses chuckled and nodded in agreement.

Further on, they came across a game room with card tables, several lounge chairs, and a library. Coffee and hot water urns sat atop a credenza along with platters of sweets.

Rachel sniffed. "Smell those fresh-baked cookies. Shall we indulge?"

"If you want."

Rachel parked Margot and returned with selection of cookies, but she waved the plate away.

"Not even a peanut butter cookie? This is so not like you."

"Cookies don't tempt me in the least. Can you believe that?"

"You must be *really* depressed."

"Wouldn't you be?"

"This isn't forever, you know; you'll be out of here in no time."

"The nurses are great—especially the two you met—and the doctors say I can probably leave in a few weeks; I'm just not used to being a vegetable."

"A vegetable? You're in physical therapy, and you're making progress, aren't you?"

"Of course, but you know patience isn't one of my virtues and . . . ."

Rachel leaned over and kissed Margot's cheek. "You may not be patient, but you've always had courage and spunk. You'll come through this just fine."

"I appreciate your faith in me, but this little jaunt has worn me out, so if you'd please chauffeur me back to my room, I'd be in your debt for at least a whole day."

Once there, the two women hugged, and Rachel made Margot promise to cheer up.

Before leaving, she said, "The next time I come, I want to see the take-charge Margot I warned those two nurses about."

A week later, The Relatives paid another visit. Rudy eased his bulky frame into a chair while Clarissa gingerly approached the bed, extending a giant box of candy.

"Auntie Margot."

Margot looked at Clarissa, quizzically. "Auntie? Where did that come from?"

Clarissa began again. "I remember you like *See's* caramels and chews."

"I love caramel and chews, but ten pounds?"

"Sorry." Clarissa laughed nervously. "You've gotten so thin since your accident, we thought these chocolates might help fatten you up."

"I appreciate the thought, but you know the saying, 'You can never be too rich or too thin.'" Margot glanced at Rudy. "Isn't that right—at least the part about never being too rich?"

Rudy glowered, shifting his shoulders back and forth.

Clarissa continued. "We're also concerned about your being able to manage your house and the bills, you know, with you still recovering from that accident, and all."

"My property management company pays the major bills."

"Even so, there must be other bills and mail; it's not safe leaving your house sitting empty either."

"My neighbor, Mirabelle, picks up the mail and keeps a sharp eye on the house, whenever I'm away."

"We could pitch in too; Rudy and I would be willing to house-sit and sort through the mail, field calls—protect your interests and all."

"You mean move into my house?"

Clarissa hurriedly added, "Only until you're well, of course."

"That's sweet and considerate." Margot forced a smile.

Sweet and considerate? Did those words come out of *my* mouth?

She turned to Rudy. "You're unusually quiet today."

"Clarissa speaks for us both; that's what relatives are for—to love and support you during tough times."

To love and support me?

"Thanks. I'll think on it and get back to you."

During his next visit, Margot mentioned the idea to Hans who still smarted from his nasty encounter with The Relatives.

"*Nej*, no! Do not, under any circumstances, let them move in." Hans exploded, "Inch by inch, they'll take control of your life. I guarantee it."

Margot reached for her migraine medication.

Hans added, "With my business experience, I'm capable of handling any problems that arise, if you're willing."

Margot considered Hans's offer and decided against it. She hadn't known him long and since Ted's death, she had become fiercely protective of her money, which she jokingly called, "My own private ATM—All to Myself."

Letting The Relatives take over worried her. She declined their offer, hoping she would soon be strong enough to return to her own home.

CHAPTER TWO

One night as Margot lay asleep in bed, loud moans startled her awake. When the moans turned to piercing screams, she bolted upright and put on the light. The clock read, 11:00 p.m. Her head began to throb, and she rang for the floor nurse.

To her relief, Sharon answered the call.

Margot covered her ears and said, "I'm so happy that you're on duty; I can't sleep with this racket."

Sharon laughed. "Help is on the way."

Margot heard Sharon's footsteps cross the hall and enter a room. In minutes, the screaming stopped.

She turned off the light and crunching her pillow into a comfortable position, she fell asleep until awakened once again by moans and screams. The time clock now read 1:00 a.m.; she repeatedly buzzed for the nurse, but no one came.

Shifting to her wheelchair, Margot followed the noise to a room across the hall where she found a patient with disheveled hair and a pinched face.

Margot extended her hand. "I'm Margot Manning; is there anything I can do to help?"

The woman stopped shrieking and struggled to sit up. In a nearly inaudible whisper, she managed to say, "Water."

Margot searched the bedside cabinet for a bottle. Finding none, she wheeled her way into the bathroom and located a cup and a pitcher. Filling the pitcher with water, Margot returned and helped the woman to the water, which she slurped thirstily.

Just then a voice demanded, "What do think you're doing?"

Margot turned her chair to see a tall husky nurse with tree trunks for legs, her face flushed in anger. She wore a badge that identified her as Helga Hasse, head nurse.

"This poor lady was absolutely parched, she's been screaming for attention all night," Margot said. "She just needed some water."

"Well you've gone and fixed her good. This patient is scheduled for a procedure at *Saddleback Hospital* today; now they'll have to postpone for another day." She approached the wheelchair and leaned over Margot menacingly.

"Oops, sorry."

"Sorry won't cut it."

"I'm only trying to help."

"I'll have a talk with the patient, after you leave, which happens to be right now."

Margot summoned an imperious stare. "I transferred to Shady Palms because of your rehab program, and because it's close to where I live. But I'm sure there are therapy centers in Laguna Hills that are quieter."

The two women locked eyes until Helga straightened up. "I *said* I'd talk to her."

On the way out, Margot turned and saw Helga towering above the patient and wagging her finger vigorously.

Wow, she thought. The head nurse is certainly bossy, and she has one king-size *derrière*.

The corridor remained quiet for a short period, but just as Margot settled down to sleep, screams again echoed through the facility. Margot heard approaching footsteps, followed by voices from the room across the hall.

A male voice said, "I'm glad you're here; I can't get her to quit shouting."

Then a woman's voice said, "You can go, I'll handle this."

Footsteps left the room.

The woman's voice continued, "I've warned you repeatedly to stop this nonsense. If you require more attention, you should hire a private nurse."

Margot found it difficult to discern exactly what followed; she thought she detected the words, "please," and "I can't."

"Don't say you can't; all the patients on this floor are complaining about you."

In a clearly audible voice, the patient said, "Want to leave."

"We'll see about that; in the meantime, I brought something to calm you."

After another series of low moans, Margot heard what sounded like retreating footsteps, followed by silence.

In the morning, she wheeled herself past the room and noted a forlorn bed, stripped bare. When Sharon appeared that afternoon, Margot asked what had happened to the screaming patient.

Sharon said, "I was off during that shift, but I heard that the woman's daughter moved her to another facility."

"I hope that's the case. At one point I got sick of the ruckus, so I took matters in my own hands; the patient was dying for water, and I got her some. Helga was furious with me, and did she ever tear into the woman."

"Giving a patient water too close to surgery is dangerous."

"If the nurses had attended to the patient or at least answered my buzzer, I wouldn't have been forced to take action. Helga didn't need to jump all over me."

"Helga comes off as being tough, but she's a dedicated nurse, and she's strict about following the rules. I've gotten to know her well since we began car-pooling."

Despite Sharon's reassurances that the woman had moved to another facility, the episode left Margot feeling uneasy.

⚊⟨⟩⚊

After that, Margot determined to work hard in physical therapy, so she could leave skilled nursing as soon as possible. In a week, she discarded the wheel chair for a walker, and two weeks later she began using a cane. She asked Ginger for a list of caregivers who could help her transition to life at home. But after developing an infection, she suffered a setback; high fever and night sweats left her feeling weak and vulnerable.

Though her condition improved over the next two weeks, The Relatives continually badgered her about transferring to residential living at Shady Palms, saying, "You should be careful—your condition could deteriorate."

Margot had become friendly with all of the nurses, but she still had chills from her experience with the screaming woman who disappeared, so she reconsidered her relatives' proposition. Moving to the residential living area would rescue her from the skilled nursing section and give her more independence.

Once, during a visit, Rudy said, "You know Shady Palms offers month-to-month stays in the residential building, depending on availability. I can check for you."

The very next day, he called, saying, "There's a vacancy—a spacious corner apartment with a lovely view."

"I don't need to be in assisted living; I can bathe and dress myself, and the therapist says that I'm nearly ready to walk without a cane."

"You can be as independent as you like."

"But I want to go home."

"This is only temporary." Rudy said. "You'll be back at your place in no time."

Although Margot had always dreaded ending up in an old-folks home, she had to admit that living there would make it easier to continue her rehab program. Moreover, Rudy had a violent temper if he didn't get his way, and she feared to cross him. The accident and the recovery had not only weakened her physically but left her emotionally fragile. So reluctantly, she arranged with them to forward the few bills not paid by her property manager and transferred from skilled nursing to the residential building while The Relatives took over her home—for what she hoped would only be a few weeks.

CHAPTER THREE

On her first morning, Margot realized she had made a colossal mistake. Rather than moving to the residential building of Shady Palms, she should have insisted on going home.

Inside the ornately decorated lobby, as she sat slumped in a faux Louis XV *Bergère,* she heard Tap...Tap...Tap...Tap...the slow sounds of the walker brigade, inching across the carpet. Some walkers were decked out with yellow or orange tennis balls to help them glide across the rich carpet, some gaily tied with bright scarves—even a Givenchy or Hermès here and there. Residents fell into chairs where they sat, mouths agape, eyes closed, legs discreetly together as taught, or indiscreetly open—not a pretty sight when the owner was wearing a skirt. Lone male stragglers shuffled in, heads down; bodies bent; hair gone missing or standing in wisps; complexions grown dim; vague remnants of handsome features. They searched to find a compatriot for breakfast. A few aging Lotharios settled contently amid the ladies, savoring the attention. Stories, all the time stories—telling who they used to be, never who they hoped to be again.

Margot repeatedly asked herself: What am I doing in this pitiful assemblage of frumpy old ladies and grumpy old men?

Her mood changed to anger, and she straightened up. Only a few short months ago she had been foremost among the beautiful people; a fashionista who had sat on boards, arranged benefits, and hobnobbed with VIPS. Adorned in elaborately beaded pendants and bracelets collected on her many trips around the world, she led the A-list of those attending important cultural events.

Initially, Margot tried reconciling herself to life at Shady Palms, deluxe by anyone's standards. The white stucco building with a red tile roof resembled a hotel. There were individual terraces outside each apartment, and the interior boasted a large, traditional lobby, bright formal dining room; well executed, if innocuous, paintings decorated the walls; other amenities included: a card room for bridge and Bunko; a be-still-my-heart special room for Bingo; a gym and a swimming pool, surrounded by lush grounds. The apartments contained all the latest electronic equipment.

What more could she want?

In truth, Margot missed certain comforts like extra towels, which she repeatedly requested and never, ever received. It had been a joke between her and Ted; whenever they checked into a hotel, he would look on bemusedly while she placed the inevitable call to housekeeping for extra towels. On a more serious level, the towel situation symbolized her loss of control.

⇥ ⇤

After feeling miserable for a week, Margot phoned Rachel and begged her to visit. Conscious of the curious stares that followed her every movement as she waited downstairs, Margot distanced herself to a less conspicuous corner, away from the smells of tired clothing and other odors she didn't dare identify.

Margot willed every person who came through the lobby door to be Rachel, until she arrived at last, gliding through the room with her own graceful walk. Tall, like Margot, Rachel had a dancer's legs. As she drew near, Margot's anxiety dissipated. A quiet, soft-spoken woman with impeccable manners, Rachel typified the perfect lady, but beneath that demeanor, there lay a will of steel determination.

I'm glad she's on my team, Margot thought.

Seeing Rachel sit down and reach for a cigarette, Margot shook her head. "Put away that poison. You know public smoking is illegal, especially here at old biddy-land."

Rachel made a face and returned the cigarette to its mother-of-pearl case; she peered intently at Margot. "How's it going in your new digs? You *look* terrific, by the way."

"I'm terrific, all right. Did you ever imagine me in an old-folks home? You remember the life I led before I landed here?" Her voice rose. "I used to be an independent woman with a real job reviewing movies. I headed committees. I gave speeches. Oh, did I give speeches. I was known for those speeches."

Margot's voice grew louder. "Do you know how many arms I twisted to raise money, how many benefits I chaired?"

Rachel squirmed with embarrassment. "Take it easy."

"I've gone from being a strong confident woman to a useless and ineffectual organism."

"Calm down. You've been through a serious accident. Blowing your stack can't be healthy."

Her face contorted in anger, she ranted. "I will not calm down. My niece, Clarissa, and her snake-in-the-grass brother, Rudy, did a number on me. They convinced me to come here and guess who's living in my house right now?"

"They're living at your house?"

"You heard me. My oversized nephew and his mousy sister are there, as we speak, enjoying the view of Saddleback Mountain from my patio. Hans warned me against letting them move in, but they took advantage of my weakened condition and the fact that I have no other family around here.

"I keep calling them to say I've changed my mind about being here, and that I want to go home."

"And what's their answer?"

"They tell me to be patient, to wait until I'm well enough. Margot jabbed her own chest, repeatedly. "It's my own fault. I've been floating along, letting things happen."

"Floating along? Don't be ridiculous. Lying in a hospital bed for weeks and fighting off an infection, it seems reasonable to take things slowly." Rachel hit her forehead. "Wait, I know the perfect solution. Why don't you live with me?"

Her anger diffused, Margot reached over and hugged Rachel. "Oh, sweetie, thanks. I appreciate your support, and I love you dearly, but bunking with you isn't the solution. I might get too comfortable; I'd lose my incentive to evict those squatters."

"I understand, but say the word, and I'll haul you away."

"Maybe all this bad stuff will disappear, and I'll be back living on my own."

"I'll root for that."

"I just hope I get my spunk back."

CHAPTER FOUR

B y the end of June, Margot had been at the residential building for a month. Physically, she felt strong again, but her body missed the regular exercise provided in the therapy program she had completed.

Her therapist had mentioned an exercise class, and one morning she debated giving it a whirl. The decision made, she pulled on a pair of sweats, eschewing her glamorous, sexy Brazilian fitness clothes.

Why bother, whom could I possibly impress?

At breakfast downstairs, she swallowed a few spoons of oatmeal, sipped the watery coffee, and headed for the large gym where she beheld a sorry group of seniors, slumped in wheel chairs or seated clutching walkers. A few seemingly alert participants occupied regular chairs, though most appeared old and in such poor shape that Margot couldn't imagine their attempts at movement qualifying as exercise. The regular instructor had not yet arrived. People fidgeted, examining their watches. Clearly the class would be leaderless for the day. The realization elicited complaints even from those who appeared to be sunk in lethargy.

An attractive woman on her right caught Margot's attention. She stood out from the rest, with her smooth, youthful complexion, light in color and tinged with pink. Layered auburn hair fell softly below her chin and framed her thin, aquiline nose and large, wide-set hazel eyes. Judging by her long legs, Margot estimated her height as five-foot ten. The woman extended her hand. "Hi, I'm Jane Driscoll. I suspect this class isn't happening."

Margot introduced herself and said, "It'd better happen; I'm going stir crazy."

"With this bum knee I need to be here, doncha know," Jane said, gesturing with her cane.

"What's wrong with your knee?"

"I am walking much better since my replacement surgery and weeks of torturous rehab, but I hate missing class. I exercise religiously so I can stop imitating the Frankenstein walk."

"Based on your "doncha know," I'd peg you for a mid-westerner. Where are you from?"

Jane slapped her thigh. "Caught out again! I'm from Wisconsin; people tease me all the time about my 'doncha knows' and 'you betcha's.' But why are you at Shady Palms? You seem more with it than the typical resident."

"After surgery, I did rehab next door, after which, I got conned into staying here; it's a long story."

The two women exchanged pleasantries until, during a lull in the conversation, Margot realized she needn't remain idle. Springing to the front, she announced she would run the class and went about checking the available CDs. She shook her head and held up a recording of *There's No Place Like Home*, mumbling aloud, "What idiot chose this?"

The Skaters Waltz with its swaying rhythms seemed a better option. She pushed the play button, instructing the group to remain seated and follow her in performing inhale-exhale deep breathing exercises.

Next, she led a series of gentle side-to-side neck movements in time to the music.

I'm doing all right, she thought.

The group performed shoulder shrugs to open up the back and twenty chin tucks. "Chin tucks not only exercise your neck muscles, but in a month, your neck wrinkles will completely disappear," she explained.

Everyone laughed.

"You may doubt me, but doesn't this feel good?"

She heard more "yeses" and a distinct "you betcha" from Jane.

"Let's try side-to-side arm swings. Begin slowly, slowly. Let it flow. Let it all hang out. Release the tension." A woman groaned and said, "That hurts my neck."

"Don't force anything; stop if it hurts and wait for the next exercise."

After she led the group in a series of arm and toe raises, she asked "Is everybody still with me?"

Again she heard "yeses."

"Fine and dandy," she said. "You're all limbered up by now, right?"

Several women shouted "right," one or two cheered, and a voice said, "This is the best exercise class ever."

Encouraged, Margot grew more ambitious. To pep them up further, she turned off the music and told everyone to remain seated. Margot instructed the class to raise one arm while holding onto their chairs with the other arm, then alternating arms, all the time chanting, "I *am* a Babe, I *am* a Hottie." The class giggled, becoming more and more animated and continuing the cheer.

Margot grew more daring. She divided the group into three separate circles, placing the mobile seniors in the front circle; next she organized the group with walkers, behind into a second circle; finally she positioned the wheel chair group at the very back, making up the third circle.

She then told all the women to move around in their respective circles, chanting, "I *am* a Babe, I *am* a Hottie; I *am* a Babe, I *am* a Hottie." The action continued for several minutes as a beaming Margot watched.

Deep into the exercise, everyone missed hearing the door open to admit Ms. Dugin, the outraged Shady Palms director. She screamed, "What's going on here?"

Startled, a few lost their balance and fell to the floor. Dugin ran quickly to help them up. Although no one appeared hurt, she turned on Margot. "See what you've done; meet me in my office right now."

One woman called out, "We were fine, until *you* interrupted."

Margot shrugged and headed for the door where she encountered Jane who patted her shoulder. "What a blast! Don't let the old bat get you down." She added, "Let's do coffee real soon. I'm in apartment 508."

Once at the office, Margot waited uneasily while the director answered a phone call. To Margot, Ms. Dugin, a squarely-built woman, had always resembled a fireplug. She changed her mind as she studied the woman's beady eyes, beak-like nose and wiry gray hair, which stuck straight up on her head. She's not a fireplug, Margot thought; she's a rooster with voluminous breasts that bounce up and down when she gets excited.

Based on the amount of jiggling, Dugin was feeling extremely agitated.

Those breasts provided daily amusement for the residents and staff each time Dugin exited the parking lot in her stick shift blue Chevy. After every gear change, her breasts would hit the car's honking mechanism, sending all within earshot into convulsions of laughter until she had honked her way onto Paseo de Valencia.

Now finished with her call, the director stared daggers and scolded Margot like a childish miscreant. She spat, "People could have been seriously hurt, and we could have been sued. What were you thinking?"

A slow smile invaded the corners of Margot's mouth; she concentrated on her long fingernails to keep from laughing.

"Since you consider your behavior a joke, effective this moment, you are banned from further exercise classes." Dugin paused. "And the board will have to approve your continued tenancy at Shady Palms."

CHAPTER FIVE

Margot chuckled all the way upstairs, but soon reality set in. She weighed the consequences of eviction from Shady Palms. If they did throw her out, the decision to leave or stay would be made for her. Where would she go? Any move to get her house back would bring the inevitable confrontation with her nephew, Rudy, who had intimidated her since childhood.

It wasn't just his enormous size. Rudy always knew facts she didn't. He had the last word in every argument, and every discussion turned into a debate where he emerged the winner. Though her junior by a few years, Rudy made her feel like the child, while he was the grownup.

A knock on the door interrupted her thoughts. Jane, the woman from exercise class arrived, accompanied by a slim woman who, at over six-feet tall, towered over both Margot and Jane.

"We've come to cheer you up," Jane said. "When my Texan friend heard what you pulled off in exercise class, she insisted on meeting you."

Nancy did a small curtsy. "Hi, y'all. I'm Nancy Ewing."

Margot remembered seeing Nancy around Shady Palms where she stood out like an exotic bird, dressed in tight-fitting jeans plus a cowboy shirt and boots. This day she also wore a tall cowboy hat.

From under the hat, Margot glimpsed short, curly blond hair and a small up-turned nose that gave Nancy's face a girlish cuteness.

Her eyes twinkled merrily. "I enjoyed that right funny tale about exercise class. Knowing Dugin, she must have been brutal."

"She threatened to throw me out—if you call that brutal."

Nancy said, "Aw don't you worry your pretty head none. We can gang up on her for you; I'll spook her with one of my scary 'looks.' Jane don't take no guff either."

"Not that look." Jane said. You might turn her to stone."

Margot laughed. "It's wonderful that you're both here. I'm better already. Make yourselves comfortable on the couch. And Nancy, take off your hat; stay a while."

"Nah," Nancy said. "I can't fix this unruly mop of mine today."

"Anyone care to join me in a friendly afternoon wine spritzer?" Margot offered.

Jane said, "You betcha. I knew, right off, you were our kind of woman."

Nancy's eyes lit up. "Sure 'nuff, ma'am."

Margot busied herself at the mini-bar, mixing the white wine and club soda; she added a squeeze of fresh lime from the refrigerator and handed Nancy a glass. "I know Jane's recovering from knee surgery. What condemned you to this evil place?"

"I went and got me breast cancer; after reconstruction, I ended up here."

"Margot sipped her drink. "That's too bad. Are you okay now?"

"They claim they got it all."

Margot said, "If that's the case, why are you still hanging around?"

Nancy removed her hat to scratch her head. "That's a right good question. They done raised the rent sky-high on my beach house;

after all that radiation, I had no energy to look for a new place. Guess now I'm too plumb lazy to move out. What's your story?"

"It's a long saga, though since you asked. . . ." Margot explained about the accident, her recovery in skilled nursing, her mistake in letting her relatives take over her house. She finished by saying, "I know what I've done sounds stupid, but I let them take advantage of my weakened condition."

Jane said, "I don't get it. Why don't you tell your relatives to scram?"

"It's complicated—you don't know what Rudy's like."

Both women seemed baffled, and Margot quickly changed the subject. "What did you ladies do before being incarcerated here?"

Nancy described her background as an artist and the Texas co-op she ran for artists, who rotated exhibiting their work.

Jane told of her long career as a fashion buyer and vice-president for a major mid-western retail chain.

"I have a lot in common with you two," Margot said. "I worked in fashion before I married, and I led tours at a local art museum until my accident." She turned to Nancy. "Do you still paint?"

"Sure do—almost every day; I also take classes. Jane here's a talented artist. Even though she has trouble walking, she drags her easel all over heck and back, painting alongside a group of die-hard landscape artists."

Jane said, "In fact, we're cooking up an art tour to LA for our fellow-captives here. You interested?"

"I'm not sure; my accident happened during a visit to an LA museum." Margot shivered. "Still gives me nightmares."

Nancy said, "How'd that happen?"

"I tripped on my five-inch stilettos."

"This time, you *could* wear sensible shoes," Jane said.

"I could, but I'm not sure I'm ready to revisit the scene of the crime. I'll let you know."

CHAPTER SIX

The next morning, while waiting downstairs for her friend Rachel, Margot perceived a distinct chill in the lobby. Before the exercise class fiasco, she had sensed an admiring buzz every time she appeared; now she heard whispers and even snickering.

What does it matter? I don't belong here, and I don't care what these people think. Margot moved to stand out front, and when Rachel pulled up, she jumped into the car. "Let's make tracks."

"Hey pumpkin, what's wrong?" Rachel asked.

"I already told you how much I detest this place, now more than ever."

"My offer stands. Come live with me."

"After yesterday, I might do that,"

"Yesterday—what happened yesterday?"

By the time Margot finished the whole exercise class saga, Rachel was laughing so hard, she begged, "Stop, I might have an accident; wish I'd been there."

"It was pretty funny, but afterwards, the director chastised me and hinted they might send me packing. I'm not sure I should tell

Hans; he's the perfect gentleman, and he might not approve of my behavior."

"Hans? Who is this Hans?"

Margot waved her hand dismissively. "Oh, someone I started dating while you were away on your fabulous world cruise."

"Are you holding out on me? Let's have it."

"I warn you, once I start, I could prattle on forever."

"Just the essentials, please; is he gorgeous?"

"Naturally, he's a true Danish specimen: 6'4, slim—with light hair, blue eyes, a straight nose. The only thing crooked is his adorable smile."

"Impressive—tell me more."

"He kisses my hand whenever we meet—he's *très sophistiquée; très romantique.*"

"I'm jealous; I never dated a man who kissed my hand. There must be something wrong with him though; I hope he doesn't wear a comb-over like my last blind date."

"No way! You know that's one of my pet peeves. My nephew, Rudy, once wore a toupee to cover his baldness. He loved shocking people by doffing it while he took a bow, but he found it hot and uncomfortable, so now he combs the few, measly strands over his huge head. It looks repulsive; he *is* repulsive."

"Forget Rudy. This Hans sounds like a keeper." Rachel paused. "Back to your problems at Shady Palms, did they truly threaten to kick you out?"

"They did, and on second thought, maybe I will accept your offer to move in; that way I won't have to tell Hans."

"Wait a minute; I get the feeling this Hans of yours is a bit controlling."

"Not at all; he's kind and considerate. It's just that manners and proper behavior are important to him, and you know how I am sometimes."

"I do know. Are you sure this Hans is a good fit for you?"

"His insistence on proper behavior *is* strange, considering his background."

"What about his background?"

"He drove racing autos when he was young, and he still rides motorcycles; mostly, though now he's into cars."

As they were talking, Margot watched the traffic zooming along PCH. "Notice all the luxury cars on the road now?"

"Yes, and it beats me how people afford them."

"Maybe they can't. Maybe they're saddled with huge monthly payments. But for Hans's sake I'm delighted to see so many Mercedes cars in Orange County."

"Why is it always such a struggle to get information out of you? What do Mercedes cars have to do with Hans?"

Margot shot Rachel an exasperated look. "Mercedes cars are his business. He distributes parts for classic cars, and he's part-owner of a Mercedes Dealership. That's how I met him, though it was Shakespeare who brought us together."

"The Bard? Is this another one of your long stories?"

"While you were away, my Mercedes kept stalling until Hans took charge. After being towed to the dealership twice in two days, I stormed the place, ready for a fight. But I melted as soon as I spotted him at the manager's desk, all Armani, in crisp black wool pants, black shirt, and black tie—no wedding band in sight. And when I heard his continental accent, I was struck by The Thunderbolt."

"You mean like in the movie, *The Godfather* where Michael Corleone sees a young Sicilian girl and falls madly in love with her?"

"I went from aggressive to meek in two seconds flat and poured out the whole sad tale about my Mercedes."

"You, meek?"

"Quit interrupting." Margot scowled at Rachel. "Hans acted so sweet and understanding, I wanted to kiss him. He asked a few questions and offered me a 'loaner,' while they ran tests."

"Where does Shakespeare come in?"

"Hold on, I'm getting there. They said the car would be ready by four o'clock, so I arrived early and brought along work for my Shakespeare Society project."

"Translation; you hung around to connect with this Hans guy again."

"I *said* not to interrupt. Anyway, when I first arrived, Hans was nowhere in sight."

"He must have shown up or you wouldn't be telling me all this."

"I was in the waiting room, working away. All at once I heard a whirring sound, and I looked up to see him, right there at the coffee machine."

"This is the juicy part, right?" Rachel tapped her hands on the steering wheel.

"To make it short: he noticed me reading Marchette Chute's *Stories from Shakespeare* and said, "I used that book to plow through all of Shakespeare's plays.""

"That's a novel pick-up line—pun intended."

"He's an autodidact, didn't finish college, designed his own curriculum."

"Must be one smart guy."

"He's brilliant and very funny. When I asked him to name his favorite Shakespearean play, he grinned and said, 'Hamlet, of course—we're both from Denmark.'"

"So he's handsome, smart and funny; what happened next?"

"The receptionist came to announce my car was ready, and I wanted to scream, 'Go away, you're interrupting this fantastic conversation.' Instead, I dutifully picked up my books and stuck out my hand to say goodbye."

"That can't have been the end?"

"Of course not; Hans offered to carry my books, walked me to the car, then leaned in and said, 'It's not often I meet a fellow Shakespeare *aficionada*. I'd love to continue this discussion.'"

"We exchanged cards, and we've been together ever since. He supported me all through my accident, and he puts up with my living at the biddy farm."

Rachel chuckled. "You just reenacted your own Danish saga; maybe you should dramatize it and put on a play for the residents of Shady Palms."

Margot elbowed Rachel. "You're a regular comedian."

At Crystal Cove, they entered the Pacific Whey Café which featured fresh and unusual food combinations.

Margot studied the menu. "I don't know whether to order the field greens vinaigrette with dates, berries, nuts, and goat cheese, or splurge on the rich, fattening, roast beef hash with Hollandaise sauce. I'm sick of watching every morsel I eat."

"Which diet of the week are you on? The beef wouldn't be too bad if you're following a high protein diet."

"Protein does make me lose weight faster, but it's boring and there are side-effects you don't want to hear about." She sighed. "I once tried eating only one food at every meal, and my weight didn't move a smidge. I loved the high carb diet, where I ate pasta and pastry, but I gained ten pounds.

"I've achieved lifetime member status in every kind of reducing program imaginable. Over the years, I bet I've lost over two hundred pounds."

"Why are you worrying? You've lost a lot of weight since your accident."

"Force of habit; with all the pain and the stress, I have dropped way down. I consider the weight loss a fringe benefit for all my aggravation."

Choosing the hash, Margot told herself she deserved comfort food after the humiliating lecture from Ms. Dugin. They dined on the patio to enjoy the Pacific Ocean breezes from across the highway. By the end of lunch, Margot had made no decisions concerning her future living arrangements, but she felt more relaxed and optimistic.

Perhaps Ms. Dugin was bluffing. If so, she had two new friends at Shady Palms to hang out with, and if she had to leave, she could move in with Rachel, or perhaps she and Hans could even . . . ?

CHAPTER SEVEN

O n her return, Margot fetched the mail, and while checking her phone messages, she rifled through the envelopes pausing to examine a letter from The Orange County Superior Court. Puzzled, she tore open the envelope and read the letter twice to make sure she understood its meaning.

The Relatives filed a petition to become my conservators?

A wave of dizziness swept over her, and she groped for a chair. She shook her head in disbelief unable to imagine what grounds her relatives had to assume control over her and her estate. Then she remembered a recent newspaper exposé on abuses in the California conservator-ship system. Countless elderly citizens had fallen prey to rapacious relatives acting as conservators to benefit themselves financially, often reducing their victims to near-poverty.

What a terrible week this has been, she thought. First the exercise class debacle and now The Relatives.

With trembling hands, she dialed Hans and begged him to come right away.

Hans, cool and suave in a beige print Tommy Bahama shirt and dark brown pants, strode through the crowded lobby, stares following his every step. He stirred up the ladies whenever he appeared—maybe even got their juices flowing. At his knock, Margot opened the door and flew into his arms. Without stopping to breathe, she stammered, "They, they filed against me. They're after everything I own."

Mystified, Hans gripped Margot's shoulder. "Slow down. Start from the beginning; tell me who is doing what to you."

After she finished explaining, Hans said, "This is sheer stupidity—an active, capable woman needing a conservator. No sane person would buy that."

Margot marched to the desk, grabbed the letter and thrust it at him. "Here read it yourself."

Carefully perusing the letter, Hans slapped his hand against the paper. "Why those crooked, conniving. . . . I've never heard anything so ridiculous."

She sniffled. "Rudy's been harboring a grudge ever since Ted dissolved our real estate partnership with him, but I never dreamed he'd try to ruin me; he's family."

When Margot began sobbing again, Hans retrieved a monogrammed linen handkerchief and dried her eyes.

The gesture ended her crying and even made her laugh. "You are a true anomaly in this day and age—a man with a handkerchief at the ready for emergencies."

"Ya, ya, my mother taught me a gentleman always carries a clean handkerchief."

They held each other until Hans checked his watch and gave a start. "Damn, of all days, I made a business appointment at five. I can try postponing it until tomorrow; or I can come around seven, and we can devise a plan over dinner. Whatever you think?"

"That's fine. You take care of business."

"Are you sure you'll be all right until I come back?"

Margot hated seeing Hans leave, but she swallowed hard, again assuring him she would be okay, but she didn't believe it one bit.

At seven-thirty, Margot sat fidgeting. A winter type, she looked smashing in her carefully chosen white linen Escada pants and shirt. She checked to make sure her make-up was on evenly, concealing the black circles under her eyes and covering the wrinkles. Each day posed a greater challenge to sustain a flawless complexion.

Margot had regained a modicum of the self-assurance she had lost after the accident; now she felt shaky and insecure. She stared longingly at her long red nails and almost succumbed to her old nail-biting habit.

Maybe I should try acrylics; they never break or chip and they're definitely not safe to chew.

She tapped her foot wondering what was keeping Hans, a man who considered punctuality a badge of honor. They had been good together, and he had supported her all through her accident. Since that time, Margot's life had changed drastically; no longer the carefree woman she had been, her problems had escalated, and with The Relatives trying to take over her estate, she needed his support more than ever.

At eight, apologizing for his delay, Hans escorted her to his '62 Corvette convertible, a favorite among the many classic cars he stored at a special facility. Her spirits lifted.

To protect herself from the wind, she wrapped a *Fendi* Jacquard Silk scarf around her black curls and donned a perky pair of over-sized *Chanel* sunglasses.

Noting the bumper-to-bumper canyon traffic on route to the ocean-side restaurant where they planned to dine, Margot said, "I forgot this is opening night for the Laguna Art Affair and Sawdust festivals."

Hans frowned. "Here we go again—the July swarm of summer tourists begins."

"I, for one, enjoy crawling along at ten miles an hour. We can add to the fun by discussing my conservator case."

"What about contacting the estate firm you used when your husband died?" Maybe they can recommend a tough lawyer experienced in challenging conservators?"

"I'll call them tomorrow. If you've read the *Time's* articles on the increasing conservator scams in this area, there must be a zillion lawyers out there who specialize in cases against the elderly."

Hans poked her playfully. "You now count yourself among the elderly?"

"I certainly do not consider myself elderly, but I'm definitely being scammed."

Hans reached over, pulling her close. "Don't worry; we'll find you a good lawyer." He retrieved his arm and tapped his cheek. "I just remembered; my neighbor is with a law firm that handles conservator cases. I'll find out."

"Thanks; I'm anxious to meet the gentleman."

⟜⊱ ⊰⟝

At *Splashes*, in Laguna Beach, the headwaiter escorted them to their usual table on an outside terrace that offered a commanding view of the waves breaking below and a magnificent sunset of rare fiery reds, bright oranges, streaks and swirls of yellow—all in combat with the disappearing deep blue sky and the blackening night.

The steady diet of bland food at Shady Palms made Margot ravenous for high cuisine whenever she dined out. Studying the menu, her mouth watered at the thought of the evening's special entrée, lamb loin with rosemary gnocci and baby turnips. She asked the waiter, "Do you serve *Lioni Latticini Bufala Mozzarella*, in the *insalata caprese*?"

"Of course."

Hans rolled his eyes.

Margot wrinkled her nose at Hans. "It's a delicacy made from premium bufala milk you don't find everywhere."

She addressed the waiter again. "And the heirloom tomatoes—are they organic?"

"Of course."

"*Kom nu*, just order."

"I love the way you kid me in Danish."

After opting for the lamb and the salad, she turned to Hans. "I bet you're having the veal medallions with Port Sabayon sauce and portobello mushroom ravioli."

"What makes you so sure?"

"Easy, you always order veal; Europeans love their veal."

"Margot, my girl, you're right. I'm confident you can also tell me what I'm having for a starter?"

"The lobster bisque."

Hans shook his head. "You must find me boringly predictable."

She leaned her head on his shoulder. "Not yet."

They enjoyed a leisurely meal, savoring the superb food and used the rosemary bread to wipe up the last bit of sauce. Hans had chosen *Silver Oak Alexander Cuvee*, an oak aged Cabernet Sauvignon. With each sip, Margot grew more relaxed.

After sharing pistachio baklava, Hans said, "How about spending the night at my place? Tomorrow morning, I'll drive you back to change, so we can surprise Rudy and Clarissa at your house.

In the morning? Since her accident, this would be their first time spending the night together. She did a quick mental inventory. The ugly discolorations had nearly disappeared and only a few tiny scars remained.

I can always throw a scarf over the lamp shade, she decided.

"It's been a long, emotional day; I'll come over, but I'm not sure I'll stay."

Hans shrugged. "You're the boss." They drove the few blocks to his home, and once inside, he acted the genial host suggesting she make herself comfortable on the living room sofa and offering to bring brandy.

She studied the large room with its highly polished dark wood floors and two over-size white leather sofas, accented by pillows in earth tones. Paintings, some abstract, others figurative, hung on the walls. Tasteful antiques and scattered Persian Rugs completed the eclectic decor. The home manifested the taste of a cultivated European gentleman.

Hans returned, carrying two snifters. "Let's move to the den; it's cozier with the fireplace."

Curling up on the couch, Margot warmed the snifter with her hands before sipping the brandy. "Very smooth."

"It's German, *Asbach Uralt*; I've been saving this for an occasion, like tonight."

"What's special about tonight?"

"You're here."

As music from *The Voice of the Violin* by Joshua Bell filled the room, he reached for a pashmina throw, tucking it around her lap and feet, before kneeling to light the fire.

The den housed electronic equipment and books—books on shelves, books on tables, books piled neatly on the floor. Margot sorted through a pile until she found a copy of short stories by Gogol and searched for *The Overcoat*, one of her favorites. She held up the book to ask Hans a question when suddenly, he sat down and began bumping her sideways.

"Hey, watch out," she said. "I'm falling off the couch."

He took the book from her hands. "Reading time is over."

"What other activity have you planned?"

"You're on the program."

Between the warm fire, the warm blanket, the warm brandy, and the warm Hans, she felt decidedly overheated—in a very nice way. They hadn't been skin to skin for these many weeks. Afterwards, she said, "Hans, you are one sexy guy."

"And you are one hot babe."

Margot's heart did flip-flops, and she snuggled close.

They remained half dozing until a realization hit her. Like college days, Shady Palms required residents to sign in and out, and she hadn't notified them she would be away overnight. By now, The Home had undoubtedly put out an APB on her.

Margot rushed to the phone apologizing for calling after midnight. She stiffened as the receptionist made a tasteless joke and chided her like a wayward teenager.

She refrained from making a sarcastic retort, but inside she was furious. I'm a grown woman—more than a grown woman. I hate to admit it, but I could be someone's grandmother.

By the next morning, Margot had forgotten the unpleasantness. She awakened to the deep aroma of European-brewed coffee and yawned contentedly. Soon Hans appeared handing her a steaming over-sized mug.

He crawled in beside her and kissed her cheek. "Did you sleep well? You must have because I heard you snoring."

"I certainly do not snore." She pushed a pillow into his face, nearly upsetting the coffee.

He moved her mug out of danger and retaliated with another pillow. "Like my brew?"

"Delicious—nice and strong; you're spoiling me rotten."

"I love spoiling you, and I love you a lot."

This was the first time Hans had said he loved her. She kissed him. "Who could help loving you? You are the sweetest man."

The cliff on which the house perched had been enshrouded with fog the night before; it now glistened in the bright, glorious morning light. Resembling a Frank Cuprien seascape, painted from the artist's hilltop Laguna home, breathtaking rainbow waves crested in gold moved slowly and rhythmically below.

"Are you game for a long, leisurely breakfast and a walk on the beach before we confront your relatives? The negative ions in sea air always fortify me."

"Maybe we should take a walk *after* we confront them. I'll need it more then. Besides I don't have casual clothes with me."

"No problem. I am a man of fashion when it comes to sweats. I can offer a choice of sweats in green, navy, black, brown, possibly even purple; I draw the line at pink."

Margot laughed. "I just bet you have all those colors. Show me."

Hans grinned. "And unless you're into wearing high heels with sweats, we can go barefoot. I *love* walking barefoot in the sand."

They walked, hand in hand on the beach, and Hans said, "You're the woman for me. I promise to stand by you and never let any harm come to you."

Moved by Hans's unusual show of emotions, she borrowed his dependable handkerchief and wiped her eyes.

Bolstered by his words and feeling brave, Margot confessed the exercise class fiasco.

At first, he chuckled. "Margot, Margot, what am I going to do with you?" Then his voice sharpened. "I love the madcap side of your personality, but sometimes you go too far. You should be careful; the court will be watching your every move."

CHAPTER EIGHT

Later that morning, when Margot and Hans arrived at her home, no one answered the bell; whichever way she turned her key, the lock refused to budge.

Hans held out his hand. "Give it to me." Try as he might, the key didn't fit.

"I know this is the right one," Margot wailed. "I can't get into my own house. I hope they didn't go and change the locks."

After peering through the lower windows without seeing movement, Hans pulled out his cell. "Here, call them at work."

Margot shifted her feet while the answering machine droned on. "They're away at a business convention, "she explained to Hans. "I left a voice message complaining about my key not fitting, and I told Rudy to call me immediately. Let's go across and ask Mirabelle if she knows anything."

A long-legged and large-boned Southerner, Mirabelle favored 'tea-party-formal,' wearing over-sized picture hats and long white gloves. She had a welcoming, sweet as honey face and freely used the word 'darlin' to address friends, neighbors, the postman, and grocery clerks.

Mirabelle spent hours producing blue-ribbon roses and orchids for garden club competitions and tours where she showed off her plantings to the ladies, who exclaimed over every blossom.

She enveloped Margot in a bear hug, and spying her pale, tear-stained face, she asked, "What's happening 'Darlin'? You look real upset."

"My key doesn't work; I'm locked out."

"Locked out? Why I declare. You two have a seat and tell me the whole story. I can fix us a nice glass of fresh-squeezed lemonade from my tree out back—unless you're hankering for my sweet tea you always enjoy so much?"

"I'm just glad you're here; I haven't heard a peep from you or nothing"

"Thanks, but we're not in the mood for a thing right now." Margot gestured towards her house. "My damn relatives went and petitioned the court to become my conservators, and I can't get a hold of them to find out why."

"Come to think of it, I haven't seen them around for a few days." Mirabelle scratched her head. "But I don't get this conservator business."

"Rudy and Clarissa claim that Margot is incapable of running her own affairs," Hans said. "They're petitioning to oversee her assets."

Mirabelle's forehead contracted in disbelief. "Are you funning me or something? Why you're the savviest gal I know."

She went to the window and pointed at Margot's house. "Your kin-folk are real, real strange. They barely say hello, won't look you in the eye, and keep to themselves most times. Some days, I have to laugh watching them struggling in and out of the car. They both should go on a strict diet—especially Rudy—maybe even do that gastric bypass business."

Margot said, "Never happen; Rudy loves eating way too much."

"I bet folks stare and laugh behind his back; it must fret him something fierce."

"Rudy copes by attacking." Margot said. "Once, at the symphony, a woman stared at him like he was some kind of sideshow until he finally barked at her, 'What are you looking at, lady?' The woman squirmed for the rest of the concert and beat a retreat, right after the orchestra played the last note. She left in such a hurry, she tripped and nearly fell. Rudy loved it. He told his lady friend, 'Now *that* was funny.'"

Mirabelle tittered, covering her mouth. "I'm glad we can laugh a little, even at the poor man's expense."

"Poor man, my eye. He's the last person you should pity, after what he's pulling on me."

Mirabelle scratched her head again. "Maybe we should get that nice sheriff fella over here and ask him to find out what's going on?"

Margot and Hans agreed, and while Mirabelle went off to find the phone number, Hans pulled Margot close and kissed her forehead. "You'll see. Everything will work out. There's probably a good explanation for the key not fitting."

Margot shook her head. "I just had a horrible thought. What if they tricked me into signing a Power of Attorney or a Quitclaim Deed? Maybe they even stole my identity? When I had that infection, I felt pretty much out of it."

"I know you're upset, but don't let your imagination go wild. They would be in serious legal trouble if they pulled those stunts."

"I wouldn't put anything past Rudy."

Hans said, "It's much simpler to pursue the conservator route. Let's wait and see what that sheriff fella finds out."

As they were leaving, Mirabelle gave Margot another big hug. "I'm sorry you're going through this mess, Darlin'. I'll keep an eye on your house, and if you need anything else, you holler, and I'll come running fast as I can."

On their way to the car, they could hear Mirabelle repeating, "Oh my goodness. Oh my goodness gracious."

⚊⬦⬦⚊

The next morning they drove to a facility in Santa Ana where they encountered deputy Ronald Ostrowski, a tall, beefy man, who made the proper sympathetic noises, and assuring them he would do a thorough investigation, he promised to contact them with the information.

When a day passed with no word, Margot phoned Hans to vent. "We'd better hear back from the Sheriff fella soon, or I'll go stark raving mad. Please do something."

Within an hour, Hans called saying that the deputy had spoken with Margot's relatives, and he would meet with Margot and Hans at Shady Palms.

A day later, as they waited downstairs in the lobby, Hans spotted the deputy six feet away trapped in the clutches of a wheel-chair-bound resident who kept yelling, "Help me, officer, they're keeping me prisoner here."

Hans rushed to free the flustered officer and signaled Margot with an overhead wave to follow them to a private conference room where the deputy removed his hat and wiped his brow. "Phew," he said. "I've faced members of the M-13 gang without breaking a sweat, but that lady wouldn't let go my shirt; I couldn't very well club her."

Margot chuckled. "I can just see the headlines—Deputy Sheriff beats to death a disabled ninety-year-old lady for groping him."

The three broke up laughing until the deputy recovered his composure and extracted a report from an accordion folder. "Sorry this took so long Ms. Manning. Seems your relatives have been away. When I finally reached them, they explained that Clarissa had left her purse containing your house keys in a shopping cart, and the purse had been stolen. She reported the lost purse to the supermarket manager, but after it didn't turn up, she called Rudy to come for her."

The Sheriff shook his head. "Your nephew, Rudy Sampson, sure carried on something fierce; he called your niece, Clarissa, a 'dimwit,' said she was the most careless person he knew, and said they had to cancel credit cards, get her a new driver's license, and replace your keys."

Margot could picture Rudy's angry face.

The deputy handed Margot the new keys along with a brief note. She and Hans exchanged doubtful looks.

Before leaving, Deputy Ostrowski opened the door to peer into the lobby. "I hope it's safe to walk through now."

"Want us to call for a police escort?" Margot said.

He laughed nervously. "I'd appreciate you folks keeping this a secret between us; the other deputies would make my life a living hell if word ever got around."

Margot smiled. "Your secret is safe with us and thanks for your help."

She opened the note from The Relatives, and as she read it aloud, the smile disappeared.

Dear Margot:

Enclosed are your new keys. I explained to the deputy about Clarissa losing her purse with your keys inside, and how we were forced to change the locks. Sorry for the mix-up. Under the circumstances, we think it best you not come to the house until your conservator-ship case is decided. Please know we have your best interests at heart.

Love, Rudy & Clarissa

When she finished reading the note, Margot screamed, "With love, no less. What nerve! I'd like to go over there and tell them a thing or two."

"Wait," Hans said. "Let's think this through. We should concentrate on finding you good legal advice for the hearing."

Though Margot argued, inside she felt relieved at not having to face Rudy, even with Hans by her side.

CHAPTER NINE

First thing the next morning Margot phoned the firm that handled her estate after Ted died. The process had been long and frustrating, but, on the whole, she'd felt satisfied.

The senior partner listened patiently while she recounted the entire saga: her accident, her confinement at Shady Palms, the conservator suit. He said, "I sympathize completely though I'm not surprised. Those shenanigans are rampant in this retirement community." He recommended five experts in conservator litigation.

Studying the list, Margot found it difficult to evaluate one attorney vs. another.

Indecision made her nervous; it would be prudent to ask around and also to see what information Hans had gleaned from his lawyer neighbor.

When Rachel arrived after a frantic call, Margot threw herself into her friend's arms and began sobbing. "You won't believe what my relatives are pulling now."

Rachel rubbed Margot's back in soothing circles. "Take a deep breath and tell me."

As she listened, her eyebrows shot up. "Rudy and Clarissa are suing to become your conservators—that's the most ridiculous thing I've ever heard."

"I'll show you the letter if you don't believe me."

"This will never fly. People will line up to testify you are one of the most competent people on the planet."

"So you'll vouch for me?"

"What a silly question. Go fix your face. I'm starved for lunch."

"Food is the last thing I want right now. I want my old life back."

Thinking that fresh air and natural surroundings would shake Margot's depression, Rachel suggested they pick up sandwiches to eat at tables beside the Marina.

But once there, Margot nibbled at her food, tossing the rest in the trash. Tears filled her eyes. "Even after my horrible accident, I didn't feel as miserable as I do now."

"I know, honey, but I'm confident you'll win, and meanwhile it's lucky you can afford to live in such a comfortable place."

"Lucky?" Margot's voice rose several octaves. "You call that lucky?"

"Shady Palms is a palace compared to those evil retirement homes they feature on *60 minutes*," Rachel said.

"Feels more like a prison."

"It doesn't need to be; you can lead a full active life there."

"Wrong. Living with people who sit around waiting to die creeps me out; they're a daily reminder that I'm getting old."

"I often feel the same way, but I don't let it ruin my life," Rachel said. "I just splurge on expensive creams that promise a youthful complexion and other miracles."

"Maybe it works for you, but remember what happened when I stupidly wore those stilettos that sent me flying down the museum steps and got me sentenced to this old folks home."

"I'll shut up for now, but I'll keep working on you."

"I won't be listening."

Later, as both women walked through the Shady Palms lobby, a hand reached out to grab Rachel's arm, and a voice said, "Stop right there. Let me see that gorgeous necklace."

The voice belonged to a striking woman wearing a stylish black pantsuit, accented by chunky silver jewelry, her white hair pulled off her face with ebony combs. She tapped her wheelchair, "Even though I'm stuck in this contraption, I haven't lost my eye for baubles."

Rachel knelt extending the necklace to provide the speaker a closer view.

The woman lovingly fingered the turquoise beads whose strands were gathered at intervals by round turquoise florets with pearl centers. She said, "Turquoise is definitely your color; it matches your eyes. Thanks for letting me admire it."

"My pleasure." Rachel stood up and smiled, introducing herself and adding, "This is my friend Margot, who lives here."

The woman held out her hand. "I'm Julia, nice meeting you both." Turning to Margot she said, "I remember now; you conducted exercise class one day; what great fun. I hope you'll be leading the class again soon?"

Margot quipped, "I've ended my career as exercise class instructor and moved on to greater glories." She fingered the necklace and turned to Rachel. "Where *did* you buy that; I want one too."

"It's free to try on—today only; otherwise it'll cost you a plane ticket to Greece."

"I saw it first," Julia said, tugging on Rachel's jacket.

Rachel bent to help Julia with the necklace. "Fortunately, this slips on right over your head. I live alone, and with my long nails I can't negotiate clasps anymore."

Julia preened a minute before relinquishing the necklace to Margot. The deep blue-green beads stood out against Margot's white skin and black curls. Julia nodded approvingly. "It definitely complements you too."

"See," Margot said, sounding cheerful for the first time since Rachel had arrived. "This necklace suits me perfectly. If you were a true friend, you'd let me keep it."

Magically, every woman in the lobby caught wind of the necklace and began chanting, "My turn, my turn."

As the necklace passed from hand to hand, remarkable changes took place; faces which previously had worn bored or tired expressions now radiated pleasure. One woman stroked the beads, purring, "This necklace makes me feel sexy—like the old days."

Back at her apartment, Margot poured two cups of *chai*, her new favorite brew.

Rachel took a sip. "Ah the pleasures of tea with a dear friend."

Now hungry after discarding her lunch, Margot dug into the triple ginger cookies she had placed on the coffee table. "That's you—a dear, dear friend who puts up with my constant whining."

"The incident with the necklace is a lesson." Rachel bit off a piece of cookie. "It's amazing how a simple piece of jewelry can bring a person to life. The major problem among aging people is that they feel unimportant, even invisible."

"Not you. You stand out wherever you go."

"Thanks for the vote of confidence, but I have feelings of insecurity too. I fool myself into thinking I still have *it*, but deep down I sometimes think I've lost my edge. Men not only don't flirt anymore, no one even notices I'm around."

Margot sighed. "These days, the 'beautiful people' are the fresh-faced young girls with their super long legs; they positively shine in their tight, sexy jeans and bare midriffs. And what do those dumb kids do? They ruin their skin with tattoos. Just imagine wrinkled skin covered in tattoos twenty or thirty years from now."

Rachel made a face. "That's their problem; our problem is how to make society realize old people matter, or should matter. We're interesting women who deserve respect and admiration instead of being treated like disposables. I bet this facility has a treasure trove of people with backgrounds in art, education, business, science . . . . ."

"I haven't noticed any." Margot thought a minute. "Wait, I did make two new friends recently—Nancy and Jane. And Julia seems like a person I might enjoy knowing."

Rachel said, "Maybe this necklace incident is saying we should reach out more."

"I suppose I could atone for my unforgivable behavior in exercise class by acting more sociable; I might even consider doing something useful for my fellow inmates."

"Any ideas?"

"Since you ask, Nancy and Jane are bugging me about organizing an art trip to LA. The question is, 'Can I stand spending a whole day with boring old people?'" She slapped her hand against her mouth. "Whoops, there I go again."

Rachel chuckled. "That's my Margot."

<hr />

The next morning, with new determination, Margot marched upstairs to meet her friends. She found Nancy bent over a work board covered by torn paper, brushes, in all shapes and sizes, along with India ink, assorted pens, acrylic paint tubes, and glue.

Margot said, "I'm here to discuss the museum trip, but you look busy."

"Oh, right, the museum trip. I've been fiddling with this collage and the time plum got away from me."

"I can come back if you like?"

"No, y'all sit down; make yourself to home. I'm almost done."

Margot studied the walls, decorated with simple abstract shapes, done in highly saturated acrylics. "Is this a new technique?"

"Yes, ma'am. I'm trying some new materials and textures. Makes a nice change."

Margot studied the paintings. "Your works are untitled."

"I like viewers to make up their own tales."

"Is Jane available?"

"She's working on a landscape for the 'Plein Air' beach competition. Nancy consulted her watch. "She should be ready for a break about now." Nancy put down a brush and dialed Jane. "Put the pot on; Margot's here. We're thirsting for your strong brew."

At Jane's apartment, the three women settled around a small dinette table to sip coffee and munch snicker doodle cookies.

Margot smacked her lips. "Yum—these are loaded with cinnamon and they taste homemade."

"They're from my darling adorable granddaughter, Janie, who takes after me, in name and beauty. She sends me a care package every month with a note begging me to move back to Wisconsin. I miss my kids, but I can't stand those freezing cold winters and hot, sticky summers."

"Admit it," Nancy said. "The real reason you can't go home again is because you're always poking fun at the Republicans. You're a disgrace to your upbringing."

"Very funny. Watch out, though; I'm the witty one around here." Biting into another snicker doodle, she added, "If little Janie keeps sending me these goodies, by the time I'm ready to walk normally, I'll be waddling. I've been packing it on ever since my surgery. It's hard to believe they elected me homecoming queen umpteen years ago."

"How many years ago, did you say?" Nancy asked.

"Don't be smart," Jane said. "You know we're all on Medicare."

"But just barely." Margot jumped in.

"What a little honey bun your granddaughter is," Nancy said. "Tell you what. I'd be glad to eat those cookies for you. Now I'm back running five miles a day, I could use the extra carbs."

"You're such a pal," Jane said, in a voice dripping with sarcasm.

Nancy looked at Margot. "You got any young-uns?"

"We tried for years with no luck. A baby would have ruined my figure anyway."

"I never did get any either." Nancy turned to Jane. "Back to being pals, if Margot knows what's good for her, she'd better tell us she'll do the art museum trip."

"All right, all right," Margot said. "I'll help because you two are the only inmates I can relate to; I can't afford losing you."

Jane said, "That's settled then. What's exciting in LA these days?"

"It's a no-brainer," Margot said. "LACMA has the best show, by far. They're showing the five Gustave Klimts, once owned by Ferdinand and Adele Bloch-Bauer."

Jane said, "I read something in the paper about those the paintings. Weren't they confiscated during the Holocaust?"

"Correct; Maria Altman and the other heirs sued the Austrian government for their return and they won. Now we can enjoy them."

"I love Klimt, but why don't we wait on that," Nancy said. "I haven't visited the Autry Center for a coon's age. They're having a special sale on Native American and Mexican jewelry; I need me some new trinkets."

Margot said, "We can catch that exhibit on our own, but the Klimt paintings will only be in LA for a few weeks before being auctioned off and possibly sold to private collections; we may never get another chance to see them."

They all agreed, and Margot said, "We should get going on this. Once we pick a date, I'll call the bus company. Nancy, can you get us a docent? And, Jane, I need you to get permission from Shady Palms."

The old Margot was back.

CHAPTER TEN

On museum day, Margot checked off the women boarding the bus. She waited while they jockeyed for seats. Once they were settled, she handed out a description of the exhibit. Even so, people kept asking questions until she said, "Read; it's all there."

Joining her friends in the back, she mopped her brow. "Can you believe I planned this trip to forget my problems?"

"Yah, brilliant," Jane said.

"Speaking of problems," Nancy said. "Heard anything from your kinfolk lately?"

"Boy did I ever; The Relatives are petitioning to become my conservators."

"No way; you're funning us," Nancy said.

"Wish I were."

"What does this conservator business mean," Jane asked. "Enlighten me."

"In plain English, it means if they win, they take control of me and every last thing I own."

"You betcha, that sounds heavy," Jane said.

"Heavy isn't the word; my hearing is set in a month, on August 15."

"I'll be danged," Nancy said. "If that could happen to a woman with your background and connections, anyone could do me dirty."

"While we're on the subject, I thought of an idea for scoring brownie points with the conservator court."

Jane said, "Brace yourself, Nancy; Margot has an idea."

Margot poked Jane. "I might volunteer in skilled nursing a couple times a week. It's right next-door. Like a good little girl, I would be helping people."

Nancy narrowed her eyes. "You can't be serious."

"I am serious, but I'm a little nervous; as a patient, I found the place kind of scary. Maybe if we all volunteered together, it wouldn't be bad. What do you think?"

"We knew you were fixing to involve us in some kind of scheme," Nancy said.

"*Moi?*"

"I'm not sure I cotton to the idea." Nancy scratched her head. "Something weird went down while I recuperated there. The cute lady, next bed over, began shouting one night, and the head nurse had a hissy fit—told her to shut up. By the next morning, the lady had vamoosed. When I asked a nurse where she disappeared to, the nurse just shrugged and walked away. I never did find out nothing more."

Margot shook her head. I had a similar experience. A patient vanished after raising a ruckus; I also asked where she had gone."

"Did you ever find out?"

"Sharon told me that the woman's daughter had moved her to another facility." Margot shrugged. "But I've always wondered if something bad happened to her."

A voice interrupted. "Sorry for intruding; I couldn't help overhearing your conversation. I spent weeks in skilled nursing, and there *is* something wrong."

The three looked up at a woman balancing her small body unsteadily on a cane. Her upturned nose, which might look cute on a more youthful face, was out of sync with her deeply carved wrinkles, grey skin, and small beady eyes.

Margot gestured to an empty seat. "Please join us. I'm Margot Manning and my two friends are Jane Driscoll, a displaced mid-westerner, and Nancy Ewing, who's obviously a Texan. After two sentences apiece, you'll figure it out for yourself."

The woman introduced herself as Barbara Turner and said she was recovering from recent hip surgery.

"It's nice meeting you, Barbara." Margot said. "I'm curious; can you elaborate?"

Barbara lowered her voice to a conspiratorial whisper. "The atmosphere in skilled nursing is poison; the head nurse, Helga Hasse, runs the place with an iron fist, and the nurses jump when she's around. She chews them out in front of everyone; she even intimidates the patients."

Margot nodded. "I remember the day she scared the wits out of my friend, Hans when she scolded him for staying too long. He said she looked like a demon out of a Nordic myth."

Warming to the subject, Barbara added, "Helga's a stickler for the nurses following orders, but if she hears the patients giving the staff a tough time, she bawls them out too."

Jane asked, "How does she get away with being mean and bossy?"

"Mr. Norwood, the Nursing Director, is a first-class wimp; he hates making decisions so he relies on her for everything. And maybe Norwood *likes* having skilled nursing run that way. Sometimes those quiet little men turn out to be control freaks."

Margot shrugged. "It is what it is, and I'm still going to check out volunteering there; I hope you three will consider joining me—safety in numbers, you know."

"We'll see," the women said in unison.

⇥⇤

With all the chatter, the trip had flown. As the group ascended the museum steps, a wave of dizziness overtook Margot. Nancy noticed Margot hanging back and joked, "Come on. Keep up."

Unable to continue, Margot sat on the steps and dropped her head between her knees. Nancy ran back down where she found Margot visibly shaken and deathly pale.

"I'm not up to this," Margot said. "I can hardly breathe, and my heart is racing. These stairs remind me of my accident."

Offering her arm, Nancy said. "Hold tight, sweetie pie, and you'll make it."

By the time they reached the entrance, Margot's color had returned, and they found the special room set aside for the five Klimts: three landscapes and two portraits of Adele-Bloch-Bauer, the young, beautiful wife of a wealthy Viennese industrialist.

The docent began by discussing Adele's 1907 portrait, painted in Klimt's best known style based on Byzantine mosaic art. In a painstaking process using real gold, he had enhanced his jewel tone palette with gold and silver paints, mother of pearl, and bits of real jewelry.

She said, "In this portrait, Klimt envelops Adele in a gold gown swirled to form the painting's rich gold background. Notice how the elaborate adornment contrasts with her lushly painted dark hair and pale white skin.

"Does this painting remind anyone of Klimt's most famous portrait?" She asked.

Several hands shot up, followed by an excited chorus, "*The Kiss*, it's *The Kiss*."

The docent nodded and proceeded to another portrait of Adele. "Klimt was an immensely talented draftsman who employed many styles. Adele is the only woman twice painted by Klimt; this one is simple following the style of Matisse. Here, and in the exhibit's three landscapes, we see impressionistic brush strokes combined with geometry, high key color, and flat modernist elements."

She allowed them several minutes to study the paintings then moved to the museum's permanent modern art collection where she pointed out similarities and differences between the five Klimts and the works of other early twentieth century artists.

≈⟵ ⟶≈

For lunch at *Pentimento*, the museum restaurant, the ladies occupied two long tables served by two waiters. Margot noticed them exchanging grim looks and heard one grumble, "Brace yourself, a table full of seniors."

The other waiter replied, "Just one juicy role, and I'm done waiting tables."

They passed out menus mechanically reciting the day's specials; a barrage of questions followed.

"How much is the halibut?"

"Is it fresh or fresh frozen?"

"Can I substitute a cream sauce for the salsa?"

"Can you leave the sauce off?"

"Can I have the salad dressing on the side?"

Several women asked to pay separately or use their charge cards, but the waiters refused to do thirty separate transactions.

Margot recalled painful lunches where the bickering had reached a fever pitch over who ate and drank what. Even though the restaurant added the eighteen percent tip, people forgot the tax, forcing Margot and her friends to make up the difference. To avoid the inevitable quibbling, Margot suggested they divide the bill evenly.

For her lunch, she debated four choices: a chicken pesto and sun dried tomato sandwich, a three-cheese chicken pasta, a chopped salad, or a lamb burger with gorgonzola cheese. Unlike others her age, she suffered no digestive or cholesterol problems, but she constantly worried about gaining weight.

Eyeing a juicy-looking lamb burger at the next table, she happily ordered one, telling herself, if I eat only half the roll, it qualifies for my low carb diet.

While waiting to be served, Margot led a discussion of the exhibit, during which the group pronounced Klimt's works as "masterful" and "fabulous;" they expressed admiration for Adele as a beautiful, romantic figure who enjoyed riches and acclaim but tragically died of meningitis in 1925 at the young age of forty-three.

The group relished Margot's description of Klimt as a painter of sensual women's portraits, clothed or otherwise. She added that he often had affairs with his models—supposedly, including Adele.

After fielding complaints over splitting the lunch check, and with only twenty minutes left for shopping, Margot made a beeline for the gift shop where she tried on several over-priced bracelets, finally leaving empty handed. More jewelry would not fix her problems.

On the bus, a head count determined that a passenger had gone missing. According to her seatmate, the woman had gone off for ice cream, and twenty minutes later, she returned licking a chocolate cone and limping badly. She had stumbled on the escalator steps cutting her knee.

Their shopping time had been cut short; now they waited grumbling and twiddling their thumbs while the injured woman underwent first aid.

To help pass the time, Margot moved to the front, and said, "How about we sing some old camps songs?" She first led the group in singing *Kookaburra* then suggested that others choose songs they remembered. By the time the bus rumbled off to creep through the now rush-hour traffic, the women were happily singing away.

Back upstairs in her apartment, Margot flopped onto the sofa and closed her eyes. Within minutes, she fell fast asleep and slept for two hours. Noting the answering machine was blinking five messages, all from Hans, she called immediately and responded to his cheery greeting with, "Sorry it took so long to get back, but I just woke up. It's been a long, long day."

"How did it go?"

"There were a few snags, but I handled them, and everyone had a great time. They fell in love with Klimt and his paintings of Adele, and lunch at *Pentimento* was delicious as always."

"You mentioned a few snags; what went wrong?"

"A women fell and scraped her knee, and we were delayed an hour coming back; I had to organize a camp song sing-along to keep the group from getting antsy."

"You didn't."

"I certainly did. They had *more* fun."

"You are something else."

"Any news on the legal front?"

Hans said, "I contacted the friend I mentioned who's a partner at Kennedy, McLaughlin and Madison; they're a top-notch firm that specializes in conservator cases. I'll bring you the information tomorrow."

Margot pictured a wise-looking, middle-aged man wearing grey pinstripes, spectacles pitched on his nose."

"Sounds perfect," she said.

CHAPTER ELEVEN

The next morning Margot received a surprise visit from Alice Marks, a former neighbor and the town busy-body. A stout, bustling woman with deeply wrinkled olive skin, a flat stubby nose, and long stringy hair—dyed punk red, she reminded Margot of a Halloween witch.

Cooing in a high-pitched voice and elongating every word, Alice said, "Maar-got, when I heard you had an ac-cident, I had to come. Sorry it took so long."

Wonder what she's up to?

"Anyway darling, you look fabulous—considering all you've been through. Are you still dating that handsome guy who lives near me at the beach?"

So that's why she's here.

"You know I ran into him yesterday." Alice tapped her cheek and cocked her head, pretending to be thinking. "Where was it?" She nodded. "I remember now; he was having lunch with Diana Kennedy on *The Cliff Restaurant* patio."

Clearly relishing every word, Alice added. "I must say they acted rather chummy, and they seemed deeply engrossed in whatever they were discussing."

Margot gave Alice a blank stare.

"That woman is so adorable; men just go crazy over her." You know who she is, don't you?"

Why does the name Kennedy ring a bell?

Then it hit her. She's the Kennedy in the firm Hans recommended.

Margot remembered Diana all right, and she didn't like what she remembered. Diana, a petite, slim woman was probably a size *two*—Margot's polar opposite. She felt like an elephant next to her.

Diana possessed the cool blonde Grace Kelly looks Margot had always envied. She wore her hair in a French knot for business and in a flippant pony tail for casual dress. Diana had to be fifteen years younger than Margot—maybe even more.

Last night's headache had disappeared; heartache took its place.

This is so high school, where "friends" couldn't wait to report spotting your boyfriend with another girl. But now it's worse. I'm stuck in an Old Folks Home, fending off conniving relatives while the man I love is involved with another woman.

Margot replied coldly and deliberately. "Oh right. Hans told me about meeting Diana; he's helping me solve a legal problem."

My life keeps getting worse.

Once rid of Alice, Margot dialed Hans, and without saying "Hello," she barked, "You didn't tell me Diana Kennedy is the lawyer you've been recommending?"

"I thought I did."

"I would remember something as important as that."

"Don't be upset. I'm just trying to help. Diana is a highly qualified lawyer and her firm has extensive experience with conservator fraud."

"And why, may I ask, did you meet her for lunch? Do you always arrange your appointments at a beachside restaurant?"

"We both live in Laguna; we chose a convenient place, that's all. I don't understand your problem."

"Hiring her firm is not a *fait accompli*; I have other law firms to check out first."

She slammed the phone and rummaged through her desk for the lawyers recommended by her estate attorney. She'd be darned if she'd give Hans an excuse to hang out with adorable little Diana Kennedy.

⇌

A few days later, Margot found herself at the conference room of Jacobs, Jacobs and Jacobs, a highly acclaimed law firm; the biblical sounding name meant she had "right" on her side.

Any thoughts on letting Diana handle the case disappeared as she studied the well-appointed conference room. A George III Mahogany conference table with its carved walnut wing armchairs, plumped in crewel-work dominated the room; a floor-to-ceiling library housed expensively bound leather law books that bespoke solidity, experience, and knowledge—the very attributes a legal firm should convey.

The receptionist showed her in to meet Gordon Jacobs, a short and bald man with a physique bordering on the stout; he had an unremarkable, but pleasant face.

In a clipped British accent, Gordon said, "I see your estate attorney, Sidney Hamilton, referred you—fine Firm his." He read through the court letter Margot had brought and gestured with his glasses. "These situations can be most difficult. Please take your time and tell me how you arrived at this bump in the road."

Normally, Margot wouldn't give a second thought to a man with an appearance like Gordon's, but his charming English accent won her over.

I might enjoy knowing this man better.

That morning, Margot had dressed carefully in a peacock blue wool pantsuit, accessorized by a chunky lapis and coral necklace. Taking care to bat her eyes, she described the accident, her recovery, and the offer of help from The Relatives that lead to her residence at Shady Palms. She added, "After my accident, Rudy said I shouldn't let my house sit empty. In my debilitated state, I foolishly agreed to let them move in; it seemed reasonable at the time."

"Most understandable." Gordon said. "I empathize, but what's done is done. You're not to bother yourself anymore. However, I need to know more about your nephew and niece, to determine what I'm up against."

"Rudy and Clarissa are extremely wealthy people. Rudy is an MBA who manages his own successful Real Estate investment firm. He's renowned as a shrewd analyst and for his ability to find and negotiate hard bargains."

"And what role does Clarissa play?"

"Clarissa has a degree in Real Estate Law; she and a small staff manage the properties. She lets Rudy push her around, but she's ruthless in navigating tenant laws.

"I should also mention that their firm is well-known in the community; they generously donate equipment and uniforms to local sports teams; their company logo is visible all over the county."

He patted her hand. "That doesn't worry me; I'm experienced in these matters. Once we research the legalities, it shouldn't be difficult to catch these chaps out."

"But the hearing is scheduled in mid-August." Margot said.

"A month from now—that does leave us a bit short. I'll see what I can sort out." Gordon escorted her to the door. "Jolly nice meeting you; I enjoyed our chat. I'll ring you up once I do some research."

Margot left feeling disquieted. She had expected the lawyer to be outraged, to tell her the hearing would be decided in her favor and that her worries would be over.

Still, the attorney did seem knowledgeable, and he presented a far safer choice than Diana when it came to Hans.

I'm sure I detected a spark of chemistry between us, she thought. It would serve Hans right if another man found me attractive.

In this mindset, she returned to her apartment where an interesting email waited.

For a lark, Margot had joined *Classmates*, the online social networking service for connecting friends. She had never expected to hear from anyone, but, to her amazement, Jim Duncan, an old college boyfriend had contacted her. She flashed to the *Classmates* site for the email, which read:

Hi Margot,

It's scary to think how many years have elapsed since we last saw each other. On a whim, while browsing through *Classmates*, I typed in your name and voilà, I found you. I read that you're a widow, living in S. California, and I thought, "Great"—not the widow part—but I've been contemplating a trip to California, and this gives me an incentive to hop on a plane. Given a little encouragement, I could be out there before you can say, 'Jack Robinson.' (Where did that cliché come from?)

You'll find me a little changed (at least my hair is; in fact it's gone) but I'm the same handsome *bon vivant* you dated; I'm sure you're still the foxy lady I remember. I'm living in Connecticut, retired from practicing law, but, these days I don't charge much for legal advice, if you need any. I hope this email reaches you; I'm anxious to hear back.

How do I sign this? Regards? All the best? Sincerely Yours?

Oh, what the heck.
Love, Jim

PS. I'm also widowed. Unfortunately, my wife died a year ago.
I've managed to keep busy, but I miss her a lot.

Since Ted's death, Margot occasionally thought about Jim. In her foggy memory, he appeared as a tall handsome guy with a slightly curved nose, a devilish grin, and twinkling brown eyes.

Jim's email certainly improved Margot's outlook on life. He hadn't lost his flair for humor (along with his hair), and he was definitely flirting.

Seeing Jim will be fun, she thought. We can bring back the old times before all the bad things that are happening. But can I live up to being "foxy?"

Maybe we'll run into Hans while we're having lunch or browsing through an art gallery—make Hans jealous.

Margot waited a few days before answering—no point sounding too anxious. She kept her answer brief, but encouraging.

Dear Jim,
What a surprise to hear from you. I often think back to college days, remembering all the fun we had—especially during Winter Carnival. I have many questions, even a legal entanglement to discuss. I see you still enjoy joking around; the older I am, the more I realize how important it is to consider the comic side of life.

Of course I'd love you to visit. Please let me know when you'll be arriving and where you'll be staying? Need any recommendations?

How should I sign this?

What the heck.

Love, Margot.

After Margot hit send, she worried.

Will Jim be shocked at how much I've aged? And should I let him see where I live? How embarrassing that could be! Perhaps if I explain the situation . . . .

I'll play it by ear.

CHAPTER TWELVE

Following the museum trip, Margot tried envisioning other ways she could help the Shady Palms residents and simultaneously curry favor with the conservator court. One morning, she sat with Nancy and Jane enjoying the sun's rays streaming through the solarium window. Margot turned to Jane. "For an aging beauty queen, you're looking pretty sharp these days."

Jane eyed Margot suspiciously. "Why are you buttering me up?"

"I've been thinking. . . ."

"Uh, oh, she's been thinking again."

"As I said, before being rudely interrupted, I'm thinking of organizing a makeover clinic for the women here. The salon in this prison is completely outdated; most residents have the same, boring wash and set, tightly-curled hairdos. And the colors: dull, mousy brown; bright blue; bleached-out-blonde; hippy-carrot red; vampire black; God-awful-magenta." She shuddered, "Those weird tints are hideous on old gray faces and they accentuate the wrinkles."

"I totally agree darlings," Nancy said. "These women need rescuing."

—⋈—

Because of her status as a *persona non grata*, Margot enlisted Nancy and Jane on her quest for Ms. Dugin's permission.

Seated in the director's office the next day, Nancy argued that a beauty clinic would lift the residents' spirits and would be excellent public relations for Shady Palms.

Ms. Dugin's first reaction, as always, was to say, "no." But on reflection, she decided the idea might have merit. "After all," she said. "My first duty is to please the residents; happy residents make my job easier."

Jane said, "I promise you the women will look and feel fabulous after a full beauty treatment and please don't forget—you're invited to join in."

Ms. Dugin turned to Margot. "You're not saying much, but I take it you're involved in this; you're probably the ringleader."

"I'm just helping out Nancy and Jane with the details."

"I'll be honest. Having you involved is what worries me. You cause trouble everywhere you go,"

Margot pursed her lips in an attempt to look hurt. "The residents enjoyed the LA museum trip, and the day went smoothly."

"Smoothly? I heard that a woman fell and cut her knee," Dugin said.

"We have safeguards to ensure nothing untoward will happen this time."

Ms. Dugin frowned and fidgeted, then instructed the women to outline the entire plan, describing Who, What, Where, When, and How. She would give them her final decision after discussing the proposal with the corporation lawyers. There were legalities to consider and permissions to grant.

She stood to shake hands. "You say I'm invited? Be sure to let me know the exact date, so I can mark my calendar."

⚊⊹⊹⚊

Before contacting salons in the area, Margot decided to seek advice from her adored hairdresser, Luigi. A man brimming with ideas, he would certainly point her in the right direction. She called immediately for an appointment.

When Margot walked through the door, Luigi's face lit up. He kissed her loudly on both cheeks and crooned, "*Ciao, Bambina.*"

Margot had always nurtured a weakness for Italian men, and the handsome Luigi fit the bill with his classic Roman nose, olive skin, thick dark hair, and soft brown eyes framed by long lashes. A man of medium height, his physique grew rounder following each dutiful visit to his mama's kitchen.

Though she knew his heart belonged to Cedric his long-term partner, Margot loved flirting with him. Luigi's mama, Maria lamented the relationship—not because Cedric was the same sex, but because Luigi's chosen one turned out to be a non-Catholic— and an Englishman to boot. She failed to comprehend how her *bambino* could love a tall, skinny man from a culture that, in her opinion, failed utterly at cooking. Cedric claimed to enjoy Italian food, but like the English Queen, Cedric disdained garlic, and for Mama, food without garlic, wasn't worth eating.

Draping Margot in a plastic cape, Luigi dabbed the black color onto her roots. "So, *bella*, what plans have you devised to escape the clutches of your relatives?"

"You'll be happy to hear I've abandoned my wicked, wicked ways, and I've embraced the cause of the elder hostages at Shady Palms."

"How's that?"

"I'm in the process of organizing makeovers for the detainees. God knows everyone there is desperate for one, and my clever little

71

gesture should please the court. We need to recruit different salons to participate; you're my first victim."

"For you, *bella*, anything."

Margot blew him a kiss. That's not my only problem; I'm having trouble with the logistics. …"

Luigi jumped right in. He prided himself on being a maven of food, fine wine, the best hotels and restaurants, choice vacation spots, top cruise lines and airlines. "It's a piece of cake," he said. "You get the ladies to sign up. Then we'll figure out how many salons we need to handle the work; we'll run a shuttle service back and forth all day."

"Luigi, you're the man. No wonder I'm desperately in love with you."

Luigi thought some more. "We can have snacks donated— coffee and breakfast pastries, maybe cheese and assorted lunch sandwiches, some vino to brighten the day."

Margot clapped her hands. "You're a genius; tell Cedric I'm out to steal you."

Following several more *bellas,* Margot slipped Luigi a generous tip. Unlike much dyed black hair, her color appeared natural, and he cut her hair perfectly—so that she only needed to blow it dry, between appointments. Luigi served as her confidante, her therapist, her guru, and her morale builder rolled into one. She left feeling more in control than at any other time lately.

⋙⋘

A veteran of the war on aging, Margot had tried nearly every known non-surgical, non-invasive beauty treatment—the age-defying, age-enhancing soaps, moisturizers, wrinkle creams and cleansers; she had undergone microdermabrasion and derma planning; photo imaging; laser resurfacing; photo rejuvenation; hydra facials; Swedish facials; aromatherapy facials.

With 'Beauty Day' set for August first—only two weeks away—Margot consulted the various clinics involved to make sure each woman received the appropriate facial treatment, the most becoming hairdo, and the most flattering make-up. She cautioned the aestheticians, hairdressers, and other practitioners not to use any aggressive procedures—no abrasions, and no new, risky, cutting-edge processes. Besides doing something special for the women residents, she had something to prove—to herself, to Director Dugin, and to the court.

On the appointed day, Shady Palms buzzed with activity. The residents lined the lobby waiting for their individual mini-busses. Margot's stomach performed flip-flops, even though she had meticulously diagrammed the plans placing each participant in a particular vehicle, at a specific time, at a specific salon.

She had co-opted Nancy, Jane and Barbara to ride shotgun on the vehicles and supervise the operations. Even her ever-loyal friend Rachel had volunteered to help. Each carried a similar diagram, cell phones at the ready. Once the first buses pulled out, Margot retreated to the Shady Palms salon, which, besides providing beauty services, would be command headquarters. Because one participant had wandered off during the museum trip, she assigned Jane to shadow her.

Soon, reports began arriving. Every woman had landed in the right place to begin with a facial, followed by hair styling, a manicure/pedicure, ending with a full-face make-up. Various juices, coffee, tea, and muffins stood arrayed for breakfast. By noon, champagne, soft drinks, light sandwiches, and fruit would be added. Great care had been taken in monitoring special diets.

Although most men would have run the other way, Hans lent his support, chauffeuring Margot to the various locations for on-site supervision. Touched by his thoughtfulness, she regretted doubting him and plotting a tryst with her old beau, Jim.

In the festive atmosphere of the salons, the women smiled and chattered—already looking years younger. Margot searched for

Ms. Dugin, the Shady Palms Director, to learn her reaction. At last, she spotted the woman in a quiet corner of one salon, happily slurping a glass of "bubbly."

Hans expressed wonder at the bizarre process of color weaving, which entailed brushing tint on individual hair clumps and wrapping each in separate foil packets. He chuckled. "I feel like an anthropologist witnessing a tribal beauty ritual."

In addition to charging the participants a nominal fee of thirty dollars, Margot had convinced the salons to donate their time as charitable contributions; her committee would underwrite any extra food and bus expenses.

A beautician, whose name tag read "Florence," finished wrapping a customer's head in giant rollers and settled her under the dryer. As Florence headed towards the food table, her eyes widened, and she told Margot, "Will you get all this food!"

"Hey, how's it going?" Margot asked.

Florence heaped an assortment of sandwiches on her plate and reached for the champagne. "It's going great. I'm having a blast working on these women. My clientele are young and hip. A snip and a spray, and they walk out looking gorgeous. This group is a challenge."

By four o'clock, the Shady Palms lobby sizzled with excitement as the women preened and showed off. A photographer stood beside a giant easel shamelessly hawking photos depicting what might be their last shot at glamour.

Amazed by the transformations, Margot shook her head. The over-bleached, dried out, unruly hair—gone; the over-powdered faces, the heavily rouged cheeks—gone; the caked eyelashes—gone; she now saw natural hairdos, soft shades, light make-up, bright shining eyes and many, many smiles.

She took her place beside the easel. "You all look fabulous. Are you pleased?"

The women cheered and applauded; they giggled and paraded around the room. Some had walkers. And some, like her new friend,

Julia, used wheel chairs, but parade they did. Margot had become a favorite. She had livened up exercise class; she had led them on an exciting art trip; now she had boosted their self-esteem. Having her at Shady Palms made life exciting.

Margot called for Ms. Dugin to step forward, but the director shrank back until Nancy pushed her to the front. Her wiry grey hair had been straightened and woven, using alternating dark and light strands of color, then swept back high off her forehead to fall softly on her face. Light make-up smoothed her creamy, white skin, minimizing her beak-like nose. Her lashes had been accented, using grey-black mascara, and a soft red gloss drew attention to her newly plumped lips. She giggled self-consciously and thanked Margot on everyone's behalf.

The day had been a great success, but something was missing.

Although everyone looked rejuvenated from the neck up, most still wore shapeless or drab clothing—either one-size-fits-all dresses or elastic waist pants with an over shirt and orthopedic shoes.

It dawned on Margot. The residents cried out for a dramatic fashion upgrade.

After Beauty Day's success, Ms. Dugin took to inviting Margot, her new best friend for drinks in her office.

The day's success gave Margot a great sense of accomplishment, but her court hearing, which loomed ahead, overshadowed her achievement.

CHAPTER THIRTEEN

T he next meeting with Gordon Jacobs took place in his office instead of the conference room. Margot nodded, approvingly, at the six-foot mahogany partner desk and the two Gainsborough chairs with old leather insets and nail heads. A six-foot English mahogany table, piled high with periodicals, stood against one wall; on the other wall, shelves contained a small library.

Gordon rushed in saying, "Sorry to keep you waiting; the Bailiff had a devilish time assembling a jury for my case and had to enlist some victims from the local supermarket. Odd system you employ in this country." His charming accent and quaint British-isms tempered her annoyance at his tardiness.

He quickly summarized the petition submitted by The Relatives. They had filed papers to become her conservators, questioning her competence based on her erratic behavior and dereliction of responsibilities.

The paper read:

a) Ms. Manning, a senior citizen, has jeopardized her person by riding a motorcycle on dangerous roads at excessive speed levels.

b) Four months ago, Ms. Manning suffered a severe accident while wearing inappropriately high five-inch heels that caused her to trip and fall down a long flight of stairs. Following said accident, she spent a month recovering in the hospital and in rehabilitation.

c) Recently, at Shady Palms, the life care facility where Ms. Manning now resides, she endangered her fellow-residents (some, extremely debilitated) by conducting an unauthorized exercise class, causing several persons to fall. Ms. Manning was reprimanded and barred from further attendance at said exercise class.

d) Ms. Manning has been delinquent in paying her bills resulting in her utilities being turned off. Only through an intervention by her relatives, the Sampsons, were the services reinstated.

e) Ms. Manning allowed herself to be victimized by deceptive mailings from Nigeria asking for money.

f) Ms. Manning has disappeared from the residence to spend the night with a strange man without notifying the facility of her whereabouts.

Tears welled up in Margot's eyes as Gordon read the allegations. When he finished, Margot complained. "I clearly remember notifying the facility the night I spent at Hans's place. I told the receptionist where I would be; she chided me and made a joke I can't repeat. As for the motorcycle riding, I discontinued the practice, long ago."

Clenching her jaws, she added, "This is outrageous. The Relatives agreed to forward any bills not paid by my management company."

She paused. "Now I'm wondering if Shady Palms has been deliberately screwing up the mail and conveniently forgetting my messages. They've been out to get me ever since the exercise class incident. They forget to change my bed or my towels; they send me erroneous bills for my stay; God knows what else they're pulling.

"My being victimized by deceptive mailings is also a fabrication to make me appear incompetent."

Gordon handed her a box of tissues. "Here, have a blow."

"Now I'm worried that my property taxes haven't been paid; my house, my real estate could be in danger."

Gordon said, "At least now we know what those cheeky blokes have up their sleeves. What they stated is patently ridiculous; we can easily sort out the bill-paying situation. And to ease your mind, my office will check out the property taxes. Please draw up a list of other matters that need addressing."

Margot slumped in the chair.

"I'll organize a set of arguments on your behalf to discuss at our next meeting." He thumbed through his desk calendar. "I'm free the day after tomorrow. And, oh yes, at the hearing, it's essential to line up some reliable chaps to vouch for you. I'll need those names beforehand."

Gordon stood up to excuse himself. "Sorry for hurrying off, but take your time to pull yourself together. When you get home, be sure to have a long lie-down and a drop of gin. Do you a world of good."

Back at her apartment, Margot took Gordon's advice and enjoyed a nice long lie-down, abetted by not one, but several spots of gin. With her eyes closed, she relived the day her short fling with motorcycle riding had begun.

Margot and Hans had been seeing each other for a few weeks when he appeared at her door and pointing to the motorcycle parked outside, he said, "Ready to hop on?"

Her first reaction had been to scream, "Are you crazy? Motorcycles are very, very dangerous."

Hans had narrowed his eyes in mock incredulity. "*Kom nu.* You're looking at an award-winning Ducati with a high performance valve design."

"Valve design—shmalve design—motorcycle riding is not in my vocabulary."

But Hans refused to be put off. He coaxed her into wearing the helmet he had brought along, and chucking her playfully under the chin, he flashed his disarming smile. "You're adorable."

At the word, 'adorable', Margot melted and agreed to give it a fling. There she was, a woman of advanced years, her arms clutching his waist for dear life while they flew through the streets.

She was terrified; she was thrilled; she was exhilarated.

She went right out and purchased a pair of black Ducati Old Times Lady Leather pants and a stunning Women's Wing Tex jacket. Admiring herself in the three-way mirror, she decided that the outfit made her look extra thin, sexy, and chic.

All that spring, they had breezed through Laguna Canyon, surrounded by the craggy hills and lush foliage, green from the recent rains; in a few months the grass would become tinder-dry, bringing about the seasonal fire threats.

Before reaching the Pacific Ocean, they parked the motorcycles near *Zinc*, their favorite outdoor vegetarian cafe for lattes and delicious pastry. Margot could never resist the buttery lemon-glazed pecan cookies. She even tried duplicating the recipe, but they didn't taste the same.

Hans always ordered his favorite flourless chocolate cake with crème anglaise. He never put on weight, a fact which annoyed Margot. Between bites, she would complain, "I'm up three pounds, if I just glance at a piece of pastry. You eat whatever please you and never gain an ounce. Not fair."

In late autumn, after attending a Laguna Playhouse matinee, they were riding their motorcycles towards Margot's house in Laguna Hills when halfway through the canyon, the rain began to fall. Unprotected by their light jackets, they soon found themselves bombarded by wild wind gusts and drenching rain.

Hans shouted and pointed. "Hold up, Margot. Let's pull over to the side and wait until the storm subsides." They stopped under a stand of Eucalyptus trees, and he added, "I'm worried we'll have an accident; the winds are whipping our motorcycles all over the canyon, and the roads are getting slick."

They had stood shivering with cold for nearly an hour before Hans felt confident the storm had passed, allowing them to safely continue the ride home.

Since that time, Margot had become increasingly worried about driving the motorcycles, especially on the freeway, and she insisted that Hans bring one of his sports models instead. The cars brought back memories of her care-free youth tooling around in the MGs and Triumphs belonging to her various boyfriends.

Remembering her current problems with the conservator court, she longed for those days and poured herself another spot of gin.

CHAPTER FOURTEEN

The next morning, life did not appear quite as grim. Margot sipped a cup of strong *Peet's* coffee and read the paper while waiting for Nancy, Jane, and Barbara, a group she jokingly called her own gang of four. It had taken considerable arm-twisting to enlist them as volunteers next door in skilled nursing, and she worried that one wrong word might send them scattering.

They would be under the head nurse, Helga Hasse, whose name conjured up images of a concentration camp matron beating the inmates into submission, but due to the perpetual scowl on her face, the nurses privately referred to her as the Austin Powers character, *Frau Farbissiner.*

Margot answered the loud knock on the door to find only Nancy and Jane.

"Where's Barbara? Did she chicken out?"

A small voice emanated from behind the two tall women. "She most certainly did not chicken out."

"Whoops, sorry. I didn't see you behind those two amazons."

"You're not exactly tiny yourself," Jane said.

Nancy said, "At least with three of us around, nobody can pick on Barbara—except for Helga."

Barbara retreated a few steps. "Helga? She worries me the most. On the way here, we discussed whether we can put up with her rules for this and her rules for that."

Bending on one knee, Margot pleaded. "Please, please, girl-friends, I'm begging you; do this for my sake. The petition filed by my relatives says I'm incompetent. I need the volunteer hours to show what a solid citizen I am."

"Competent, maybe; a solid citizen would be a gross exaggeration," Jane said.

"I'll ignore that remark. And to say 'thank you,' I prepared a lit-tle surprise in my apartment after the meeting today."

Barbara said, "This will cost you a lot more than one little surprise; you owe us, big time."

⚊⚊

The four women walked across the lawn to skilled nursing where Loretta, the receptionist, greeted them. "So you're the new recruits. I remember you as patients. She pointed them towards the head nurse's office, adding, "I certainly wish you luck."

A few doors down the hall they entered a large, scrupulously neat room with standard office furniture; a swivel chair behind a utilitarian metal desk and three chairs on castors. Grey aluminum mini-blinds covered the large window overlooking the parking lot, blocking the strong morning sun. A wall of book shelves contained medical texts; on an opposite wall hung diplomas from two different Nursing Colleges, one diploma showing a Bachelor's degree, the other a Master's, in nursing.

Margot leaned against the doorjamb, while the others took the three available seats. She said, "Will you get this place—no paper-work in sight, not one vase, no family photos—no evidence, whatso-ever, of human habitation."

Helga arrived and seeing they were missing one chair, she bellowed, "Loretta, bring another chair, fast."

Mr. Norwood, the nursing Director happened by and grimaced before scurrying into his office across the hall without stopping to say 'hello.'

Once the volunteers were seated, Helga said, "As former patients, you know that I'm the head nurse at this facility. I thank you for volunteering. Your duties will involve visiting patients, fluffing pillows, helping them with phone calls, and generally assisting the staff. If you follow the rules, you'll have no problems. Break them and you're out."

"Rules, rules, what did I tell you." Barbara whispered.

Margot said, "Shush—she'll hear you,"

Barbara said, "Nah, she's deaf in one ear and losing it in the other; she won't wear a hearing aid because she's worried the administration will give her the boot."

"What about a boot?" Helga cocked her head.

Everyone stared straight ahead, trying not to laugh.

Helga took a thick manual from her desk. Inside were several pages entitled Volunteer Rules. She handed each woman a copy, which she proceeded to read aloud.

Loud whispers and snide comments followed every rule. From time to time, Helga stopped reading and stared hard. "Quiet down. This is serious business."

Before she could continue, Loretta appeared, announcing an emergency. Helga rushed away, saying, "You're off the hook, but you need to study these rules carefully. There will be a test tomorrow."

"A test? She must be kidding." Barbara made a face and discontented murmurs sounded until Margot quickly ushered the group to her apartment where she held up a cocktail glass. "I bought myself a cute little blender, which I hide in a secret location. Let's order Mexican take-out and wash the food down with Margaritas while we study for our test."

After a few whirs of the blender, Margot proposed a toast, "Here's to following Helga's rules—our way."

Jane fingered through the booklet and read the rule on submitting requests in triplicate. She said, "I don't object to making three copies, but I draw the line at having to kowtow first."

"And not sitting on the patients' beds. Where else would I nap?" Nancy said.

Barbara said, "Did you take a gander at those God-awful scrubs?"

Margot sneered. "I sure did; the material feels cheesy. But tell me daahlings, you were maybe expecting Chanel Scrubs?"

"Seriously, though—the woman is so anal;" Barbara said, "she hasn't omitted one thing. We can't share any personal information. We can't give or accept gifts. It's surprising she didn't give us guidelines for our own regularity."

Nancy said, "Don't fret your purty, little head, honey bun; once we're finger printed and chips are surgically implanted, we'll know the rules automatically; they can track our every movement."

Margot grabbed hold of a sofa pillow and stuffed it in her pants to expand her *derrière*. Imitating Helga, she wagged her finger up and down. "These are the rules—there are no exceptions to the rules. Break the rules and you die."

As Margot continued her performance, the women laughed so hard they fell to the floor and struggled to stand. Jane said, "Help me Margot, I'm like that women in the 'I've fallen and I can't get up' commercial."

Margot yanked Jane to her feet. "Old ladies should know better than to get down on the floor. You could lie there for days before anyone would find you."

Once the Margarita buzz had dissipated, their moods turned somber, and the women repeated their objections to volunteering. Worrying about losing them, Margot said, "Listen, girlfriends, my court hearing is tomorrow; it's crucial I impress the judge. Let's give this volunteering a trial; if we're not happy, we'll chuck the idea."

The women looked uncertain, but agreed.

⋙⋘

The next morning, a disturbing nightmare awakened Margot. She vaguely remembered Gordon scolding her for appearing at the conservator hearing wearing a mini skirt along with black net stockings and stiletto heels; a lace-up blouse with the top laces untied revealed an ample bosom. She had argued saying she knew perfectly well how to dress, having been a fashion maven her entire life.

What a depressing way to begin such an important day, she thought.

She dragged herself to the bathroom and stood before the closet, crowded and inadequate compared with her spacious walk-in closet at home. She had utilized a color-coordinated system to organize the tight space, but, even so, she spent hours frantically searching for clothing eaten by the closet goblin. Days later, the item might mysteriously turn up on the floor or tangled with another garment.

For the hearing, she needed to strike the right note. She considered a red print *Diane Von Furstenburg* wrap dress that caught her eye.

Too busy, too short, too much cleavage. Undoubtedly a *Loehmann's* bargain reduced three times and too cheap to resist.

She shoved the hangers aside for a better view until she found a smart, business-attire, grey silk *Valentino* pantsuit and donned reading glasses to check for cleanliness. Finding a tiny spot, she dropped the garment like an old friend turned traitor.

She rummaged further and hit on a black wool *Armani* that would be perfect with a crisp white, open-collar blouse—for a no-nonsense, schoolmarm effect.

While buttoning the blouse, one loosened and fell to the carpet. She fumbled in her dresser for a sewing kit and struggled with her long nails to thread the needle. Then, after she pulled the thread around the button one last time, she pierced her knee-highs and had to search for a snag-free pair.

From her jewelry box, she selected a silver link bracelet with matching necklace and hoop earrings and a plain wedding band. Last, she chose a classic *Chanel* logo handbag, completing the outfit with sensible low-heeled *Ferragamo* pumps.

She studied herself, hoping the court would see her as a mature and capable woman.

In the small hearing room, Margot eyed Judge Garrote suspiciously. Margot had worried that the judge would appoint The Relatives as interim conservators, following the common, nefarious practice of calling emergency hearings without the person being present and without being interviewed by an investigator.

That didn't happen, but during their last conversation, her attorney had let slip that the Judge reputedly favored plaintiffs petitioning to become conservators. A recent *The LA Times* series was equally disheartening. In reviewing 2,400 cases, they found that more than 500 seniors and dependent adults had been entrusted to for-profit conservators at hearings lasting scant minutes. *The Times* also mentioned that 500 conservators currently were overseeing 4,000 clients and controlling over 1.5 billion dollars in assets.

She shifted uneasily until Hans arrived for moral support along with friends there to testify regarding her competence.

Arriving late, The Relatives evoked titters as both heavy weights tried to enter the narrow doorway at the same time. Immediately, Rudy chided Clarissa, "Watch it; you're in my way." Rudy always had to be first. He could behave politely, though never to his sister.

Margot knew they both supported the popular fat acceptance movements, which financed ads using plus size models proudly posed in the latest extra-large fashions. Lawyers sued to end discrimination against fat people; organizations issued information debunking the myth that fat people were unhealthy and could lose weight if only they tried. They warned against yoyo dieting and weight loss surgeries as the true dangers, maintaining that many fat people exercised rigorously and practiced sound nutrition.

Clarissa habitually concealed her ample body under loose, flowing skirts or caftans. She never exercised, but she wore sweats or warm-ups, until Rudy once barked, "For God's sake, you look like a plumber. I see your crack every time you lean forward."

Since then, she chose tailored slacks, and to hide her bat-wing upper arms, she favored long-sleeved shirts. But this day, a new Clarissa appeared sporting a stylish pantsuit, her newly waved hair, falling softly around her face.

Margot hugged Clarissa warmly. "It's wonderful seeing you. You look great." Given Clarissa's size, Margot immediately regretted using the word great.

"I've been working out at Curves a few times a week; I've already lost a few pounds. Can you tell?"

"You're definitely thinner, and I love your new hairdo."

"I had it cut and styled by your hairdresser, Luigi. He's a genius. I also found a personal shopper at Nordstrom's who helped me select several flattering outfits. They have an excellent plus size department."

Growing flustered, she added in a confidential tone, "I want you to know, I'm not entirely on Rudy's side about this conservator business. I think I sometimes let him influence me too much.

"Lately, I've started keeping things from him. I didn't even tell him how I voted in the last election. Enrolling in a self-esteem workshop helped me a lot."

"Good for you, Clarissa. It's time you stood your ground. Let's sneak away for lunch someday soon, so we can catch up."

Before Clarissa could answer, Judge Garrote wrapped his gavel for quiet.

Hans quietly told Margot, "This judge looks like trouble; he could be a charter member of NAAFA."

"What's the NAAFA?"

"The National Association to Advance Fat Acceptance; maybe he and Rudy belong to the same chapter."

After shuffling through his papers, the judge read aloud the petition for the conservator-ship of Margot's estate and asked Herman Myers, the attorney for The Relatives, to state their case.

Margot whispered to Hans. "Bet their lawyer hasn't missed a meal either."

Attorney Myers said, "My clients, the Sampsons, have bent over backwards, supporting Ms. Manning throughout her recuperation, overseeing her property and handling her affairs. For all the reasons stated in the petition, it is with great sadness that they ask to become conservators of their beloved aunt's estate.

Margot nudged Hans. "Beloved Aunt?"

Attorney Meyers, repeated each and every slander—the motorcycle riding, her accident at the museum, the exercise class fiasco, her delinquency in paying bills, the contribution to African scams, and her failure to notify Shady Palms of her stay at the home of a stranger.

Gordon Jacobs continually voiced objections, resulting in a reprimand to wait his turn. At last he rose to address the judge.

"Your honor, Margot Manning is a fine, upstanding citizen. Several witnesses will attest to her competency and to her countless contributions to the community. But first I want to address the allegations."

He gestured towards Rudy and Clarissa. "Regarding Ms. Manning's bill paying: the Sampsons moved into her home and agreed to forward any bills not paid by her management company. Any unpaid bills are due to their dereliction."

Gordon waved his hand dismissively, "As for the motorcycle riding: Ms. Manning did so for a short time, but realizing the dangers involved, she discontinued the practice."

He glanced at Hans. "And Mr. Jorgensen, the gentleman with whom Ms. Manning is allegedly cavorting, enjoys an excellent reputation in the community as a successful businessman."

"Regarding her alleged failure to notify Shady Palms of her absence overnight: Mr. Jorgensen witnessed her call to the residence informing them she would not be returning on the night she stayed at his home. The fault lies with inaccurate record keeping. If she had *not* notified Shady Palms, they would have reported her as missing. That didn't happen, and on her return, the facility never mentioned her absence. I move that the motivations behind this charge be investigated."

"The mail fraud charge is completely bogus. My client contributes regularly to several African Relief Funds—all legitimate charities. I have canceled checks and acknowledgements as proof. She deserves praise for her generosity, rather than condemnation."

Gordon first called Margot's neighbor, Mirabelle, her neighbor for fifteen years. She and Margot's friend, Rachel, testified as long-term witnesses to her competency before and since her accident.

Nancy and Jane, new friends from Shady Palms friends, spoke glowingly of her intelligence, her organizational skills, her creativity, her empathy for fellow residents, her efforts to organize volunteers in skilled nursing. They described Beauty Day, how successful it had been, how much it improved everyone's morale.

For his final witness, Gordon Jacobs called Margot herself. He had cautioned her to keep her testimony brief and simple.

She chronicled her life before the accident, citing her past community service, her organization of charitable events and finished by saying, "I thank Your Honor for the opportunity of speaking. I am fully capable of handling my own life; I ask nothing more than to return home and continue making contributions to the community."

Judge Garrote listened intently during the entire hearing. At the end, he postponed his decision for another month.

After the judge's ruling, Gordon told Margot he felt optimistic. He said the decision to postpone signified the judge's doubts on the case's merits. He added that his staff would check whether or not the records at Shady Palms did indeed reflect her call saying she would be gone overnight.

Nonetheless, Margot complained that the facts had been distorted to make her appear incompetent, and she expressed disappointment that the judge did not immediately settle the case in her favor.

Sounding hurt, Hans said, "I suppose I'm the gentleman you're allegedly cavorting with. Thanks a lot."

"I'm sorry; they're dredging up anything to disparage me."

"If Diana Kennedy were handling the case, this never would. . . ."

"That makes no sense. How could Diana stop all this muckraking?"

"Anyone would be better than the pompous British lawyer you hired."

"Pompous British lawyer? You're being grossly unfair. He came highly recommended, and he's been extremely diligent."

"Unfair or not, I'm going to discuss your case with Diana and investigate the judge on my own."

CHAPTER FIFTEEN

As a thank-you for their support during the hearing, Margot invited her friends to Kitayama, a restaurant renowned for its sushi, its architecture, and its setting which overlooked Newport Bay. The building, an exotic Zen design, used shoji screens and mats in a composition of line, texture, and the play of light. It included a sushi bar and a tranquil private Japanese tea garden with soft moss, feathery plants, trees, rocks, stone lanterns, and raked sand—an atmosphere reflecting simplicity that allowed the viewer's imagination free reign. The extensive menu featured sushi, sashimi, shabu-shabu, sukiyaki, tempura, and *kobe* steak.

Despite the peaceful surroundings, Margot couldn't help venting about the deliberate misrepresentations made during the hearing.

Mirabelle patted her hand. "Honey don't you pay those fools no mind. The good Lord will make this come out right."

Making a temple with her palms, Margot raised her eyes to the ceiling in mock piety and bowed her head, saying "Thank you, Lord."

That done, she settled down to sipping her miso and delicately tipping the pieces of tofu into her mouth with chopsticks.

Seeing Hans's number listed when her cell chimed, she excused herself and took the call out on the gazebo.

Hans said, "I knew that Judge was crooked. Diana's law firm is positive he's on the take; she says if we find evidence of contributions from your relatives, we may have cause for removal."

Diana again.

"I'm glad you called. I was feeling rocky about the hearing; your news should bode well for my case."

"Diana may have more definitive information soon."

Margot's stomach muscles tightened. "I hope you realize how much I appreciate your help."

"I'm trying to do something constructive after a morning full of lies and innuendos. I nearly lost my cool."

"Don't know what I'd do without you."

"Let's plan something interesting—maybe check out the mummies exhibit at Bowers—lunch on the terrace. What do you say?"

"I'd love to do Bowers, but first I want to grab Clarissa; when I saw her in court, she seemed sympathetic to my cause, so I said I'd call. I want to ask her why Rudy has it in for me."

Hans said, "Good idea; I'm anxious to hear what she has to say."

Margot returned to the table and covered her face with her hands.

"More bad news?" Rachel asked.

"The good *and* bad news is that Hans asked Diana, his young and beautiful neighbor/lawyer to investigate this morning's Judge. Her firm is sure he accepts bribes. Of course this gives Hans a reason to hang around Diana."

"Oh fiddlesticks!" Rachel said, "I know Diana, and you have it way over her."

Everyone nodded and lifted their wine glasses. "We'll drink to that."

Margot held her glass high, but deep down she didn't feel the least bit confident—not with a young, attractive, smarty like Diana in the picture.

Early the next morning, Margot dialed Clarissa. "I've been dying to ask you some questions. Is this a good time or would you rather do lunch?"

"Lunch would be better. I'm free today, if that works for you."

"Can you suggest a place near your offices?"

"We're still in that building across from the Design Center. Have you been to their restaurant?"

"Many times when I used to shop for furniture." Margot bit her lip and thought, furniture for the house *you* now occupy.

"How about twelve-thirty?" Clarissa said.

"It's a date."

≒╪ ╪≒

At twelve-thirty sharp, Margot seated herself on the café patio and looked around. Noting the several vacant showrooms, she sighed, wondering how long before the economy would improve.

She browsed the menu which featured two favorites; tortilla soup and tarragon chicken salad with pecans, as a soup and salad combo.

Clarissa arrived, breathless from rushing, and plopped into a chair. "Sorry I'm late, but we're swamped. So many clients are asking for help with loan modifications."

"That should be good for your bottom line."

"We're barely staying in business."

Now that's a piece of information, I hadn't expected, she thought.

Margot handed Clarissa a menu. "I'm having the soup and salad combo with iced tea."

"Sounds good." Clarissa ordered for them both and turned to Margot. "You mentioned having questions for me."

"I'll be blunt. My relationship with Rudy hasn't always gone smoothly, but I can't figure out why he's petitioning to become my conservator. That's downright mean, and I don't deserve it."

Clarissa hung her head. "I usually side with my brother, but I'm mortified by his actions on this one."

"So why *is* he doing this to me?"

"Bottom line; he's desperate for money."

"He can't be desperate for money; you've always had a booming real estate business."

"We did until the economic crisis of '08."

"But that happened almost four years ago."

"We're still hurting from all those sub-prime mortgages the banks made. The government bank bail-outs were supposed to fix the problems, but people are still upside down on their loans, and foreclosures are happening right and left."

Clarissa continued, "Even with the bail-out money, Wall Street and the banks are holding tight and not investing in loans; it's almost impossible to get funds."

"Why?"

"They're worried about forthcoming regulations."

Margot's eyes widened. "I think I get it now; Rudy wants control of my assets to save his business."

Clarissa's silence spoke the answer.

"What a dastardly thing to do. If he needed money that badly, he could have asked me for a loan."

"A loan won't do it; we need a large infusion of capital."

Margot felt sick; she pushed her plate away, paid the check and stood to leave. "I still like you, Clarissa, but this is too much."

As soon as Margot reached her car, she dialed Hans and in a voice filled with cold fury, she told him what Clarissa had said.

"So Rudy wants the money from your estate to save his own neck—why that dirty, rotten guy."

"Yup."

"I can't believe this; we have to stop him. I'm going to hang up and call Diana."

"Wait," she said. "Don't do that. I need to talk to my own lawyer first."

CHAPTER SIXTEEN

Gordon's reaction to Margot's news surprised her. She had advocated approaching the judge and telling him about Rudy's financial difficulties as the motive behind his petition to become her conservator. Gordon had cautioned her to hold back; he argued that they had no way of knowing if Clarissa would corroborate the story and bringing the matter to light could alienate her niece against Margot. Clarissa not only lived with Rudy, but the pair ran the real estate company together.

Gordon suggested, "Let's sit on this for now; Clarissa might be useful in the future as a source of additional information. "

When Margot repeated the conversation to Hans, he said. "Your lawyer does make some cogent arguments against jumping in with Clarissa's story. I think you should wait and decide after we hear back from Diana about whether or not the judge *is* receiving paybacks from your relatives."

"I guess you're right, but I'm disappointed; I thought we had the goods on them."

"I know how you feel; I've always been a man of action."

He paused. "My suggestion about visiting Bowers Museum still stands. Why don't we go tomorrow—take your mind off your troubles."

"I guess we could. What time?'

"The museum opens at eleven so pick you up at ten-thirty?

"I'll be ready and thanks for being there for me."

≈⊹ ⊹≈

A visit to Bowers offered a return to the early days of California, with its Spanish Mission-style architecture; bright, white buildings, red tile roofs, a courtyard and a bell tower. The next morning, Hans and Margot strolled alongside the garden, enjoying its many bougainvillea plantings among the palms and the cacti.

Since its opening in1936, Bowers had held world-class art exhibitions displaying artifacts and buildings from throughout the globe. The current exhibit Mummies: death and the after-life in Ancient Egypt, offered an intimate look into mummification; it had been drawn from the largest collection of mummies and funerary objects to ever leave the British Museum.

Margot and Hans spent three hours viewing centuries-old corpses and tomb artifacts created to accompany the dead in the next world: jewelry, jars, shabti sculptures, busts and figurines, a five-ton sarcophagus lid, even a boat. Every object had been scrupulously labeled; scholarly didactic texts explained the seven thematic sections.

Margo sighed. "I'd love to tour Egypt again, but with the revolution and the ouster of Mubarak, who knows what will happen to the country. I just hope they don't break into the Cairo Museum again.

"What a dingy and poorly lit building! I could barely see the objects, and many of the labels were either missing or falling off. I hear the museum's first rate since it's been refurbished."

Hans said, "I saw the Tut exhibit three or four times when it came to LA."

"That was a mere fraction of the 120,000 artifacts at the Egyptian Museum. And there's so much more to see in Egypt: the Pyramids, Aswan, the tombs of lower Egypt, Abu Simbel."

"When it's safe, I want to visit Alexandria too. It gives me goose bumps to think that they resurrected the Ancient Library after almost 2,000 years. Let's go together once my court mess and the Egypt mess straightens out."

"We'll do it."

For lunch at *Tangata,* the museum restaurant, Hans ordered Duck Two Ways- crispy duck steak in a sour cherry sauce, duck confit ravioli, and Savoy cabbage.

"That sounds delicious," Margot said. "But it's probably fattening." She settled for a low-calorie fire-grilled chicken breast with almond caper salsa and balsamic cippolini onions, substituting mashed potatoes for the roasted vegetables.

Hans laughed. "You're having grilled chicken to save calories, then you go ahead and order mashed potatoes?"

"Stop making fun of me. One day, I'm going to dive into a huge bowl of luscious, creamy, garlicky mashed potatoes for my main course and skip the rest."

After the entrees, Margot's mouth watered at the dessert menu. "I suppose now you're going to gorge yourself on a decadent dessert?"

"I'm ordering the triple chocolate threat; it has milk chocolate mousse, covered by a dark chocolate mirror and a malted milk chocolate sauce; I'm confident you'll help."

"You *would* do that to me."

Savoring spoon after spoon of the rich chocolate, she said. "In my next life, I'm coming back as a tall, slender Danish man with a high metabolic rate."

"To me, you are a goddess."

"That's a compliment? Weren't Greek and Roman goddesses rather *zaftig*?"

"*Kom nu,* you're not fat; you're pleasingly round in all the right places."

The day had been the perfect antidote for yesterday's humiliating court hearing until Hans broke the mood, saying, "You know the faster we settle your case, the sooner we can make a trip to Egypt. Hiring Diana's firm gives us a much better chance. They have the expertise."

Through gritted teeth she said, "Hold up Hans. Just yesterday you agreed with Gordon's suggestions; you even said we should wait to see what Diana's firm digs up on Judge Garrote. So don't pressure me."

CHAPTER SEVENTEEN

Orientation the following day provided a welcome distraction from Margot's problems. Having forgotten her previously threatened test, Helga introduced the staff.

Three rows ahead, Margot spotted a burly man with a shaved head and a small diamond earring in his left ear; he turned, exposing a darkly, handsome face, a roguish smile, and gleaming white teeth. His eyes twinkled merrily as he bowed his head. "*Bienvenidas bellas muchachas,* welcome beautiful women. I am Ernesto at your service." Helga glared at him before continuing.

After the head nurse suggested the group get acquainted, Margot introduced herself and rattled off a greeting in Spanish. In a high-pitched, girlish voice, she fluttered her hands. "Please forgive my terrible Spanish; I have a fairly decent vocabulary, but I get nervous when I talk, and my pronunciation screams *gringa*. If you help improve my accent, I'll be your best friend."

He laughed. "Anything for a *guapa*, beautiful woman, like you."

Margot noticed that the nurses flocked to Ernesto. Helga's body language, on the other hand, screamed antipathy for him.

At lunch, Margot sought out Betty, a garrulous blonde nurse, to ask about Ernesto.

"We love having him around; he makes us feel attractive and sexy. But Helga hates Latinos—especially Ernesto. She's positive he's a former gang member."

"And is he?"

"We don't know much about him; Ernesto talks a lot and makes jokes, but he keeps his personal life to himself. A good-looking stud like him must have a voluptuous *muchacha* tucked away; if so, she certainly doesn't interfere with his flirting."

Betty finished by saying, "Anyway, Ernesto's days here are numbered; Helga forces out anyone who gives her trouble, and Ernesto is high on that list."

⇥⇤

The first day on the job, the volunteers fluffed pillows, poured water, and delivered flowers. They searched for the latest magazines, read to the patients, and tracked down nurses. Obeying Helga's strict rules, the volunteers dared not sit on the beds or discuss politics. Nevertheless they found it impossible not to trade personal information or listen to jokes from patients like Joe Dally, nicknamed Joe the Jokester for his large store of 'knock-knock jokes.'

When Margot entered his room where Joe sat playing solitaire, he stood up to shake hands. "Aha, a new victim," he said, with relish, "Want to play Knock, Knock?"

"It's been a while, but I'll bite; who's there?"

"Leena."

"Leena who?"

He bent to kiss the top of her head. "Leena little closer, honey, and I'll tell you."

Margot grinned. "Got one for *you* now—Knock, Knock."

"Who's there?"

"Abby."

"Abby who?'

She sang, "Abby birthday to you. I heard you turned seventy this week."

"Not bad for an amateur."

"You're not bad yourself for an old guy. How come your hair's still brown? Have you been hitting the bottle?

"Good genes. You seem like someone I'd enjoy schmoozing with."

"Sorry, can't stay—It's my first day—*must* make a good impression. Catch you another time."

Joe pouted. "All right for you but don't disappoint me."

In making the rounds for the rest of the day, Margot decided that volunteering might be a pleasant experience, after all. Still, she sensed a negative current following in Helga's wake; even the patients seemed to grow agitated when Helga entered a room. She made a mental note to poke around a little—maybe ask Sharon, one of her favorite nurses during the time Margot had been a patient in skilled nursing. Sharon had said that she car-pooled with Helga and that they had become good friends.

Seeing Sharon signing in for the afternoon shift, Margot asked her to lunch, and they made a date for 11:30 the following day at *California Pizza Kitchen* in the nearby Laguna Hills Mall.

Before keeping the appointment, Margot browsed at a men's fashion store looking for a present for Hans. Sorting through a large selection of *Aspinal* leather goods, she chose a tri-fold wallet, the style of wallet Hans carried, and had it gift wrapped. Why a man as fastidious as Hans persisted in using a beat-up old wallet remained a mystery.

She hoped that Diana, his lawyer/neighbor, would disappear from the scene once she delivered the information about whether the conservator judge was on the take from The Relatives. In the meantime, Margot planned to shower Hans with gifts and attention.

At *California Pizza Kitchen,* Sharon was already perusing the menu. She laughed and pointed to the salad listings. "I see that the Original Chopped Salad is listed as gluten-free—this year's latest dietary fad."

"A nutritionist once told me that for a gluten-free diet to be beneficial, *all* foods containing the gluten protein should be eliminated," Margot said. "She claimed that eating just one gluten-free meal is a total waste of time."

Both women decided that the chopped salad, beneficial or not, with a cup of artichoke and broccoli soup would make a delicious lunch. While waiting for their orders, Sharon filled her in on the recent happenings at skilled nursing.

Before Margot could raise the subject of Helga's negative behavior, Sharon startled her, saying, "I'm glad we're getting together for lunch before I leave next week."

"You're leaving?"

"We're moving to North Dakota."

"Why North Dakota—of all places?"

"My husband's been unemployed for a year; the oil shale industry's booming there and they have a shortage of workers for all kinds of jobs.

"Finding a nursing position should be a snap; what type of work is your husband looking for?"

"He's in construction; the building industry in California sucks, to put it mildly."

"I'm happy for you, but not for us. How did Helga take the news? You two seem to be good buddies."

"I told her at lunch one day, and she actually broke down and cried."

"Helga cried? She doesn't seem like the type."

"She's a lot more sensitive than you think; she told me a long story about her lonely childhood. Apparently, the other kids used to make fun of her for being so big and clumsy. She finally made a friend, but after six months, the girl moved away."

Margot took a bite of salad. "So she feels like you're deserting her too?"

"That on top of her husband taking off on her six months ago."

"I didn't even know Helga was married."

"Yes, for a few years."

"Did they divorce?"

"Apparently, he bought a boat—a forty-foot Bayfield Cutter Ketch that he moored in Dana Point; Helga used to complain that he spent all his time scraping, sanding, painting, and staining the damn thing."

Margot nodded. "According to my friends who own boats, it's not as glamorous as people think; it's supposedly ninety-percent hard work and ten percent pleasure."

"I suspect the boat gave him an excuse to get away from home. I like the woman, but we both know how bossy Helga can be."

"For sure."

"The boat was rigged for solo sailing—had a bunk, a kitchen, a head, a shower—all the amenities. And one day Helga found a note saying he was leaving on a trip."

"Did he mention when he'd be back?"

"Apparently not."

"I wanted to ask if you knew why Helga had been acting more mean than usual, but I think you've given me the answer."

"Seems so," Sharon said.

⇒⊹ ⊹⇐

After the two women hugged and made their final goodbyes, Margot was feeling down. Knowing who could cheer her up, she stopped by Joe's room and found him reading *Penthouse*. "Why you whipper-snapper, she said. "I see you're still into 'racy' magazines. Are those what keep you looking youthful and unwrinkled?"

Joe laughed. "I bet you don't know what I did in my younger days."

Margot shook her head. "I can't even guess."

"You're looking at a former management trainee for *Playboy Clubs*. We used to party at Heff's place every week."

"The Chicago mansion on State Street?"

"Yup, those were the days. They would set out buckets of *Kentucky Fried Chicken*—a novelty in those times—along with booze galore. We would stand on the bottom floor, below the two-level indoor pool, to watch what the swimmers were up to."

"This another joke?"

"Honest, it's the truth. I had a great job there, inspecting the Bunnies' tails to make sure they were on straight."

"And you called that work?"

"I toiled mightily"

"I could weep for you."

From then on Joe's room became a favorite stop to hear him describe his stay at *Playboy*. One day he told her, "They spotted me right off as an outgoing guy, so they set me up emceeing shows and announcing celebrities who visited the club. The local gangsters hung out there; we used phony names for them: Mickey Mouse, Bugs Bunny, Donald Duck."

During one visit Margot asked Joe, "Did you make *Playboy* your career?"

"Are you kidding? I worked into the wee hours of the morning, on an erratic schedule—ten, twelve days straight without a break. The wife rebelled and made me quit; I took a job as a head-hunter while I attended law school at night. The wife divorced me anyway—too many lonely nights; she ditched me for some 9 to 5 nerd."

"I suspect you deserved it."

"Her loss; my *Playboy* experience definitely helped my practice though; I became a successful entertainment attorney. Ready for another knock, knock?"

"Save it. Helga will be wondering where I am."

"She might even fire you—if you're lucky."

———

Only a week after that conversation with Joe, Margot found the skilled nursing staff standing in small groups, talking. A tangible pall hung over them.

She tapped Ginger on the shoulder. "Why is everyone upset?"

"Joe, the guy who loved knock-knock jokes, died last night."

Margot covered her mouth. "Not Joe? I'm shocked."

"He suffered from Brittle diabetes; it can be very serious."

"I never heard of Brittle diabetes."

"People with the disease often experience large swings in blood sugar levels."

"Couldn't they give him meds to control it?"

"They tried, but. . . ." Ginger shrugged.

Margot dabbed at her eyes. "I still can't believe it. Just a few days ago, he cornered me with another silly knock-knock. I told him I had patients to see, and he said, 'Screw that; make an old man happy; it'll only take thirty seconds.'

"And what did I do? I left him flat to obey Helga's commands."

Ginger put her arm around Margot's shoulders. "It's tough; I know."

Margot twisted one of her curls. "Did they remove his body yet?"

"The Coroner's office took him away early this morning. Since you're here, will you help me box up his belongings?"

Margot followed Ginger to Joe's room where they began removing clothing from the closet. Among the garments, she found an old sweater. "Can you believe this, an argyle cardigan, probably from the year one? I bet we find matching socks."

From under the empty bed, Margot fished out a pile of girlie magazines, along with an anthology of classic knock-knocks. "So that's where he stashed his treasures."

Ginger bent to rummage through the bedside table and removed Joe's personal items; reading glasses, a comb, keys, a wallet. She ran her hand along the drawer to ensure she hadn't missed anything. Tucked back in the corner, she hit on a small hard object which turned out to be a silver hip flask, and held it up. "What have we here?"

She unscrewed the top, sniffed and frowned. "Why the old tippler; alcohol is a definite no-no for diabetics." Ginger handed Margot the flask. "Can you tell what kind of alcohol was in here?"

Margot sniffed a few times and added the flask to the small pile. "Beats me; I wonder who smuggled in alcohol for him?"

Once they finished packing up, Margot said, with sadness, "So this is all that's left of Joe, the Jokester."

She stood staring into space until Ginger asked, "What's wrong?"

"It's just that Joe's death doesn't add up."

Ginger said, "I'm sure the alcohol helped him out of this world."

"Someone mentioned that Joe had a daughter; do you know if she lives around here?" Margot asked.

"Doris. I think she lives nearby. Why?"

"Just wondering . . . "

CHAPTER EIGHTEEN

Later Hans phoned, saying he had tried her earlier.
"Cell's off when I'm volunteering."

"You sound upset."

"One of my favorite patients, Joe the Jokester, died suddenly."

"Joe the Jokester?"

"We nicknamed him that because he loved knock-knock jokes."

"Sorry to hear he passed away."

"He just turned seventy—a young seventy, but he did suffer from diabetes."

"Diabetes can be serious."

"There's more to it; when we were packing up his belongings, we found a hip flask that smelled of alcohol and . . . ."

"Sounds like a matter for the Coroner."

"I agree, but I want to contact his daughter first."

"Why would you do that?"

"I just want to ask a few questions."

"Remember the trouble you got into—the time you took over exercise class?"

"This is different."

"Have it your way," Hans said. "You always do."

"Thanks a lot."

"The main reason I called is that Diana's firm has information for us on Judge Garrote. If you're free tonight, I'd like to come over and discuss it."

"I'm here."

Uh-oh, Diana again; I need ammunition.

Margot rushed to the closet to find a smashing outfit and immediately rejected an alluring black silk ensemble as inappropriate for a casual get-together. She searched until she hit on a cozy fleece set that showed off her long legs; the jacket unzipped to reveal however much cleavage she wanted. To that, she added a stylish *Natori* shawl.

While waiting for Hans to arrive, she checked her email and found a message from Jim with his flight information; he added how much he looked forward to his visit.

"I'll show Hans," she muttered.

Thirty minutes later she admitted Hans, who gave her a fierce hug. "You feel deliciously soft and warm tonight. Why do we say things that drive us apart?"

"Not my fault; I'm always the epitome of calm and reason."

Hans opened his mouth to reply and quickly shut it. He settled on the sofa, while Margot brought a tray of green apple Martinis.

"So, what did you find out?"

"A lot; Diana's firm has dealt with Judge Garrote many times. There's no direct evidence that he accepts bribes, but he does receive campaign contributions from people who come before his court, and your relatives are among the heaviest donors."

"Why am I not surprised?"

"Diana thinks we should ask for a new judge on the basis of prejudice." Hans removed a document from his brief case. "I'm impressed by the way she laid out a comprehensive legal approach.

When you study this proposal, I'm sure you'll be convinced to switch to her firm."

She bit her lip and set the document on the coffee table. "I'll need to show it to my lawyer."

"We can go over it together first."

"Right now let's enjoy the evening." Margot snuggled close, embedding his face in her fluffy, warm wrap and took away his drink, kissing him long and hard. Then she led him to the bedroom where they made love.

As they lay side by side, talking lazily, he propped himself up on one elbow. "Have you ever considered moving out of here?"

"Of course, but . . . ."

"That way I could visit you any time without all those nosy-parkers in the lobby watching my every move. I could even stay overnight. What do you say?"

"The idea's tempting, but I'm worried that moving out might damage my case with the conservator court. Right now, Shady Palms is my chaperone, though why a woman my age needs chaperoning is beyond me"

"The situation is preposterous"

Margot checked the time. "Preposterous or not, it's almost four a.m. You'd better leave before the 'lobby-sitters' resume their posts downstairs." She added, "Maybe I'll get lucky, and my case will resolve itself soon."

Hans pulled on his shirt. "It's not luck; success hinges on competent legal representation. Take my advice. Change law firms."

"Stop badgering me. And as for Diana, I still don't understand why you two had lunch without including me. This is my case, not yours.

"Are you harping on that again? What did I do wrong?"

"I already explained that you should have invited me along."

"I live near Diana. We run into each other occasionally, and we had lunch on the spur of the moment. Do I need your permission for everything?"

"Spur of the moment, yah, right."

"Grow up, will you?"

"Don't tell me to grow up."

They glared at each other until Hans picked up his clothes and headed for the bathroom. On his way out, he paused. "Earlier, didn't you describe yourself as the epitome of calm and reason?"

He left slamming the door behind him.

Margot broke into tears. The Relatives are bribing the Judge, and I'm driving Hans into Diana's arms.

—+ +—

In the morning, Margot brightened at Jim's voice on the phone, saying, "Hi, just checking in."

"Glad you called; I've been wondering where you'll be staying."

"I thought maybe I could bunk at your place?"

"Uh, my place? I'm not equipped for guests."

"I don't take up much room these days—ever since I went on Jenny Craig."

Margot laughed. "You haven't changed one iota. I can suggest a few places. Want something simple or something luxurious?"

"Something simply luxurious."

"Joking aside, *The Montage* hotel fits the bill—it's simple but luxurious.

"It's built in early 20th century craftsman style; If I remember correctly, you've always been interested in architecture."

"Still am."

"And it's right on the beach."

"Must be pricey if it's on the beach."

"Prices *are* a little steep, though compared with the tariffs back east, you may not find them too bad."

"You're paying, I assume?"

"I'm ignoring that. They offer bungalows, suites, or guest rooms. You tell me."

"A guest room, if I'm paying; that way I'll have more money to spend on you."

"Good decision; you'll love it. The hotel's close to downtown Laguna which is loaded with art galleries and good restaurants. If you want theatre, there's a playhouse, and the Performing Arts Center is only twenty minutes away."

"All those perks and seeing you too. How lucky can I get?"

"I'm even willing to come fetch you."

"Are you going to carry a sign with my name in big bold letters?"

"In real gold leaf."

They chatted a few minutes more before hanging up.

It would be fun showing Jim the sights; maybe they'd even dine at the hotel's posh restaurant, *The Studio.*

Jim had restored her good humor, but her excitement over seeing him abruptly turned to worry. She counted the years since they last met.

Would he be disappointed? Would she?

⇥⇤

Late afternoon, the receptionist rang to say that Margot had a floral delivery. Would she pick up the flowers or should they deliver them to her apartment?

Anxious to show off her bouquet to the lobby sitters, she said, "Be right down."

Were they from Hans, atoning for the argument, or from Jim, courting her in advance? Margot hurried downstairs, and once at the desk, she tore open the box. She gasped and held up the vase for everyone to see. Sniffing the bouquet, she declared loudly, "Casablanca lilies—my favorites. What a heavenly smell. I can't imagine who would splurge on these gorgeous blooms for me?"

The receptionist grinned. "Must be from your handsome boyfriend; if you ever tire of him, toss him my way, would yuh?"

Margot searched the floral papers and found a note from Hans that read:

Dear Margot,

Sorry we argued. Let's do dinner tonight and kiss and make up. Or we could forget the dinner part and . . . .

Seriously, there's a new dine and dance place where we can practice dipping. Remember how? Put on a sexy dress and bring a change of clothing because I'm not going to let you run off at the stroke of midnight.

Margot certainly remembered dipping. In her youth, how far down you dipped might indicate the way the evening would turn out. Nowadays, young couples didn't even dance close; they often spent the night together without giving it any thought.

Just then, Nancy and Jane walked into the lobby, dragging their art supplies behind them in carts. Eyeing the flowers, Nancy asked, "What have we here?"

"They're from Hans."

She shot Margot a wicked smile. "And what did you do to deserve those?"

Ignoring the question, Margot said. "You both look disgustingly bronzed and healthy; I take it you enjoyed the workshop in Coronado."

"It went great," Jane said. "We painted every morning and spent the afternoons swimming and sailing."

"You're trying to make me jealous, but I'm not because Hans is taking me dining and dancing tonight." Margot thumbed her nose. "So there."

"Not bad, sweet pea," Nancy said.

Jane bent to sniff the petals. "Not bad at all."

That evening at Harry's, they enjoyed a delicious dinner and danced to '50's music played by a small combo. Hans moved smoothly, holding her tight; he laughed as he dipped her practically to the floor.

Once at his house, she notified Shady Palms that she would be away overnight, carefully noting the receptionist's name in case anyone claimed she hadn't checked in.

They did kiss and make up. But the next morning, over coffee, Hans said, "It's time we had a heart-to heart. Willing to hear me out?"

"Go ahead."

He kissed her hand. "I know you've been through a lot, but I've been suffering too. I worried sick about you after the accident; then, I not only had to put up with your relatives treating me discourteously, but their lawyer insulted me at the hearing."

"I'm truly sorry your feelings were hurt."

Hans continued, "And the old-folks home where you live. . . . I have to sneak off like a criminal if I stay one minute past ten o'clock."

Margot gulped. "Again, I'm sorry, but I'm not ready to make a change."

"And speaking of changes, I think you should give Diana's firm a try."

Diana again.

"I know I acted thoughtlessly, meeting her without you. But please don't let my mistake keep you from obtaining the help you need. Diana is one sharp lawyer."

Margot forced a smile; inwardly she winced. "I already said, I'd give her firm some thought."

"That's all I ask; I only hope you won't take too long; I'm anxious to get this conservator business over with."

"We've had our heart-to heart, now do I get breakfast? I'm starving."

"You most certainly do, and we're taking a field trip."

"With binoculars, and pith helmets, and mosquito netting?"

"Such an imagination the lady has."

Hans drove up the coast and parked at a beachside lot where they boarded a shuttle down to Crystal Cove State Park with its newly renovated beach cottages, recently opened for rental.

After breakfasting on beignets and macadamia nut pancakes at the Beachcomber restaurant, they took the morning tour of the twelve-acre historic district, dating from the 1920s. Of the original forty-six cottages, thirteen had been renovated; funds from the restaurant were being channeled into further restoration.

Besides the guests who stayed in the cottages, families had camped on the beach in tents or cabanas where they held *tiki* parties and luaus. Some cottages had even served as movie sets for silent films, and rum runners once used the area as a drop-off spot.

"Let's reserve a cottage for a long weekend." Hans suggested.

"I'd love it."

They spent the rest of the day walking in the sand and sitting on the beach, discussing their favorite subject—books.

Margot no longer wanted to make Hans jealous. Worrying that Hans would find out, she regretted her exchange of flirtatious emails with Jim and his coming visit.

CHAPTER NINETEEN

Preparations for Jim's visit began long before his scheduled arrival. Margot camped out at her favorite day spa for the works: a full body salt scrub to produce baby-soft skin; an herbal moisturizing facial that left her cheeks rosy and her face glowing; a relaxing Swedish massage; a pedicure; a new set of nails. Margot had scheduled a few days off from volunteering, and she felt good to go.

On the appointed day, she donned her most slenderizing pantsuit and headed for the airport. She smiled, remembering Jim's last email.

Dear Margot,

I'm sending a recent photo, so you won't be shocked when we meet. An integral part of me is missing—namely my hair. Yes, it's all gone; I don't know where it went. I woke up bald one morning, and that's who I am now. I'm not thrilled, but it's better than waking up and finding I've turned into a gigantic insect. Hope you think I look okay. Can you also spare a photo, or should I wait to be surprised?

Love, Jim

Margot chuckled at Jim's reference to Kafka's, *The Metamorphosis*, the story where Gregor Samsa wakes to find himself transformed into a cockroach. Jim's self-deprecating humor, peppered with literary references, had endeared him to her when they were dating. She replied in the same joking manner.

Dear Jim,

It's lucky I recognize your smile; otherwise I might have thought Yul Brynner was coming to visit. Since I always considered him a sexy devil, I know I will adore the new you.

Love, Margot

After pulling into the parking structure at the airport, Margot made her way to the baggage carousel. She searched for Jim and noted that several men waiting for their luggage were bald or had shaved their heads. Most wore jeans or casual attire along with the usual disappointing array of baggy shorts and flip-flops.

Dress for airplane travel certainly had changed for the worse. During her long ago European honeymoon, she had spent every day wearing dresses and trussed up in a tight girdle, along with stockings and heels, to traipse through cathedrals and museums.

The information board showed the plane had already landed, and within minutes, a jean-clad man stopped beside her. Smiling broadly, he doffed his fedora hat to reveal a totally bald pate.

"Hi Margot, It's me, Jim. What a handsome woman you've become."

She frowned. Handsome? Become?

"You're pretty snazzy yourself. I can't believe you recognized me."

He reached into a tote bag and retrieved a page of computer-generated photos featuring Margot at various charity events. "Cheat sheets."

She slapped his hand. "You devil."

Jim rocked her in his arms. "But I would have known you anywhere."

"Liar."

They retrieved his luggage and rolled it to the parking garage. Catching a glimpse of her Mercedes convertible, he whistled. "Sharp car."

"Glad you approve; want a ride?"

On the drive along the scenic coastal route, Jim admired the abundant, lush foliage everywhere: the vibrant fuchsia bougainvillea, interspersed with the yellow gazania ground cover, running down the slopes.

He sniffed the air. "What's that pungent fragrance?"

"Oleander; the blossoms are red, pink, yellow, salmon, white; they thrive in this hot, dry climate. Just don't go chewing on them; every single part of the oleander is poisonous."

Jim chuckled. "Like women I've known."

"You're a cynical man."

"These sandy beaches against the mountain backdrop are spectacular. Are you sure this isn't a fake movie set?"

"You're welcome to get out and touch," Margot said.

"I bet I could ski and swim on the same day; I'm speechless, after the miserable, freezing weather I left behind."

"You speechless? That'll never happen. If you're impressed by this, wait until you see your ocean front room; it even includes a concierge to fulfill your every wish."

Once Jim checked in, they followed the bellhop to his room where he removed his hat and plopped on the bed, "Man oh man, I call this living. I can order a beer on the patio and watch the waves or ogle the bathing beauties fifty feet to my right."

"The hotel will drive you down to the beach with your very own towel and umbrella, if you desire. Should you prefer golf, there's a course across the way."

"Right now, I need food; I'm ravenous. I forgot to pick up take-out before the flight and the junk the airline had for sale. . . ."

"Feeding you is first on our agenda." They linked arms and strolled over to *Mosaic*, the poolside restaurant. While waiting for lunch, they caught up on the important events that had occurred over the years.

Margot enjoyed laughing and flirting like old times until Jim said. "I'm anxious to see where you live, meet your friends, maybe crash some parties. Can we do that?"

She drummed her fingers on the table nervously. "There's a lot to tell you first."

"Sounds mysterious."

"Not at all." She stood up. "Right now I have errands to run. I'll leave you to unpack, relax—maybe catch a snooze, adjust to the time change."

"I am a little drowsy; I'd love you to sit by me until I fall asleep?"

"Sorry, no can do. I'll be back here at five for dinner."

This is going to be dicey, she thought.

Despite having the spa works the week before, Margot had no intention of cheating on Hans. Aware of the admiring glances he received wherever they went, she had decided that if Hans remained faithful, she would do the same.

Still, having a new admirer. . .

On the way to the parking garage, Margot sat on the bluff relishing the ocean breezes and the natural seaside plantings. On her right, Catalina stood out in the brilliant sunshine; on her left the rugged coastline edged in and out down to Dana Point, the city named for Richard Dana, Jr., author of *TwoYears Before The Mast.*

Her cell rang and hearing Hans's voice made her jump as though she had been caught misbehaving.

"Margot, how are you? I haven't heard from you today."

"I sat down to call you this very minute; I've been busy."

Busy hanging out with my old boyfriend.

"I'm calling about my plans for the coming week," Hans said.

What do I do now?

"I'm leaving for D.C. tomorrow; I'm thinking of selling my old condo there."

Perfect timing.

"I thought you had a good tenant—a reliable government guy."

"I did, but he gave notice this week. He's sick of commuting between D.C. and Arizona; I can't hack the process of finding another tenant."

"How long will you be gone?"

"For a few days—maybe even a week."

"This is important; better not rush it."

"The thing is, I hate leaving you stranded while you're dealing with your conservator problems."

"Don't feel bad; I'll use the time for researching my case."

"I'd like to get together before I go. Are you game for an early dinner tonight?"

"Sorry sweetie; I'm not feeling great today. I may order something light sent to my room and curl up with a book."

"Hope it's nothing serious."

"I think my body's saying I've been running around too much."

"Be sure you get plenty of rest. I want you in tip-top shape when I return. I'll check up on how you're doing?"

"Have a safe trip."

Phew, that was close.

⟞⟝

Late that afternoon, she found Jim in his room looking red-faced and bleary-eyed.

"What's wrong?"

"I don't know, but suddenly I feel beat."

"It's the time change; you've been up since dawn. That's why I suggested a nap."

Jim reached for her hand, "You are my guru; I followed your every command and relaxed on the patio with a few drinks to enjoy the gorgeous sunset."

"Want to order in or go out?"

"Out—if there's a place close by for a bite?"

"*La Sirena Grille,* right across the highway, has delicious tortilla soup and an avocado lime salad to die for."

Jim pointed to his shorts and tee shirt. "Dressed this way?"

"This is the beach; anything goes."

At the crosswalk, they waited for the long red light to change and scrambled across PCH, barely avoiding the oncoming rush hour traffic. Jim held up his hand and shouted, "For crying out loud. Give us a chance, will you."

"Traffic is king around here. If you don't move fast, you're toast."

In the small restaurant, they studied the blackboard menu, and Margot said, "Everything is fresh and healthy, with a spicy edge."

Jim squeezed her arm. "I dig spicy; that's why I like you."

"Okay, but don't say I didn't warn you. I'm having the blackened shrimp tacos and sweet corn soup. Want to try the tortilla soup and the salad I mentioned?"

"Sure, why not? Plus a Margarita."

The waiter brought the drinks to their patio table, and Jim slurped his down.

"Guess you didn't enjoy that."

"Me approve; me ordering another."

By the time the tacos came, Jim had downed his third Margarita and was loudly proclaiming that the restaurant served the best damn Mexican food he had ever eaten.

"How many drinks did you imbibe before I arrived?"

"A few beers—uh, plus the complimentary champagne in my room."

"Please don't tell me you drank the whole bottle."

Jim hung his head.

Margot grimaced and paid the tab. She pulled Jim all the way across the busy highway, through the long arcade and crowded lobby, into the elevator and over to his room, where he flopped on the bed; immediately he began snoring. She removed his shoes and sat fanning herself while she caught her breath.

Leaving a note to call her in the morning, she tiptoed out and collapsed into a patio chair.

No wrestling Jim tonight.

CHAPTER TWENTY

The next morning, Jim awakened Margot at six a.m. declaring himself ready for sightseeing and demanding, "When are you picking me up, anyway?"

"You're nervy calling this early, all bright and cheery and expecting me to pop right over there."

"Sorry, I'm on East Coast time; I've been up since four."

"That's because you passed out at eight last night."

"Sorry."

"I had a devilish time hauling you back last night."

"A thousand pardons. That should cover any past and future sins."

"Not accepted."

Jim asked, "Want breakfast together?"

"It's way early to even think of food. Be outside your hotel at ten. You said you like exploring historic places, so we're touring *The San Juan Capistrano adobe Mission.*"

"Why are you being good to me?"

"Don't know; I must be having an off day."

At exactly ten, Margot pulled into the hotel's circular driveway. With Jim nowhere in sight, she handed off the keys and went inside where she found him seated at the lobby bar, sipping a Bloody Mary.

He grinned. "They make a mean drink here; care to join me?"

"I certainly do not; finish up and let's get moving."

Jim signed the check, stood and kissed her forehead. "Smile. No tip unless the tour guide makes me happy."

"I'm the one who needs appeasing."

During the thirty-minute drive to the Mission, Jim chattered happily asking questions, which she answered in clipped mono-syllables. But as they walked through the lush Mission gardens, Margot's mood softened. For her, the Mission had always exuded an aura of serenity.

Jim said, "It's like I'm back in the 18th century. Even with all the scaffolding and reconstruction, the buildings seem timeless."

"This Mission is the oldest building in California," Margot said. "Repairing and maintaining a 200 year-old complex costs a bundle, what with earthquake damage and general wear."

At the stone church and the cemetery that contained the unmarked graves of the *Juaneño* Indian workers, Jim nudged Margot. "Catch this sign. Fray Junipero Serra actually celebrated mass in the chapel."

Further on he said, "Look at these miniscule cells. There's barely room for an iron bed and a crude wooden chest. Those Padres sure lived a Spartan existence."

They spent the rest of the time, visiting the soldiers' barracks, which exhibited uniforms and firearms; the industrial areas held water pumps, tools for milling, and corn to feed the natives who made goods for every day living.

"Missions are a first for me," Jim said. We don't have any back East. Is there a store nearby that carries old Spanish bells? I want one to hang on my patio."

"This street, Camino Capistrano, used to be lined with antique shops; luckily, *The Barn* is still here; it's a block-long antique mall. We can browse after lunch."

"And when *is* lunch?"

"I'll feed you when we finish exploring; I promise."

They crossed the railroad tracks to enter Los Rios, California's oldest residential street, where Margot pointed out the single-wall board and batten adobe homes and wooden structures. Stopping in front of the old Rios adobe with its shingle reading 'Law Office,' she said, "This is one of only three remaining structures that housed the Mission builders and ranch workers."

"What a neat place for a law practice. Sure is a far cry from my office on the top floor of a Manhattan skyscraper."

They strolled along the quiet street, shaded by eucalyptus, willows, and palms; cactus and wildflowers nestled among the bougainvillea. Next they browsed the Ito Nursery and children's petting zoo.

As they passed the *Tea House* restaurant, Jim said, "To my mind, tea does not comport with missions and Spanish architecture."

"You underestimate me. Following today's theme, we are dining at the *Ramos House Café* in a charming, old adobe."

"Now you're talking my language."

"The serve breakfast and lunch on the patio under an old mulberry, and all the food is made from scratch; they grow their own herbs, and they hand-turn the ice cream out back. The owner lives and works at the house."

As soon as they were seated, Jim zeroed in on the patrons sipping a pink liquid from canning jars. "What are those drinks?"

"Mimosas, made with pomegranate juice."

"Pomegranate juice—that's a new one on me; I think I'll try one."

Before even finishing his drink, Jim smacked his lips and signaled for another.

"You've had plenty already; save some drinking for tonight."

"That cute little jar didn't even dent my thirst."

"Try water; it's healthy for you."

Jim made a face. "Spoilsport."

Margot studied the menu. "I should try something new, but I'm hooked on the southern fried chicken salad with buttermilk dressing and hush puppies." She rubbed her stomach. "So-o good."

"I'm ordering the potato, corn and buttermilk crab cakes; they're different from the ones back home."

Savoring his meal, Jim said, "I love this place; I love this whole day. The mission, lunch in an historic house, fantastic food, a ravishing companion—it's perfect for an old guy like me."

"Where did that old guy stuff come from?"

He scratched his head. "I don't know; getting old has been on my mind lately. Tell me the truth; do I look much older than the last time you saw me?"

Before Margot could respond, he said, "Forget I asked; I'm afraid of the answer."

Margot laughed. "What a crazy idea. You're still quite the handsome dude."

Inwardly she shuddered. If Jim's old, what am I?

Her thoughts were interrupted by her cell ringing. Checking it wasn't Hans, she answered.

On the other end, Nancy said, "How're y'all doing? Having fun with your old beau? Wait til Hans hears what you've been up to."

Margot could feel the warmth spreading on her cheeks. "Now Nancy, you behave. We toured the mission and we're just finishing lunch."

"Remember to keep your socks on."

Margot blushed again.

"All funning aside," Nancy said. "I have two hot bulletins for you."

"Shoot."

"Joe's family ordered an autopsy on him."

"An autopsy? How do you know?"

"I get around."

"Seriously—how?"

"I overheard Norwood telling Helga; they both sounded pur-ty darn upset."

"Interesting. What else?"

"Jane said she noticed two detectives in Helga's office this morning."

"And?"

"That's it, honey bun."

"I wonder what they're after."

"Dunno; I'm fixing to poke around more."

"Good work, girlfriend."

When Margot finished talking, Jim asked, "Did I detect a blush cross your maiden cheeks?"

"My friend Nancy loves kidding me."

"The conversation sounded intriguing."

"I'm a volunteer at a skilled nursing center, and a favorite patient recently died under strange circumstances; Nancy, another volunteer clued me in on the latest."

"I heard you say the word autopsy."

"You heard right, and I, for one, am relieved. I've been suspicious about his death ever since we packed up his belongings and found a hip flask that sure smelled of alcohol."

"Wouldn't be the first time someone boozed it up in a medical setting."

"But Joe suffered from diabetes."

"That does make a difference; alcohol and diabetes don't mix, but the question is did the alcohol cause his death?"

"It's what I'm trying to find out."

"What are you some kind of lady detective?"

"Just curious."

"Did you tell the higher ups about the hip flask? I'm sure they'd be interested."

"In fact, Nancy just said that two detectives came to the facility this morning; now I'm wondering why."

"All the more reason to let them know about the hip flask."

"I will, but first, I want to interview Joe's daughter—once I get her address and number. The hip flask should be with his belongings that were sent to her."

"The authorities may not appreciate your meddling."

"I'm not meddling, I'm . . . ."

"Take my advice; tell the powers that be what you found and let them handle it."

Margot took a deep breath. "This reminds me; I haven't told you about the legal difficulties I mentioned in my email."

"Did you commit a heinous crime? Fess up."

"No, but I have a long, boring story for you."

"Speak. I am your captive audience."

Margot filled Jim in on the details: the accident, The Relatives, Shady Palms, her lawyer, the hearing—everything except her relationship with Hans—though she did mention that a friend had advised her to change attorneys.

Jim scratched his head. "That couldn't happen to a smart cookie like you."

"It did happen, and it's still happening."

"What's the name of the law Firm you hired?"

"Jacobs, Jacobs and Jacobs."

"Easy to remember—and the firm recommended by your friend?"

"Whittaker, Justice and Appleby; both firms handle conservator cases."

"Two law school buddies live in Orange County; I can ask what they think?"

"That would be great."

After lunch, they spent an hour, meandering through *The Barn*, where Jim found an old school bell.

"That's pretty hefty. How are you ever going to haul that home?"

"I buy antiques for a hobby; I'm an old hand at having goods shipped. While I'm here, I want to check out more of your West Coast treasures. Want to be my tour guide?"

"I'd love it, but I've done enough running for one day. I'm going to drop you off and take a nap before dinner.

"Napping together at my place saves driving and gas."

"Negative—*rest* is the operative word."

"You're no fun."

⟞⟝ ⟞⟝

Back at Shady Palms, Margot took Jim's advice and tried locating the homicide detectives who had visited skilled nursing, but with only scant information from Nancy she had no luck. After dialing several phone numbers, she found herself connected to the Orange County Sheriff-Coroner's office in Santa Ana, and using a mixture of flattery and cajoling, she succeeded in setting up an appointment for the following day.

That accomplished, she snuggled under a warm comforter while she returned Hans's many calls. He answered on the first ring.

Margot said, "Hi, it's me. How are you?"

"The question is, how are *you*? I phoned several times; when you didn't answer, I worried—especially since you didn't feel well yesterday."

"I'm much better now. I spent the day with a friend, touring the San Juan Mission and antiquing."

"That was a fast recovery."

"I probably overdid it a little; I just crawled into bed to rest. Any luck selling your condo?"

"Keep your fingers crossed; my agent may have a solid buyer—a cash deal, no less. I should find out tomorrow."

"Hey, good luck. I hope you make a bundle, and everything goes smoothly."

"I could wind up the deal tomorrow—possibly be home the next day."

"Terrific—can't wait to see you."

Hans back in two days?

⊷ ⊷

At eight sharp, Margot found Jim waiting outside *The Studio* restaurant, a small freestanding craftsman bungalow on the hotel grounds. Rather than choosing the chef's table menu where diners could watch the food preparation, they had reserved a cozy table away from the other diners to enjoy ocean-view dining through the tall windows.

As the waiter filled the water glasses Jim whispered, "Let's see if this is really a top drawer restaurant." He asked, "Do you offer *Glenfiddich* 40 year-old Scotch?"

"Yes sir, we do. We also provide 50 year-old *Glenfiddich*."

"Very good; make it a double on the rocks."

Margot grimaced. "I thought we'd try the tasting menu with a different wine for every course. That's way more than enough alcohol."

"I rarely get the chance to taste the 50-year-old vintage; "I'll be *fine*—my bungalow is only twenty giant steps away."

Margot shrugged. "But speaking of fine vintages, since you like old collectibles, what became of the turquoise and cream Chevy you drove in college?"

"You mean my 56 Bel Air with wings? Did you know that model broke the Pike's Peak record the year it came out?"

"Can't say I did."

"You have no idea how many times I've kicked myself for selling the beauty."

"So why did you sell?"

"I put myself through NYU law, and to save money, I ditched the car which I didn't need in New York; besides parking around Washington Square was impossible. Back in the fifties, who knew it would become a hot classic worth big money today?"

"Why don't you buy one now? I don't know how much red tape would be involved, but during my visit to Cuba, I saw old American cars all over downtown Havana."

"Messing around with Cuba? Not the best idea. The prices on The Net are up around a hundred grand, and it costs thousands more to modernize the cars. I'll admit it though; I've thought about blowing a wad for the right one."

"My former neighbors, an old couple, had the exact same car. I think they had owned it ever since the sixties."

"Hey, let's change the subject before I get depressed." Jim picked up his drink. "This Scotch is so-o smooth. Here, take a sip."

Margot shook her head.

"Did you know Scotch is making a comeback?" Jim said. "Even the Chinese are drinking it. They love mixing Scotch and green tea—of all things. Isn't that a kick?"

At that point, a platter containing tender, juicy Maine scallops arrived along with French Bordeaux. Next, they sampled *Foie Gras* on lightly toasted bread, served with a rare full-bodied Côte Du Rhône white wine.

Margot nibbled at an heirloom tomato and beet salad; she offered the rest to Jim.

Jim declined, though he offered to finish her glass of Sauvignon Blanc.

Margot took a small sip of the French Burgundy, the next wine, and ate several mouthfuls of Mahi Mahi, which she usually found bland. "I'm getting full," she said. "But this is superbly flavored."

A beef filet arrived, topped off by creamy polenta and a wild mushroom red wine sauce and accompanied by an Australian Cabernet Sauvignon. Margot could feel her pant waist tightening.

"This is the best beef I've ever had," Jim said. "I thought only old-line restaurants in Chicago and the East Coast served this quality of meat."

"Laguna is not a frontier town. Easterners are such snobs; you're always looking down on the West Coast."

"Don't get all het up. I didn't mean to be insulting." Changing the subject, he said, "For dessert let's try this Ouray cheese with fennel marmalade and toasted walnuts."

Waving away the dish and a glass of 40-year-old Madera, Margot squealed, "Help, I can't touch one more thing."

But when the molten chocolate cake with candied kumquats and sesame ice cream arrived, she couldn't resist a small bite. She declined the Hungarian Tokaji wine; Jim happily obliged by draining her glass. He had been finishing his wine and hers throughout the meal.

By this time, Jim had grown quite tipsy and began sloshing his words. The waiter brought the check and stood discreetly aside while Jim struggled to focus his eyes.

"Sheesh Margot, thish bill is obshene," he bellowed. "Where'sh my credit card, anyway?"

"Quiet down, will you. Just sign and write your room number."

As though the situation couldn't worsen, she spied her nemesis, Alice Marks, a few tables away. Margot tried hiding her face behind a menu, but the wretched woman had already spotted them.

She came bouncing over. "Nice seeing you again, Margot dear. Last time I called, you said you were extremely busy—too busy for lunch, and now I know why." She held out her hand. "Introduce me to your handsome friend."

Jim struggled to stand and weakly shook her hand. Groping for his chair, he plopped back down.

I hope she hasn't noticed how drunk he is, Margot thought.

Alice said, "So, do you live nearby or are you visiting?"

"Jim's an old college friend."

"Are you at the hotel?"

Jim had been leaning his head against the chair. He opened his half-closed eyes "Yesh, right here."

Margot stood and yanked Jim to his feet. "Sorry to run off, Alice. Jim's exhausted, and he needs his rest."

"Alice purred. "I hope we meet again soon." She paused a minute. "I'm having a party tomorrow night. Why don't you both come?"

"Jim has plans with his former classmates tomorrow; I'm tied up as well."

"Oh, what a shame," Alice said, as she flounced off.

With the horrid woman gone, Margot hoped for a quick exit, but Jim commenced a slow drunken, stagger through the dining room. As they passed Alice's table, Margot said loudly, "You poor man; this is the worst case of jetlag I've ever seen."

For the second night in a row, Margot dragged Jim back to his room and removed his shoes, leaving him passed out on the bed. She stopped at the lobby bar for an espresso cappuccino and stared at the black ocean through the window, wondering why she had been fooling around with Jim since Hans was the man she loved.

CHAPTER TWENTY-ONE

The following day, Margot took the 5 freeway to Santa Ana's Civic Plaza and pulled into the large, multi-leveled parking structure. The attendant directed her toward a sleek, modern office building, which, disappointingly, bore no resemblance whatsoever to the buildings pictured in the old L.A. Noir films.

Once at the Coroner's office, Margot half-expected to be turned away as a frivolous, nosey body, but the uniformed receptionist merely motioned Margot to follow her down the hall, stopping outside Cornelia Hatchett's door.

Aside from the usual sterile furniture and innocuous art reproductions, one wall displayed diplomas from several eminent scientific institutions. Unlike some Coroners in other parts of the country, the Orange County Coroner had been well-schooled in forensics.

At over six-feet tall and black, the Coroner cut a striking figure. Her wide, almond shaped eyes twinkled as she smiled warmly, displaying full sensuous lips and large white teeth. She extended her hand, motioning Margot to take a seat. "Hi, I'm Cornelia. You look startled."

Margot managed to say, "Not at all; I'm just happy you agreed to see me."

"I understand you have information about the recent death of Joe Farelli, a patient at the skilled nursing center where you volunteer."

"That's right." She briefly outlined her suspicions about Joe's sudden demise and finding the silver hip flask when they packed up his room.

"A hip flask? Containing alcohol?"

"The flask appeared empty, but we detected a whiff of alcohol; Joe suffered from diabetes, so the alcohol set off alarm bells."

"Do you know where the hip flask is now?"

"I assume Joe's daughter has it."

Cornelia tapped a finger against her cheek. "This hip flask business should interest Homicide. According to what you told my secretary, two detectives interviewed the head nurse at the facility where Joe died; it seems Homicide is already working the case. They generally take the lead, but somehow you convinced my secretary to give you an appointment with me."

"I'm sorry to take up your time. Initially, I called in to report the information about the hip flask, but I wasn't sure which department I needed, and . . . ."

"Sounds like our communications system needs straightening out, but now that you're here, please tell me more."

"Joe and I became good friends, and I worried that his passing might be sloughed off as the death of yet another old man. Then I heard that Joe's family had ordered an autopsy, and that made me think I had some basis for my suspicions."

"I get the picture." She pressed a buzzer. "You'll need to make a statement to Homicide; my receptionist will walk you over there."

"Before I leave, I have a small favor," Margot said. "I'd like to send Joe's daughter a condolence card, and I need her address. Could you possibly . . . ?"

"Sorry, we're not at liberty to release that information."

Standing quickly, the Coroner ended the interview by extending her hand. "Thanks for coming forward."

Margot likewise thanked Cornelia for her time and left.

At Homicide, a deputy took down the information she had given the Coroner and promised to pass it on to the detectives investigating Joe's death.

Since the Coroner had refused to disclose the address of Joe's daughter, she would have to poke through the files at skilled nursing for the information. As soon as she reached the lobby, she phoned the facility to say that she would be cutting short her vacation and working a few hours every day.

CHAPTER TWENTY-TWO

Before exiting the civic center, Margot debated whether to check on Jim or leave him to his own devices.

Check on Jim won, and she dialed his cell. "Hi, it's me. You don't deserve my attention after your binge last night, but I'm feeling generous today."

"You're more than generous; you're fantastic, gorgeous, brilliant, and . . . ."

"Enough with the fake compliments. Tell me how you're feeling."

"Like I've been run over by a golf cart. My room slave, a super nice guy, brought me a hangover concoction. It helped a little, but I've been holed up all day with a killer headache. Where've you been?"

"I took your advice and visited the Orange County Coroner."

"And?"

"I'll tell you when I see you."

"What time are you coming over?" Jim asked.

"In a while; let's take it easy tonight—maybe relax over an early dinner on your patio, okay?

"Suits me—I can't wait."

In the past two days, both Jim and Hans had said they couldn't wait to see her. She wondered how she could continue juggling two men.

As she handed the garage attendant the parking fee, Hans phoned, saying he had signed the papers to sell his condo.

"Congratulations. Did you get your asking price?"

"Sure did; I'm rich. Let's celebrate tonight."

"Tonight?"

"I hopped an early plane; we landed at John Wayne a few minutes ago."

"I didn't expect you until tomorrow. I made plans with a friend, who's visiting from Connecticut."

"Let's make it a threesome for dinner; I want to meet her."

"Sorry, I can't talk right now; the 5 is jammed. I'll call when I get home, okay?"

"I'll be waiting."

He'll be waiting; Jim is waiting. I'm in trouble.

She made kissing noises. "I'm glad you're back."

What now?

Once home, she sipped a glass of wine for courage and punched in Hans's number. "Hi sweetie, traffic took forever. Listen, my friend isn't feeling great; we'll probably grab a quick dinner. Can I come over, afterwards? I'd rather spend time with you alone anyway. What do you say?"

"Okay with me, if you promise to spend the night; I've missed you."

"I promise; I've missed you too."

Margot changed quickly into slenderizing black linen capris, black and white striped T-shirt, silver thongs, and a large silver medallion necklace. She tied a black cashmere sweater around her shoulders for warmth against the cool night air. Still worrying how she would string both men along, she headed out to meet Jim at *Mosaic,* the hotel's poolside bar & grill where they lunched on the first day.

Jim bowed and held out her chair. "You are as glorious as tonight's sunset."

"Why thank you sir; you seem fully recovered from your hangover."

"I am a man of great resiliency." Jim handed her the cocktail menu. "Ever try a black and tan?"

"Can't say I have."

"It's half light beer and half dark beer. I heartily recommend it."

"I'll order a cappuccino; unlike you, I drank much too much last night."

"Very funny."

"I hope you're having only one beer."

Jim grimaced. "Starting already?"

"I thought you were going easy tonight."

"I don't recall swearing a blood oath. Tell me about your visit with the Coroner."

"She's a tall black giant and one sharp lady."

"What went down?"

"She lit up when I mentioned the hip flask we found, and she sent me to Homicide to make a statement; I guess it's up to them now."

"At least you got things rolling; you're a regular Miss Margot."

"We'll see what happens."

"Did you get the address you wanted?"

"Negative."

"As I predicted."

"I'll get it."

During the next hour, Jim downed beer after beer until she exploded. "You've had three beers since I sat down and who knows how many before I arrived. I'm cutting you off before you get drunk again."

Jim shot her a dirty look. "Stop nagging me." He called over the waiter. "Another black and tan, please."

"That's it," Margot said. "One more beer, and I'm gone."

Relenting, he asked for the check and signed his name. Then he stood and took a few wobbly steps, latching onto Margot for support. They slowly descended the steps to the pool area below where, to her horror, Hans waited, shock written on his face.

"Oh, Hans, it's…. it's you. What are you doing here?" Pulling herself together, she added, "This is Jim, the old college friend I told you about." She gestured from one to the other. "Jim, this is Hans. Hans, this is Jim. We're headed for dinner on his. . . . I mean, we're on our way to dinner. Won't you join us?"

Jim moved to shake hands but lost his balance and fell into Hans's arms. Steadying him, Hans said, "It's okay, old man; I've got you now."

Each taking one arm, Hans and Margot helped Jim back to his room and deposited him face down on the bed.

"That makes three nights for three," Margot muttered. She waited outside while Hans helped Jim undress and sat holding her face in her hands, wondering how to bluff her way out of the mess.

In a few minutes, Hans closed the patio door and sat opposite her. "So this is your *girlfriend*. What are you doing with this drunk?"

"I never said my friend was a woman. Uh, I planned to tell you about Jim when I came over to your place; I haven't seen him since college. He'd been planning a trip out here, and after he found me on *Classmates*, he contacted me. It's only natural."

"Is Jim the real reason you couldn't have dinner before my trip, the time you pretended to be sick?"

"I truly didn't feel well, but it would have been mean to leave Jim all alone on his first night here. We ran across the highway for a bite."

"Meaner than not having dinner with me?"

Ignoring the question, Margot said, "How did you know where to find me?"

"Alice Marks invited me to a party and mentioned seeing you two looking chummy at that fancy restaurant, *The Studio;* she said the fellow you were with was staying at the hotel; I figured him for the *friend* you ditched me for two times in a row." `

"Alice loves carrying stories and making trouble."

"Never mind Alice, it's you who's causing trouble. How could you treat me this way when I've been there for you during all your problems?" He rose to leave.

"Hans, please let me explain. Jim means nothing to me. We had fun reminiscing; that's all. And you're right; he does drink too much. Being with Jim made me appreciate you all the more."

"I've had enough for one night. I need time to reconsider our relationship. Don't bother calling me. If I decide to get in touch, I'll call *you*."

⟞⟝ ⟞⟝

The next morning, Margot awoke to the sound of loud knocking; her head throbbed from crying all night. She struggled out of bed to admit Jane, who quickly took in the scene and said, "What in the Sam Hill happened to you?"

Still half-asleep, Margot mumbled, "Happened?"

"You have big ugly black lumps under your eyes." Jane lifted one lid, "And red rivulets covering this eyeball; must've been one awful night."

Margot nodded.

"Got any teabags?"

Margot gestured lethargically toward the kitchenette, "Try the canister beside the toaster."

Jane grabbed two teabags and soaked them in cool water, then held them gently over the swellings until she realized the bags were dripping all over Margot's robe. "Woops, sorry; I hope you can get the stains out."

Margot shrugged. "Whatever."

Jane checked beneath the bags. "They're not working." She thought a minute and said, "Preparation H, for hemorrhoids, is supposed to reduce puffiness under the eyes by constricting the blood vessels or something."

"Huh?"

"I have a tube somewhere; be right back."

Jane returned, brandishing the ointment and dabbed a spot on the swellings, carefully avoiding Margot's inflamed eyes.

A strong, medicinal odor assailed Margot's nostrils. "Yuck, what a horrible smell. Is there at least any improvement?"

"Not yet; maybe we need more time."

"Nah, I give up; I'm too far gone."

Jane said, "So how about cluing me in?"

"Let me get dressed first; I'll tell you the whole sad story at breakfast."

Once downstairs, Margot gnawed a piece of toast; avoiding the usual weak coffee, she dunked a bag of breakfast tea, until the liquid turned black.

Heaven forbid the old folks should be stimulated, she thought.

The mug shook in her hand as she told Jane, "I can summarize last night in two sentences: Hans found me at *The Montage* with my drunk, out-of control, former boyfriend; Hans helped put Jim to bed, then bawled me out and stormed off, saying he needed to rethink our relationship."

Jane said, "Things could be worse."

"I doubt that, but thanks for your tender loving care this morning. I'm headed to *Starbucks* for the real stuff before I drag myself off to skilled nursing. Maybe work will take my mind off this fiasco."

CHAPTER TWENTY-THREE

Later at the facility, Margot spotted Ernesto, the sexy orderly she relied on to brighten her day. His eyes narrowed in surprise, and he cupped her chin gently, "Hey, Senorita, *que paso?* Tell Ernesto your troubles."

"Oh, Ernesto, I screwed up royally. My boyfriend caught me hanging out with Jim, my college beau."

"That's good. Make him *celoso.* Stir the pot a little."

"You don't understand. I told Hans a white lie about why I couldn't have dinner with him. And when he saw us together at the hotel, Jim was so drunk, he tripped and fell into Hans's arms. Hans was completely disgusted. Tell me how to make it right."

"*No problema.* Fix yourself up; put on a low-cut dress and those platform shoes, like the ones my girlfriend wears to make her legs look long and sexy. Oh, Senorita, I am *loco* thinking about it. Then go see this Hans *hombre.* Say you're sorry and . . . you know what to do after that."

"Maybe, I'll try that, once my nerves settle down. Did you hear that two detectives interviewed Helga yesterday?"

Ernesto closed his eyes and shook his head, "I am right next to Helga's office, and I don't like what I hear."

"Why?"

"I can't make out too much what the detectives say, but I catch every word from that loud-mouth Helga. She keep yelling 'Joe died of natural causes; that's all there is to it.' Then she say, 'But if you have any suspicions, you should interview Ernesto, the orderly who works here. He argued with Joe all the time.'"

Margot's eyes widened in surprise.

"She's after me since the first day. Joe and I are friends. We never argue. We laugh together every day. I love his little knock-knocks."

Margot swallowed hard. "Yah, me too."

"I am plenty worried. The *policia*, they hate people from the barrio."

"Tell you what. I'll nose around and see what I can find out—maybe visit Pete Peterson; I've heard he and Joe were buddies."

Margot headed off to Pete's room, where she found him playing solitaire and watching baseball on TV. "Sorry to interrupt. May I come in?"

"Sure, sure; I'm always available for pretty ladies, especially when I'm in bed." He winked, raising his eyebrows up and down like Groucho Marx and patted the bed for Margot to sit.

Margot pulled up a chair instead. "How are you today, Pete?"

"I had such a bad toothache this morning I became abscessed with it. I made a dental appointment, but changed my mind because I already know the drill." Looking pleased with himself, he added, "How are you, lovely lady?'

"Not well." Margot bantered back. "I tried exercising today, but it didn't work out."

Pete squeezed her hand. "Good one. We're going to get along fine."

"Now I understand why they call you Pete the Punster. What are you here for?

"A broken hip; I can't stand to be without it."

Good one for you too. "Tell me Pete, how did all this punning begin?"

"In high school, my parents thought I should learn a musical instrument, and when the band needed a piccolo player, I volunteered. Once the music director heard my name, he loved the idea of having Pete Peterson playing piccolo. Then, after he discovered I had perfect pitch, he began introducing me as Pete Peterson, the piccolo player with perfect pitch and a potential Philharmonic performer."

"You were like a walking Peter Piper nursery rhyme."

"I had a ball punning around with that handle; it worked as a real chic magnet."

"I'm sure your being a tall, blond Viking helped a lot."

"Since then, my whole world has become alliteration; words are music to me."

"My friend Hans is musical too; he plays the viola in a local symphony."

"The lady has a boyfriend. I'm not surprised seeing what a smart doll you are."

"You two would get along. Hans isn't into puns, but he loves playing pranks on me. He once pulled a doozy."

"Let's hear it; maybe I'll get a couple of new ideas."

"We had been dating for only a few weeks when he said he had tickets for a concert? I readily agreed; I love music."

Then do you know what he did?"

"I'm certain you're going to tell me."

"After he escorted me to a seat in the auditorium, he vanished."

"Did you think he abandoned you?"

"I imagined all kinds of scary scenarios."

"I assume he turned up."

"I finally spotted him in the string section wearing a huge grin and proudly holding up his viola."

"That *is* a good one. I may try something similar once I blow this joint. "

"Careful. You could give someone a heart attack."

"I only choose victims in top physical condition."

"Speaking of physical conditions: were you shocked that Joe the Jokester died? I heard you two used to be friends."

"Friends? We grew up together, for God sakes."

"How awful for you."

"I couldn't believe it; one day he seemed perfectly healthy." Pete snapped his fingers. "The next day he died. Everyone liked him, except for Helga, the head curse—I mean nurse."

"But Joe didn't seem to care; he told me when Helga hollered at him, he found it a hoot. A hoot and a holler—get it?"

"I get it; I get it. You're not just another handsome face; you're a funny man."

"And you're a champion flatterer."

"What did Helga have against Joe?"

"I'd rather trade compliments, but if you insist, I'll tell you. Apparently, his habit of pinching the female patients infuriated Helga; Joe maintained that the women didn't mind because, at their advanced ages, they enjoyed the male attention. He thought he was doing the ladies a favor."

"Did Joe ever mention his daughter Doris?"

"Yah, once or twice, I guess."

"Do you know Doris's full name?"

"Yes, Doris what's her face."

"Come on Pete, stop kidding around."

"Doris, what's her face; I swear that's her name."

Margot threw her hands up in the air. "I surrender." She stood to leave, fluttering her arms and imitating a ghost-like voice, "But I'll be baa-ack."

"Promise?"

"How could anyone resist you?"

Having had no success with Pete, Margot decided her next move would be to quiz Betty, the petite, blonde, go-to person, for information. Margot approached her at the nursing station. "Quick question, Betty, if you don't mind."

"I don't mind, but I'm trying to escape Helga's long claws before she finds more work for me." Taking Margot by the arm, Betty pulled her down the corridor into a small supply alcove.

Margot asked, "Do you know where I can find the address for Joe's daughter?"

"Why do you want it?"

"I want to send her a sympathy card."

"I'm not sure she'd appreciate that," Betty said. "The last time his daughter visited, I heard her reading Joe the riot act."

"About what?"

"Sounded like it involved Helga."

"Helga?"

"I shouldn't have mentioned that; I honestly don't know."

"So about Doris's address, can you get it for me?"

"That's privileged information."

"What's the harm?"

"Sorry, no can do."

CHAPTER TWENTY-FOUR

Following her shift, Margot headed over to Jim's room where she found him asleep on the patio.

"Wake up Jim." She shook him roughly. "Your body is as red as your eyes—from guzzling so much last night. You should be arrested for self-abuse."

Jim sat up. "That's a fine greeting. I looked forward all day to seeing you, and when you get here, you manhandle me."

"Frying your body is not smart. My late husband died of skin cancer."

"Sorry, I didn't realize."

"And another thing; I've had to put you to bed every single night since your arrival. I'm tired of your sophomoric behavior."

Jim cupped his chin. "I'm in such a fog, I need you to explain what went down last night. I vaguely remember a tall stranger helping me undress and throwing a blanket over me. Who was that masked man?"

"Always with the jokes; that 'masked man' is my friend Hans. You literally ran into him as we were leaving Mosaic."

"What do you mean?"

"He reached up and caught you when you tripped on the steps; we both had to haul you back to your room. I bet you emptied your mini-bar before I even arrived then had several beers at the restaurant."

"Just a couple on the patio."

"A couple? Whether you own up to it or not, mister, you have a serious drinking problem. Have you ever considered getting help?"

"There you go again, butting in. I have a question for you too. Is this guy Hans your boyfriend?

"He's a close friend."

"I bet he's a lot more than a close friend; that's why you're so ticked at me."

Margot didn't reply.

"And I bet he's the guy who's been crabbing about the law firm you hired."

Margot nodded.

"Want to hear what my law school buddies told me?"

"Of course."

"Whittaker, Justice and Appleby specialize in defending the elderly against would-be conservators and other crooks that prey on the senior community around here—but they did also say complimentary things about the firm you're with."

At least that last part bodes well for Gordon's law firm, she thought.

Margot answered in a slow, clipped voice, "Thanks for the information. I appreciate your help, but my legal problems don't change the fact you drink too much."

"Listen, Lady. I've managed fine without you all these years, so if you don't like the way I am, that's too bad. I'll hang out with my friends for the rest of my stay."

Margot found her car keys and started down the path toward the parking garage.

"Margot, I'm sorry," Jim called out. "Come back and let's talk."

She hurried on without turning around and backed her car up so quickly, she nearly hit a Porsche, parked behind her.

Take it easy, she told herself; all you need is an accident to add to your problems. You've fought with Hans and Jim; you're unsure about the firm handling the conservator case, but you don't want Diana anywhere near Hans. You could lose everything.

She phoned Hans and listened until the recording came on. Then she clicked off, vowing to try him again, maybe take Ernesto's suggestion—wear a sexy outfit and bring along his favorite port wine.

━+ +━

That evening Margot dialed Hans's number over and over again; from nervousness she reverted to her old habit of picking her fingers. Maybe she *should* give Hans breathing space, time to miss her? But visualizing a young, adorable Diana waiting to snatch Hans away, she nixed the idea. By ten o'clock, she stopped dialing and fell asleep to the mellow sounds of classical guitar.

At six a.m., Margot awakened; she had slept on the sofa still fully dressed. She took a leisurely shower, forced down a breakfast of toast and eggs, and drove over to surprise Hans.

When no one answered the door, she stood on tiptoe to peak through the garage windows and found his Chevy convertible missing.

Had Hans been out all night and with whom?

She unlatched the side gate and walked around to the back where a thick fog had created small puddles on the deck and penetrated the furniture cushions, making it difficult to find a dry spot. As soon as she sat on the chaise, the wet soaked through to her skin. Minutes passed; the dampness filled her sinuses, and she began sniffling. Every time she swallowed, daggers of pain attacked her throat. Shivering from the cold, she gave up and left, then slowly drove down the street, hoping to meet Hans along the way, but he was nowhere in sight.

Stopping only to buy a decongestant, Margot headed back to Shady Palms, where she bundled into a warm chenille robe and fixed a cup of peppermint tea. Every sip brought more pain, and the shivering persisted long after she crawled into bed.

Hans called at last, saying, "By any chance, were you at my house this morning? On my way home, I thought I recognized your car headed in the opposite direction."

"I waited on your deck for what seemed like a week."

"We probably missed each other by seconds; I went out for coffee and bagels."

"I hung around until the fog got to me."

"It's lifting now, and the sun should be out soon. Come on back."

"I can't; I caught a chill from the dampness, and I'm in bed trying to warm up." She put down the phone and blew her nose.

"I heard that. Can I do anything for you?"

"No, thanks; I just need to stay put and doctor myself."

"It's too bad we didn't connect because I have a week-long convention in Vegas, beginning tomorrow," Hans said. "We're overdue for a long talk."

"I suppose the talk can wait until you get back. It gives us both time to think."

"If you're feeling better later, I could stop by."

Margot sneezed again.

"Never mind; rest. I'll check on you tomorrow."

After that, the decongestant knocked her out, and she awakened with a full-blown head cold, which laid her low for days. At first she slept for hours, but by day five, she found herself wide-awake, bored by reading and TV'd out. Then Nancy called, saying Helga would be leaving on a week-long vacation. Margot resolved to get herself up and moving; Helga's absence presented a rare opportunity for some strategic snooping.

CHAPTER TWENTY-FIVE

The next morning, although still feeling low on energy, Margot reported to work eager to implement her plan. She would loiter near the front desk until the receptionist took her morning coffee break. From there, Margot would have easy access to the file cabinet in a small adjoining office.

A few minutes before ten, she sat down across from Loretta, who launched into a long story about her sister's illness, the various hospitalizations, the incompetent doctors, the unfeeling and inattentive husband.

Every few minutes, Margot would nod, pretending to listen. Losing patience, she said, "I don't think I'm contagious; I'd hate for you to catch this rotten cold."

Loretta jumped up right away. "Sorry if I seem rude; this is my break time."

"How long do you usually take?"

"Fifteen minutes—sometimes longer—depends how busy we are."

"Don't rush; I'll keep an eye on things."

Loretta strolled off, calling over her shoulder, "Thanks, that would be great."

Once Loretta disappeared from view, Margot rushed to the file cabinet. She opened the top drawer which contained the patient files arranged alphabetically and searched the F's but found none for Farelli.

Strange—Joe had died only a few weeks before.

On a hunch, Margot tried finding Pete's file and located it easily. Apparently, the drawer contained only files for current patients. Her watch indicated five minutes had elapsed since Loretta had left.

Searching further, she pulled out the second drawer and saw a pile of folders lying horizontally and rubber-banded together. Near the bottom, she located one marked, Farelli, Joseph.

Success.

Another five minutes had elapsed; Loretta would be returning shortly.

Hearing voices, she froze. Two visitors chatting animatedly passed by; they stopped and said, "Good morning," before moving on.

Margot opened Joe's file. Seconds later, footsteps click-clicked in her direction; her heart thumping, she quickly closed the drawer and moved back to the reception desk where she encountered two more visitors. She said, "May I help you?"

"That's all right; we know which room our Aunt is in."

The third time she accessed the drawer, she grasped the edge for support; her legs ached and her entire body felt weak. The recent illness had taken its toll.

From a distance, Margot heard Betty, the same nurse who had refused to give her the information about Joe's daughter. She slipped behind the reception desk in case Betty came her way.

By the time Betty arrived, Margot had busied herself flipping through the calendar and looking as though she belonged.

"Hi, covering for Loretta today?" Betty asked.

"I suggested she take a long break today; she deserves it."

After Betty moved on, Margot breathed a great sigh and continued perusing Joe's file. The first page listed Joe's personal data but contained no information on his daughter. Margot scanned the next two pages and there on page three, under "next of kin," she saw the name, Doris Gooding, followed by relationship, daughter, along with an address and phone number.

Mentally scolding herself for not being prepared, she rushed back to the desk and fumbled to locate paper and pencil then returned to the file cabinet and quickly jotted down the information.

Then, seemingly out of nowhere, a hand reached out and slammed the drawer shut with a loud bang, sending shock waves through her body. Ashen faced, Margot jumped and turned to find the head nurse looming like an avenging she-devil. Her features distorted in anger, Helga asked, "And what business brings you to the file room?"

"Um, um, I thought you were on vacation."

"And you decided this would be a good chance to snoop."

"I wasn't snooping, I . . . . ."

"You what?"

Collecting her nerves, she casually slipped the paper with Doris's information into her pocket. "A patient asked me to find his son's phone number; you know how forgetful older people are."

"What did you just put away? Give it here."

Margot jumbled the papers in her pocket trying to conceal her jottings beneath a wad of tissues.

"I'm waiting, hurry it up," Helga snarled.

Margot extracted the crumpled tissues praying the information lay hidden on the bottom.

Eyeing the wet tissues in disgust, Helga said, "I don't believe you; which patient?"

"Pete. He asked me."

I'd better warn Pete, before Helga questions him, Margot thought.

Helga latched onto Margot's arm. "Let's go ask Pete right now."

Not knowing how Pete would react, Margot's heart sank until Loretta arrived, breathless from running. "Mr. Norwood needs you in his office right away; the health department is inspecting the premises in three weeks."

"I know all about it," Helga bristled. "That's why I had to interrupt my vacation."

Glaring at Margot, she said, "You've had a reprieve, Missy. Even so, you are *never* to search the patient files without permission. Understand me? And remember, I'll be watching you."

Margot sat for a few minutes to recover then hurried away to Pete's room where she found him inching his way out the door on crutches. "Hey there, Margot, did you know that when the doctor applied this cast, he drank so much, he became plastered too?"

Margot had been saving one up for Pete. "Well my plastic surgeon became so successful, he raised a few eyebrows."

"Oh, you're getting better all the time. Let's prance down the hall together; I'll introduce you to my pretty Polly?"

"Hold up. I need a favor."

"I always say 'yes' to a proposition, but favors are iffy."

"Seriously, Pete. If you don't back me up, I'll be in trouble with Helga."

"The hell with Helga, I say."

"Please, will you listen?"

"Okay, tell me your sins."

"Remember the time I asked you for the name and address of Joe's daughter?"

"Yeah, Doris Gooding, in Lake Forest."

"*Now* you tell me. Thanks a whole lot."

"What's the problem?"

"You wouldn't give me a straight answer, so I had to snoop through the files and Helga caught me."

"Naughty girl."

"You're the naughty one; now you need to cover for me."

"How's that?"

"I told a tiny little fib and used your name when Helga caught me poking through the files."

"I hope you didn't get me in Dutch with that dame."

"No, I just said you asked me to find your son's phone number."

"I have a son?"

"Stop it, Pete. You told me you did."

"Come to think of it, maybe I do."

"Will you back me up, or not?"

"Oh, all right, but this will cost you big time. I need to cogitate on the particulars."

"You're a pal."

"Do I owe you palimony?"

Margot frowned. "Enough already; I'm beat. I've been under the weather for days."

"I did notice that rain cloud hanging over your head."

"Seriously, I need to go home."

"What about meeting my Polly?"

"Next time; I give you my solemn vow."

He gestured down the hallway with one crutch. "Go if you must."

Margot bid Pete goodbye and fingered the information in her pocket. After all the trouble she'd gone to, she hoped Doris would see her.

Exhaustion overtook Margot on the way back to Shady Palms where she fixed a strong cup of tea laced with whiskey. She inhaled the aroma before taking slow, healing sips, after which she collapsed and slept for several hours.

Early the next morning, Margot phoned to set up a visit with Doris who warmed to the idea. "Any friend of my father is welcome." They arranged a meeting for the following afternoon.

Stopping to purchase a white *dendrobium* orchid plant, Margot headed toward Lake Forest and entered the tree-lined development where Doris lived. Visitors unfamiliar with Eucalyptus would express shock at the peeling bark and drooping leaves and inquire what blight had attacked the trees. But they thrived in the Southern California climate, providing much needed shade during the hot summers.

As she negotiated the endless speed bumps, placed at intervals to protect the neighborhood children, Margot rehearsed ways of approaching Doris. She might begin by expressing her condolences, raise the question of Joe's health—the diabetes and his medications; she would mention Helga and gauge Doris's reaction.

Doris might even tell her the findings of the autopsy. Only then would Margot mention the hip flask.

Several speed bumps later, she arrived at a split-level rustic home accessed by a long flight of steps; when she finally reached the top, her heart was pounding. Months since her accident, she still found stairs daunting.

A woman with short blond hair who appeared to be in her mid-thirties answered the door and gave Margot a blank look. "May I help you?"

"I'm Margot, a volunteer from the Shady Palms skilled nursing facility; we made a date for two o'clock."

"Oh, right. I've been a little distracted lately."

On close inspection, Margot saw that the woman looked deadly pale, and her eyes were red and swollen. Margot hesitated then extended the plant. "My condolences for your loss."

"How sweet; I love orchids."

Margot shuffled from side to side uneasily. "If you're not feeling well, I could come back another time."

"Since you drove all the way up here; I can at least offer you tea."

"I hate being a bother."

"It's no bother." Doris gestured to the living room. "Please make yourself comfortable while I get the tea, unless you'd rather have coffee or a coke?

"Tea would be great."

She excused herself and disappeared into the kitchen.

Margot chose a sofa flanking the fireplace and remarked the myriad shells, pots, and carvings scattered around the room. She tapped on a small hollowed-out boat, an alligator, shaped like a drum—similar to one she had purchased while visiting Papua New Guinea.

In a few minutes, Doris returned carrying a tray with two cups, a hot water carafe, and an assortment of blends, which she placed on the coffee table. "Please choose whichever you prefer."

Margot selected lemon-mint herb tea and let the bag steep until the liquid darkened. She took a sip. "The orchid fits right in with your other tropical artifacts."

Doris sat down on the opposite sofa. "We shopped like crazy on our trip to the Philippines; the goods there are hand-carved and so exotic."

"Nice collection."

"Now we're glad we spent the money; we may never get back."

"As I told you on the phone, I volunteer at the nursing center where I got to know your dad. We all enjoyed his sense of humor so much; it's a shame he passed away."

Doris's eyes teared up. "Dad *was* a kick and a great father; he would come by to fix things and play games with my three kids. They adored him."

"How lucky to have Joe in your life."

Doris wiped her eyes. "It's only been three weeks; we're still not used to his being gone and now this."

"Meaning what?"

"The autopsy report came yesterday." Large teardrops ran down her freckled face, and she began emitting great gulping sobs.

Margot crossed the room to sit beside Doris and put an arm around her shoulders. She reached the other arm for a napkin, handing it to Doris, who wiped her eyes.

"I can't talk about it; I'm too upset."

"Go ahead, if you want; I'd be glad to listen."

"Ever since Dad died, I've felt completely guilty." Doris picked up a fresh napkin and dabbed at her eyes again.

Margot said, "Guilty? Why?"

"For the way I acted toward him."

Margot patted Doris's arm and waited.

"I'm embarrassed, carrying on this way in front of you."

"Don't be embarrassed. You'll feel a lot better if you get it all out."

"You're sure you don't mind?"

"I'm sure."

"It happened the morning I found Helga standing by his bed screaming at him."

"Screaming at Joe?"

"I'll never forget it; she yelled, 'I'm sick of you behaving like a dirty old man; if you don't stop pinching the women patients, I'll fix you good.' She made such a commotion I'm amazed no one came running."

"What did Joe say to that?"

"He just laughed."

"That's typical Joe. Why do you feel guilty, though?"

"After she left, I jumped all over him for acting like an over-sexed tomcat, and I called him a disgrace to our family. He tried passing it off as nothing, but that made me even angrier, and I said things I regret."

"During an argument, people often say things they're sorry for later."

Doris buried her face in her hands and shook her head.

Margot gave Doris a moment to pull herself together before asking, "How did Joe react to what you said?'

"He gave it to me good, and I stormed off."

"Did you visit with your dad after that?"

"A few times. He still seemed angry with me."

"Did you discuss it with him?"

"I tried, but then he changed; he became uncommunicative."

"I never thought of Joe as uncommunicative," Margot said.

"It seemed to happen overnight, and right afterwards, I received a call saying Dad had passed away. People his age die all the time, but the meds seemed to be working, and . . . ." Doris broke into new sobs.

Margot squeezed her shoulder. "I know this is hard for you."

"Since reading the report, I feel guiltier than ever. I should've paid more attention."

"What could you have done differently?"

"They were giving him Glucophage to control his blood sugar, and they insisted it was not only effective but safe, but I should have been more watchful. I felt so uneasy about his death, I asked for an autopsy; the report said Dad asphyxiated in his sleep."

"Did it mention what caused the asphyxiation?"

"A combination of alcohol and Valium."

"How could *you* could have prevented that?"

"I should have checked every few days to make sure they were monitoring him correctly.

"I still don't understand what made you order an autopsy?"

"I just had a funny feeling—maybe because he was so subdued the last time I saw him, not at all like the Dad I knew. As it turns out, I was right to be suspicious; the Valium probably quieted him down."

Margot said, "If anyone's at fault, it's the facility. Did you contact them?"

"I tried calling Helga, first thing, but so far she hasn't called back. Do you think she may be hiding something?"

"It's possible."

Doris scratched her head. "I can't figure out how Dad got a hold of either the alcohol or the Valium."

Margot took a deep breath. "I may have a partial answer to the puzzle."

Doris's eyebrows shot up in surprise.

"When we packed Joe's belongings, right after he died, we found an empty hip flask that smelled of alcohol."

"A hip flask?"

"At the time, we wondered how it got there."

"I suppose my dad could have brought the hip flask with him."

"Or someone else did; any ideas who?"

"I haven't a clue. Even if we figure that out, we still don't know how he obtained the Valium."

Margot shrugged. "Did anyone else visit him besides your family?"

"Only his golf buddy, Rick Mathews, as far as I can tell; he dropped by here, after Dad passed and told me he had seen Dad three days before he died."

"Did he mention that Joe acted sick or anything?"

"No, he didn't; he just said he felt terrible dad had died."

Margot asked, "How well do you know Rick?"

"Not well; he and dad would often golf together at the La Mesa country club; I think Rick's a pro there."

Margot filed the information away. "Back to the hip flask, it should be among Joe's things. Did you ever receive them from the facility?"

"The box came ten days ago; I haven't had the heart to open it yet. What should I do with the flask if I find it?"

"I'd keep it, in case."

"In case what?"

"Could be evidence."

"Do you think I should involve the police?" Doris wondered.

"Definitely."

"I plan to ask Helga about the flask when she calls me back."

"She might not know anything about it."

"Anyway, thanks for telling me about the flask and also for letting me vent."

Margot picked up her purse to leave. "I hope our talk helped; there's absolutely no reason to feel guilty. You were a loving and attentive daughter."

"Do you really think so?'

Margot nodded. "Absolutely."

Doris hugged Margot and opened the door to peer out. "My kids are getting off the school bus; if you wait, I'll introduce you."

"Sorry, I have another appointment." For Margot, going down stairs proved more frightening than going up. She envisioned herself lying sprawled on the ground in front of Doris's laughing children. "Perhaps I'll meet them another time."

Gripping the railing tightly, she maneuvered her sensible Mephisto walking shoes, step-by-step, to the bottom where she gave silent thanks for having descended without a mishap.

On the way home, Margot congratulated herself on learning the cause of Joe's death. But new questions had arisen: How did Joe obtain the alcohol? Who might have given him Valium and why? Maybe Joe's friend, Rick, could provide the answers.

CHAPTER TWENTY-SIX

That evening, Margot found herself at loose ends. Nancy had gone on a date with her eighty year old boyfriend, the proud owner of a bright red 59 Cadillac convertible with tailfins, an icon of Detroit's excess. Nancy loved the attention whenever they drove through Laguna—the honking cars and people calling out "way to go" or whistling.

Jane, too, had a date with a new prospect from an online website. As Jane modeled possible outfits, she told Margot, "I've given up on finding love; these days, I'll settle for a half-way presentable guy who does more than grunt."

Margot laughed. "In your entire on-line dating experience, has anyone ever measured up to those minimal standards?"

"Not even close. Provided my knee stops acting up, I may join a dance club, for fun without the romantic entanglements."

After the third outfit, Margot said, "Stop right there; those black slacks make you look skinny, skinny, and the low-cut blouse shows off your boobs."

"You convinced me, but if he doesn't call again, I'm blaming you."

"I think I'll follow you downstairs and check him out."

"If my knee were strong enough, I'd give you a swift kick."

Margot wished Jane Godspeed and scanned the Laguna Beach papers for somewhere interesting to go. The *Coastline Pilot* displayed an ad for the Laguna Beach Old Pottery Place, formerly known as The Pottery Shack. In the past, browsing the aisles that contained pots of all sizes and shapes had been a favorite pastime. Over the years, she had accumulated assorted glassware and cloths from the large home entertaining section. When *The Shack* closed, Democratic headquarters briefly occupied the site during the '04 National election.

The new development on the corner of PCH and Brooks Street now housed a mix of shops: shoes, clothing, home furnishings, chocolates, and Laguna Beach Books – a rare, independent bookstore. Sapphire, a five-star restaurant, with an adjoining gourmet market, headlined the center. Margot would browse the bookstore and relax on the restaurant's patio with a glass of wine.

On her way out the door, Hans called explaining that he had just returned from the convention. During the week he was away, he had only called twice to see how she was feeling. She choked back her resentment, and when she mentioned her plans for the evening, Hans suggested they meet at the bookstore.

Reaching Pottery Place, she noted the gnome-like *Greeter* statue had been returned to its former place on the corner. She parked and walked past *Sapphire*, now crowded with tourists and Laguna residents happily imbibing food and wine. At *Tootsies*, a shoe and handbag store, she considered a bronze handbag that would work in all four seasons, but remembering that she already owned three similar handbags, she returned the purse to the display rack.

She proceeded to *Laguna Beach Books* which, although small, offered a mix of everything from the classics to bestsellers, mysteries, and even a children's corner. Nothing made Margot happier than fingering and leafing through books.

She chuckled at a note card that read, "If it wasn't for the last minute, I'd never get anything done." That would make the perfect gift for several people I know, including me, she thought.

Books had always been precious to Margot. During the cold winters in Boston, they became her stalwart childhood companions. She could hardly wait for Thursdays when the Bookmobile pulled into the shopping center near her house. Margot would race down the oak-lined sidewalk, often tripping on the cracked pavements and uneven lumps lifted up by the encroaching tree roots. She would climb the steps to the place she considered heaven on wheels to peruse the shelves.

The librarian would look the other way as she reached up to the top shelf which housed the adult books off limits to pre-teen children. That forbidden access lent adventure to her weekly visits.

Margot loved that she and Hans shared a passion for reading. They spent hours discussing literature, music, the arts, and politics, and she despaired that losing him would also mean losing their companionable interests.

Growing alarmed at not seeing him in the bookstore, she checked her watch. At last, a tall man emerged from the back, carrying a small volume of Yeats.

Her heart jumped; he had come after all.

Grinning widely, Hans pulled her close. "Margot, I'm happy to see you looking so well. You must be fully recovered."

Without stopping to breathe and running her sentences together, she said, "I'm fine, but I've missed you. I haven't seen you since that awful night at the Montage. Let's not fight anymore—please."

He replaced the Yeats volume. "I completely agree; ready for a drink next door?"

By way of answer, she took his arm and they walked to the restaurant patio where they found a table.

"Do you still prefer *La Crema Chardonnay*?" Hans asked.

She nodded.

Hans ordered two glasses. "Tell me what you've been up to besides trespassing on my property last week."

"You wouldn't have known I'd been there if I hadn't confessed."

"I found a few plants missing from the deck: I figured you for the thief."

She tapped him playfully on the cheek.

"And what other trouble have you been into lately?" Hans asked.

"You know I behave impeccably."

"That patient who died, the guy you called Joe the Jokester, any luck investigating his death further?"

"I saw the coroner, Cornelia Hatchett, and told her about finding the hip flask."

"Hatchett—good name for a coroner. Did she show any interest in your information?"

"Definitely; she had me give a statement to Homicide.

I also found out that Joe's daughter, Doris, asked for an autopsy of his remains."

"How did you accomplish that, or am I asking a silly question?"

"Doris confirmed it when we met at her home in Lake Forest."

Hans shook his head in disbelief. "You drove up there to see her?

"Her house is only ten minutes from Shady Palms; the trip proved to be worth the effort. She told me that Joe died of a combination of Valium and alcohol."

"My, you've been a busy lady." He shook his head again, "I'm surprised you even missed me. Don't you think you're taking on a lot? That's Homicide's job."

"They don't necessarily do it right. Think they care if another old geezer kicks the bucket?"

"What do you hope to accomplish by your investigations?"

"I'm trying to clear Ernesto."

"Who is this Ernesto?"

"He's an orderly at skilled nursing; Helga, the head nurse, sicced the sheriff on him. She has it in for Latinos—especially Ernesto."

"This sleuthing could be dangerous."

"I'll be careful."

Hans threw up his hands. "After we finish our drinks, let's head over to my place; I need to catch up on the hugs I've been missing."

"Hugs are good; I like hugs."

Margot relaxed for the first time since their argument at *The Montage*. She had taken a last sip of wine and put on fresh lipstick, when she spotted three men, pointing and waving. Recognizing one as Jim, she braced herself as the trio approached the table.

Jim stopped and bowed. "These are my friends, Tony and Rob, from N.Y.U. Law. You said this is the hottest scene in Laguna, and here you are to enhance my cultural experience."

Margot gave Jim a cold stare. "I see you're still hanging around." Nodding towards the other two men, she said, "This is my friend Hans. He and Jim met the other night, but Jim won't remember anything until he sees the bar bill."

Tony chortled, "Yeah, that's Jim for you. In law school, he had the distinction of being the class guzzler; I don't know how he managed to graduate."

"With his ugly mug, I never understood how he attracted the best chicks," Rob added." He knelt on one knee beside Margot. "I see he hasn't lost the magic touch."

"Jim says you're his old college girlfriend." Tony clapped his hands against his mouth, as though stricken. "Whoops, I didn't mean *old*, *old*; I meant his *former* college girlfriend."

All three men began guffawing, and Margot wondered why men often behaved like clowns when they traveled in packs?

Hans, for his part, was not laughing; his face became a stony mask, his eyes narrowed to slits, and his body stiffened. Gesturing to a waiter, he said, "Check, please."

"Don't go. We need to talk," Margot urged.

Tossing some bills on the table, Hans stood to leave.

"Wait, I'll go with you."

"Another time, Margot, enjoy yourself."

She picked up her purse and stood to follow when Tony grabbed her by the shoulders and sat her back down, "Oh, don't *you* leave; we're just getting acquainted."

She glowered at Jim. "Tell your dweeby friend to stop manhandling me!" Then pushing Tony away, she fumbled her way out of the chair.

"You're not being very friendly," Tony said.

Jim shrugged. "That's the way she's been ever since I got here. She never acted this way in college."

"And you weren't a drunk in college."

"Women." Rob threw up his hands.

Margot rushed after Hans, who had disappeared from view. At her car, she rummaged around to find the parking ticket and handed ten dollars to the attendant. "This enough?"

"Plenty; you got change coming."

"Keep it."

He saluted her. "Thanks—my lucky day."

Not mine.

She drove as fast as she could through the heavy coastal traffic to Hans's house, but he wasn't home, and she had no idea where to find him.

CHAPTER TWENTY-SEVEN

Once back in her apartment, Margot replayed the evening's events.

What an annoying coincidence, being at the same restaurant the exact time as Jim and his friends.

Admittedly, she shared blame for the misunderstandings between her and Hans, but every time she tried to put things right, an incident would prevent them from reconciling—a pattern now becoming the norm for their relationship.

To forget her problems, Margot dressed and went to the care facility where she encountered Ginger, the bubbly nurse, who had become a friend during Margot's convalescence.

In those days, when Ginger's frustrations became overwhelming, she would often sit beside Margot's bed and vent. Now Ginger radiated anger; she asked if Margot could spare a few minutes to talk. They repaired to the kitchenette where Margot offered to make a fresh brew of coffee.

While they waited, she massaged Ginger's neck. "You're all knots. What got you so riled up today?"

"Helga's been on a tear ever since Norwood interrupted her vacation; this time I let her get to me."

"What went down?"

"I had been checking Polly Parker's vitals, and . . . ."

"Oh, Pete wants me to meet her."

"You'd like her. Anyway, I sat down for a minute to chat when Helga walked in and started bawling me out—right in front of Polly."

"Our Helga, ever gentle and full of grace. What set her off this time?"

"She said that other patients needed attention and that I should get a move on."

Margot continued massaging Ginger's neck. "How mortifying."

"Poor Polly immediately apologized for keeping me, and Helga, in that phony-sweet voice of hers, said, 'Oh, Polly dear, it's not your fault.' Then she grabbed my arm and yanked me out of the room."

"She yanked you? What did you do?"

"I told her to keep her hands off of me and never to speak to me like that again in front of a patient"

"What did she say to that?"

"Nothing; she just strode off without saying a word."

Margot said, "You could sue her, or at least file a complaint."

"I'm giving it a think; her behavior is totally inappropriate for a nurse. We've asked ourselves repeatedly why such a mean-spirited person would choose care-giving for a career."

"I've wondered that myself."

"I think she chose nursing because she loves being in charge," Ginger said. "Most patients are helpless and needy, and, as head nurse, she also has a staff to boss around; it makes her feel all-powerful."

Margot washed her hands at the sink and poured herself a cup of coffee. "Next time she acts up, you could accidentally bump into her really hard or step on her foot; then you could apologize for being clumsy. "

"Good idea. Or even better, maybe I could slip her an interesting medication; I'll have to figure out what I can get away with."

They both laughed and Ginger seemed to snap out of it.

"Tell me about Polly; why is she here?"

"She developed a serious case of shingles; she was in the hospital for a full month before coming here."

"I know someone who was also hospitalized with shingles for several weeks; she hasn't ever fully recovered her strength. When I found out, I had myself vaccinated; the doctor said I could still contract the disease."

"The chances of that happening are slight. Even though Polly's prognosis is for a complete recovery, Shingles attacks the nerve endings, and it's not only extremely painful, but she has purple spots all over her body."

"How awful," Margot said. "I'd die if that happened to me."

"Polly's worried there might be permanent scarring, but the spots will disappear; maybe you can help cheer her up."

"And I thought I had problems. I'm tied up today, but I'll make time to visit her tomorrow—maybe bring a bouquet." She caught herself. "Nix that; flowers and gifts are verboten. I'll find something small enough to sneak past Helga."

⇌ ⇋

The following morning Margot entered the room where she found Polly lying in bed and Pete lounging in a chair next to her. Margot introduced herself and extended a decorative notebook with a jeweled clasp, "Pete suggested we meet; I brought you a little welcome gift."

"Polly held up the notebook. "How pretty! Thanks. I can use it for sketching."

Pete gestured towards Polly, "Did I tell you how mad I am about this woman? The first time I saw Polly Parker lying there, pallid but pretty and recovering from shingles, I picked her as the perfect pal for me. Right sweetheart?"

Polly laughed. "There you go again."

"People may accuse me of being partial to the p's in her names, but I would be a particularly peculiar pinhead, if I picked her for the p's pervading her person."

"It's true; I'm Polly Parker—the patient with shingles, and I'm positively perturbed about the problem."

Margot joined in. "I'm pleased as punch to have popped by to participate in this palaver with the pair of you."

Pete struggled to his feet. "Pardon me, precious ladies; I do perceive the need to depart." He bent and kissed Polly's forehead before hobbling off on his crutches.

Margot shook her head. "What a character."

"He's been wonderful for me. It's impossible to feel depressed with him around."

Margot tapped her volunteer badge. "My assignment is to cheer you up as well."

"You're kind to spend time visiting patients stuck here."

"Listen. I can relate to being stuck. I'm over at the residential section and not by my own choice. What brought you to this facility?"

"I came to visit my daughter in Dana Point and, on a lark, I looked up old friends who, it turns out, are thinking about starting a new Fashion Magazine on this coast; they wanted to toss around a few ideas."

"Did you work in fashion?"

"I started out as a fashion editor with *McCall's*, which is now defunct. Then I moved over to Condé Nast for work on *Glamour* and *Vogue*; I'm retired now."

Margot's eyes widened. "That's impressive. Before I married, I had a job as a 'prop girl' on ad shoots for a New York agency. I bet if we played 'geography,' we'd find we know the same people. But continue your story; I didn't mean to interrupt."

"My friends and I camped out at the Ritz Carlton to spend time on the beach and tour the area." Polly stopped mid-sentence. "Sure you want the whole gory story?"

Margot nodded.

"We had a ball until the morning I woke up with a burning sensation. I tried ignoring the whole thing, but my skin became hypersensitive; even wearing clothes hurt. Then I developed blisters, and they kept multiplying until I thought I would go mad. I'll spare you the rest; it's so gross!"

"What's the treatment for shingles?"

"Anti-virals. Lucky they put me on them immediately; otherwise I could have developed cellulitis."

"Cellulitis?"

"It's a bacterial infection that can be serious.

"South Coast Hospital, where the Doc sent me for treatment, recommended this place. I still felt weak, so since my daughter, Susan, is always busy socializing, I thought it simplest to come here."

"Are the drugs working?"

Polly crossed her fingers. "So far."

"If there's any way I can help, let me know; I'm a regular around here."

"Meeting you and remembering the old days makes me feel better already.

Margot stood to leave, "Sorry I can't stay, but I'll be back for a nice long visit as soon as I can."

On her way down the corridor, Margot ran into Ginger again. Grabbing her by the arm, she said, "I met Polly today. What a knockout she is. I love her gorgeous, creamy complexion and grey hair with those subtle black streaks. But the purple spots on her arms are scary. Are you sure they won't be permanent?"

"I told you they'll disappear."
"And you said that chances are I won't develop shingles."
"Stop worrying. Trust me."

———

Since Beauty Day's success, Margot had been mulling over a fashion project for the residents of Shady Palms. A few weeks back, she had noticed a newspaper article describing a drop-in sewing lounge, called Stitch, owned and run by women. Stitch supplied the tools and also offered classes and professional advice.

Her discussion of fashion with Polly renewed her interest in the project, and she phoned the sewing facility. Margot spoke with one of the owners, a woman named, Dagmar, who said that Stitch would welcome the idea of a group visit; she went on to explain that Stitch offered designer-taught classes at different levels, depending on the number of attendees and their various needs.

At first the idea sounded appealing, but thinking about the many details involved brought her back to reality. She would need to generate interest, set a tentative date, post sign-up sheets describing Stitch and ask for information on past sewing experience.

Bus rental, class fees, lunch, snacks, all had to be calculated; she would need the help of Nancy, Jane, and Barbara in order to pull it off. Her friend, Rachel, was always good at organizing events; maybe Margot could enlist her expertise.

The next morning, Margot entered Polly's room and found her staring out the window. She patted Polly's hand, "You seem down; shall I fetch Pete to cheer you up?"

"Not even Pete could do that. My recovery is maddeningly slow; I have ugly purple spots all over, and I itch like crazy. This must be payback from the gods, for my wicked ways in a former life."

"I doubt that very much, but I'm working on a project that may help you atone." She told her about Beauty Day's success and described the plans for visiting Stitch.

On hearing this, Polly's mood seemed to brighten. "Sounds perfect for anyone who enjoys sewing."

"It does, doesn't it? There's also a designer boutique where we can shop."

"If I muster the courage to show my face in public, I'd love to tag along."

"I know this is short notice, but I wonder if you have any design suggestions."

"Maybe I can sketch out one or two ideas." She found the notebook Margot had given her. "Post menopause, our waists disappear and our stomachs pop out, so designers know special tricks for adding style to the shapeless house dresses or muumuus our mothers wore."

"Not mine; *my* mother dressed like a fashion plate way into her eighties."

"So that's where your glamour comes from." After sketching a few minutes, she held up the page. "For comfort plus style, besides traditional A-line dresses, we can expand garments, using hidden elastic, or to achieve a more tailored look, we use pleats and darts. Home sewing is adaptable to all body types and sizes."

Polly continued sketching, "The bloused style is hot right now; it's comfortable and it definitely provides a younger look, but I prefer higher necklines and a little more sleeve, for hiding the bad stuff."

Over her shoulder, Margot studied the drawings. "What you're sketching is a vast improvement. I just wish manufacturers offered more shirts in all-cotton. Because of my 'hot flash' problem, I die of the heat, wearing synthetics."

"I'm the same way. In summer, I wear cotton or linen tops with small cap sleeves; I carry a shawl for the times my fickle body alternates between freezing and roasting."

"I sure asked the right person. May I keep your drawings and add a few notes?"

"Keep them. Having you around makes me forget my problems. Come by whenever you can."

"Of course, I'll visit every chance I have." She kissed Polly's forehead and hurried away for a golf lesson with Joe's friend, Rick. She had called him, briefly mentioning Joe and that she had met his daughter, Doris. Once there, she would bring up the hip flask and ask about its possible involvement in Joe's death."

CHAPTER TWENTY-EIGHT

For her appointment with Rick, Margot chose a tight, peacock-blue polo shirt and a short white skirt that displayed her still smooth and unblemished legs. Some teases to her curls for more bounce, and off she drove to the golf course.

With time to spare until her lesson, she popped into the Pro shop where Tim, the blond, crew-cut clerk, proved a welcome distraction as he restocked the shelves.

Not one extra ounce of fat and no tush.

Margot browsed through the clothing and golf accessories until a sage green shirt caught her eye as a possible let's-make-up gift for Hans.

If I ever see him again.

At the driving range, Margot watched Rick pivot his lean body and exccute a perfect drive toward the 300-yard flag. She applauded. "Well done."

"Why thank you, Ma'am."

Rick's white shirt showed off a deeply tanned body and strong athletic arms; his demeanor radiated confidence in himself as a fine human specimen. He smiled as he introduced himself, revealing deep dimples.

They eyed each other approvingly.

"Right on time; I appreciate that. You can't believe how many people keep me waiting, especially women."

Strike one against you, but I'll play nice.

"I didn't want to be late for my first lesson."

"Are you a new golfer or here to improve your game?"

"My golfing career began and ended the day my husband took me on a round with two friends."

"Let me guess. You whiffed the ball. You played too slow. You drove into a sand trap. You lost a ball in the water hazard."

"All of the above; we agreed never to set foot on a golf course together again."

"Did you let your husband hang around very long after that?"

"Ted and I had a happy marriage, partially due to his playing golf without me. He passed away a few years ago."

"Sorry to hear that."

For the first few minutes, they worked on Margot's stance. Next, Rick demonstrated a proper swing and follow-through, before wrapping his arms around her from behind and guiding her through several shots.

Just like in the movies, but sure feels good.

Rick patted her shoulder, "Excellent. Shame you let your husband scare you off."

"No regrets. The time feels right for something new."

After she practiced several more swings, he said, "Make sure you finish your drive all the way through. That's important."

He lined up several balls at various distances from the hole, demonstrating the stances and grips used for putting. Following his instructions, she sank the ball about a third of the time.

"You're definitely a natural. With more practice, I can have you on the course by the next lesson."

"Can we set up some times?"

Rick pulled out his *Smartphone,* and they agreed on several dates.

She said casually, "I'd like to hear more about your friendship with Joe; are you free for coffee?"

"My next appointment's in an hour; we can go to the clubhouse."

"Lovely."

As Margot followed him, she gestured to the stunning vista of grass stretching from the Olympic-sized swimming pool all the way to the deep purple-blue ocean. "My word, what glorious surroundings."

"Did you say 'my word'?" That's an expression I haven't heard in a while. Do you also say, land sakes or land sakes alive?"

Margot blushed, wondering if her vocabulary gave her age away. She lowered her eyes in mock modesty, "I'm just a shy, old-fashioned girl."

He winked. "Oh, I'll bet you are; I'm partial to old-fashioned women."

Once seated on the patio, he asked, "Ever tried a pomegranate margarita?"

"Pomegranate anything sounds great to me."

Rick ordered two. "So Margot, how did you meet Joe?"

"We met at the skilled nursing facility where I volunteer. I enjoyed Joe a lot during the short time I knew him; he always made me laugh, and I'm so sorry he died."

"Me too; we go all the way back to Chicago when we were both management trainees for Playboy Clubs."

"Joe told me all about his stint at Playboy; must have been a wild scene."

"Not too wild; we never got to touch the Bunnies, but I hear 'Heff' still helps himself plenty at age eighty plus."

"Did you work there long?"

"Joe and I both burned out quick. We ditched the place and headed out West where I ended up on the golf circuit. You may know that he became a mouth piece, the perfect profession for a guy who loved to talk and argue."

After the drinks arrived, Margot said "salud" and took a sip. "I recently paid a condolence call on his daughter, and, speaking of arguing, she told me you visited Joe at skilled nursing. Did he ever mention arguing with Helga, the head nurse there?"

Rick scratched his head. "He once said she bawled him out for pinching women patients; he didn't seem to take it very seriously. Old Joe never could resist a bottom—big or small."

"I can just imagine Helga's reaction; I hear that anything related to 'sex' makes her uncomfortable."

"I met her once—moose of a broad."

"When did you last see Joe? Was it close to the time he died?"

"One or two days before, I think; I remember because he acted way too quiet for Joe. Made me uneasy. I called to check on him a few days later, and they told me he had died."

"I'm curious; can you be more specific about why you were concerned?"

"It's hard to say; he just wasn't his usual joking around self."

"No more knock-knocks?"

"I'll never hear another knock-knock without thinking of Joe."

"Ditto for me. Want another round, my treat?" Margot said.

"No, mine." Rick signaled the waiter.

As they sipped their drinks and chatted amiably, Margot said, "I'm hoping you can clear up a mystery for me."

"A mystery; I love mysteries."

"It's no big deal; while we were packing up Joe's belongings, we found an empty hip flask in the chest beside his bed. By any chance, do you know where it came from?"

A shadow crossed Rick's face.

"It definitely smelled of alcohol."

Rick frowned. "That's what hip flasks are intended for."

"But a diabetic, like Joe, shouldn't be drinking; we're wondering how he obtained the hip flask?"

Small drops of sweat appeared on Rick's brow. "Beats me."

Margot bore in. "I only mention it because Joe's sudden death puzzled the staff, and his family."

"I couldn't believe it either."

Margot slowly ran a finger across the salted rim of her drink. "I'm not sure his daughter told you, but she felt so unnerved, she ordered an autopsy."

"Doris didn't mention it."

"It showed that a combination of alcohol and Valium caused Joe's death."

Rick blanched. "I know nothing about that." He motioned for the check, signed quickly without reading it and stood to leave.

Margot raised her now empty glass. "Thanks for the lesson and for introducing me to a pomegranate margarita."

Once more his charming and affable self, Rick, smiled. "I love teaching pretty ladies, especially old-fashioned ones."

They both laughed and said, "Goodbye."

On the drive back to Shady Palms, Margot ran over the conversation in her mind. Mentioning the hip flask and the autopsy results had definitely hit a nerve.

What could Rick be hiding?

Taking lessons from him would be fun; he was certainly easy on the eyes. If Hans stayed mad, they might even . . . .

CHAPTER TWENTY-NINE

A week passed without word from Hans. Margot left several messages, but there was only silence on his part.

In the meantime, Jim called to say goodbye. He said how much he enjoyed seeing her again, adding, "I'm sorry for being such a consummate jerk. You must be disgusted with me."

"It's too bad your visit ended on such a sour note; we once had a special relationship; perhaps we'll meet again—either here or on the East Coast."

"I hope I didn't screw you with your friend, Hans. He's a real sport, helping me the way he did. You should hold on to him."

"That might not be easy; currently he's not returning my phone calls."

"If it's because of what I did, I could phone him, try to smooth things over.

"Oh don't do that."

"I won't, but before I leave, tell me how your conservator case is going?"

"I'm waiting for a court date."

"Same lawyer you started with?"

"Same one."

"Maybe you *should* hire the firm Hans and my buddies recommended."

Margot stiffened. "I'm good."

"I could ask my friends for other referrals?"

"I told you, I'm good. Have a safe trip home and take care of yourself."

Jim said, "Hope I see you again soon."

"Me too," she lied.

The next call came from her attorney, saying, "Gordon Jacobs here, I trust you're well and staying out of mischief."

"I'm fine; my volunteers and I are working like little elves in skilled-nursing."

"Good for you, old scout."

"Oh, and next week, I'm taking the residents to a sewing workshop."

"Proud of you."

"Trying my best."

"I'm calling for two reasons: First, I checked out the information you passed on; Rudy and Clarissa *are* major contributors to Judge Garrote's campaigns, and I've made a motion for his dismissal from the case based on extreme prejudice."

"Hallelujah."

"I'm also notifying you that His Honor has set up another hearing on Tuesday, the third of October, at 10:30."

"Why the hearing if he's being dismissed?"

"I'm hoping for his removal beforehand, but to be safe, phone my secretary for an appointment, so we can work on a strategy. And don't forget to document your good deeds to impress the court."

My case is moving right along, she thought. There's no reason to change law firms.

Margot hung up and dressed hurriedly to meet Rachel at *Sapphire*, the restaurant where she and Hans had the unfortunate encounter with Jim and his friends. Afterwards, she and Rachel could shop in Laguna. Perhaps they would luck out and run into Hans.

Margot arrived at *Sapphire* first and requested a patio table to avoid the deafening music inside. Though the rumbling PCH traffic intoned its own cacophonous sound, the patio afforded a ring-side seat to watch the comings and goings in Laguna Beach. She scanned the menu to discover what new global dishes the chef had devised. The restaurant still featured the Five-Surprises Bento box, but they had discontinued the deliciously rich lamb sliders, the kind of comfort food she craved these days.

Soon Rachel appeared, apologizing for being late.

"I don't mind; I'm enjoying my pom iced tea; it's . . . ."

"Not that pomegranate/anti-oxidant spiel again." Rachel lit a cigarette and waved it in the air. "All right, I surrender; order me one."

"How can you smoke in the same breath you mention anti-oxidants?"

"They're your obsession, not mine. Anyway I just saw Hans next door."

Margot leaned forward. "You saw Hans—where?"

"Buying cheese at *Sapphire's* Pantry."

"Do you think he's headed here to the restaurant?"

"Don't know, but he said hello and asked about you."

"That's promising. Tell me exactly what he said—word for word. Maybe…." She stopped mid-sentence, letting out a gasp.

Rachel raised her head, in surprise. "What's wrong?"

Margot gestured to the couple sitting down two tables away. "Quick, get the check."

Spotting them, Diana waved and called out, "Hi Margot, hi Rachel."

Hans gave them a half salute and quickly looked away.

Rachel blustered, "Why that brazen hussy; she's waving with a big smirk on her face. Did you notice the cool and sophisticated pantsuit to match her baby blues? I could go over there and pull her blonde hair out by the dark roots."

"I may throw up, right here in front of everyone."

"Come on honey." Rachel pulled Margot to her feet. "This calls for heavy duty lifting. Wine or something more serious? Your place or mine?"

⪥ ⪤

Early the next morning, Margot woke with a throbbing headache and fumbled in the night table drawer until she found aspirin. She struggled to open the bottle, and with no water handy, she choked down the bitter tablets. En route to the bathroom, she shuddered at the white apparition flashing from the mirrored walls.

Throwing cold water by the handfuls onto her face, she noted she hadn't felt this wretched since her youthful five-Martini days.

She wagged her finger. You're nothing but a bedraggled old hag boozing it up because you saw Hans with his little friend.

Margot remembered rushing out of the restaurant, but she had no memory of paying for the drinks. Embarrassed, she promised herself to visit Sapphire, pay up, apologize profusely, and leave a generous tip.

They had retired to Margot's apartment where she broke out a stash of Grey Goose, replenishing their glasses again and again. She had no idea how much vodka they had polished off or how Rachel had made it home.

Now, to check the day's schedule, she thumbed through her date book, and read, LUNCHEON, DINING ROOM, SKILLED NURSING STAFF, 1:00 P.M. MUST GO. Two weeks earlier, Ginger had urged her to attend the luncheon, saying, "You can't miss seeing Helga in action with our eminent director, Mr. Norwood."

"The luncheon's in an hour," Margot wailed. "I'll never have time to repair the damage."

All at once, she heard loud knocking; was it the door or her head? She dragged herself off to admit Nancy and Jane, who looked at her and both gasped.

"What happened to you, sweet pea?" Nancy asked. Taking in the empty bottles and wine glasses, she said, "Never mind; we get it."

Immediately they went to work. Stripping off Margot's robe, they forced her into the shower where they held her under an icy cold spray. Ignoring her loud protests, they followed up with hot, steamy water until the color crept back into her face.

While Nancy applied Margot's make-up, Jane slid open the closet door and pulled out a lavender pantsuit. "This color flatters every-one, doncha think?"

As they dressed her, Margot rehashed the whole mess; Hans and Diana, Hans and Jim, the Judge, The Relatives. It came out sounding like gibberish, and she began to cry.

Jane screeched, "Oh, don't get so worked up; you'll smear your mascara."

Nancy fiddled with the collar of Margot's jacket. "This is all catty-wampus. You sure do clean up purty though."

She smoothed Margot's jacket one last time. "Don't move, ya hear. Don't go doing anything foolish and ruin how we fixed ya up so nice. We'll be back to fetch y'all to lunch after we go dress."

Margot raised her eyes to the ceiling. *Thank you Lord for my women friends.*

Downstairs, the dining room, now transformed, held round tables set with white damask cloths, simple gold-rimmed china, and lightly-etched fancy goblets, to mark the special occasion. White and yellow daisies, purple lisianthus, pink alstromeria, and yellow carnations comprised a festive centerpiece on each table. The formal drapes were drawn back from the tall, narrow, mullioned windows to reveal the lion's head fountain, centered in the expanse of lawn, edged by flowerbeds containing seasonal blooms.

A special table had been reserved for Helga and Mr. Norwood along with a retinue of staff doctors forced to witness Helga's cloying attentions to the Director.

Margot, Nancy, Jane, and Barbara, joined by Ernesto, Ginger, and Betty were perfectly situated at a table close enough to observe and overhear the happenings at the head table.

A large buffet offered the usual pedestrian cold turkey, ham, assorted salads, cheeses, and breads; for dessert there were pick-up squares or cookies. Soft drinks, coffee, and bottles of wine stood at the ready.

Ernesto, the lone man at Margot's table, announced, "As El Padre, I will pour the wine." Noticing that everyone but Margot held out a glass, he asked, "No vino today?"

"I drank more than enough last night."

"You need, how you say, hair of the dog. What means hair of the dog, anyway?"

"It's a hangover cure." Betty answered. "Supposedly, when someone drinks too much, the cure involves drinking more of the same."

"We have similar customs."

"Besides," Margot said, "I'm here for an education. Ginger told me I shouldn't miss the Helga and Norwood show."

Said show, now in full swing, they watched as Helga brought Norwood a glass of water, followed by a heaping plate of food, all the while bombarding him with questions: "Is white wine all right, or do you prefer red? Do you need more turkey or ham? Would you like mustard or mayo? I can bring both. Want me to make you a sandwich?"

On the way for more food, Helga stopped at Margot's table and, ignoring Ernesto, she said, "Hello ladies, are you enjoying yourselves?"

"I see Mr. Norwood, he have has his own private waitress today," Ernesto said.

Helga glared at Ernesto. "*You* must be having trouble finding something to eat; there are no tacos and enchiladas on the buffet."

Ernesto lifted up the end of the table cloth and pointed to the floor. "I bring my own; want some?"

Helga left in a huff and continued loading more plates, which she took to Norwood. "I brought you mixed green salad, Caesar, and coleslaw. Also, chocolate cake and three kinds of cookies."

Margot gestured towards the pair. "Will you catch Helga, running here, running there; she's a regular little energizer bunny."

Betty said, "I'm half expecting Helga to salute and say, "Reporting for duty, sir."

"Do you think she'll cut up his food, feed him, hold a straw to his mouth, and help him drink?" Margot asked.

Ernesto puffed out his chest. "My *novia* does those things for me. That's the way a woman *should* treat a man."

Unmoved by the loud boos and hisses, he shrugged. "*No me importa;* you can boo all you want. I'm the hombre surrounded today by all you beauties."

"Now I get it," Margot said. "Helga plays Norwood's devoted slave, all soft and submissive, and in return he gives her absolute rule."

"Let's drink to our own absolute rule."

Ernesto held up a bottle of Pinot Noir and filled Margot's glass, "Come, join us."

Margot shrugged and accepted, sipping one glass after another. By the time Norwood stood to deliver a long-winded speech, the room started spinning, and it had become increasingly difficult for her to stay awake.

Norwood droned on and began introducing the new volunteers. Then came her turn. "Will Mrs. Margot Manning please stand up?"

Through an alcoholic haze, Margot thought she heard her name but found herself incapable of responding. "Margot, will you please stand?" he repeated.

Ernesto tugged at her hand. "Psst, Margot, get up." He yanked her from the chair, forcing her to stand. She grasped the top rail for support, bobbing her head up and down a few times then fell into her seat. The crowd tittered.

Immediately, Nancy jumped up. "I'm fetching black coffee."

The next thing Margot knew, she found herself upstairs on the bed with a cool cloth on her forehead.

"Please let me sleep," she begged Nancy and Jane who rolled their eyes and tiptoed out, leaving her sprawled flat.

They returned at dinner time to shake her awake. "Listen here, girlfriend, you need to get your act together." Nancy said. "You're not helping yourself any."

Margot whimpered, "I know, but bad things keep happening."

Nancy wagged her finger. "Stop being a cry baby. What's happened to the tough gal I reckoned you for?"

Margot stood up, and tucking in her shirt, she promised herself to reform: no more drowning her sorrows with booze when things went wrong; she would work hard volunteering. And she would quit her sleuthing—once she found out how Joe died.

CHAPTER THIRTY

The next day, Margot wakened before the alarm, determined to keep her new resolutions. Arriving at work earlier than usual, she found Betty and Ginger huddled together and whispering. "Hey you two is something wrong?" She asked.

"I'll say," Ginger said. "First thing this morning, two detectives barged in and took Ernesto to headquarters."

"What's all that about?"

Betty shrugged. "We'll have to wait and ask him."

Late in the day, Margot found Ernesto in the lunchroom and noted that his dark skin had lost its usual robust color; there were new dark circles under his eyes.

She sat down and reached for his hand, "*Que paso, amigo?*"

Barely lifting his head, he said, "Oh Señora, you'd look this way too after hours with *La Policia,* asking the same questions over and over: When did I last see Joe? What did I have against him? Did I bring him any alcohol?

"I would never give no liquor to a diabetic; I'm not e*stupido.*"

"What else did they ask?"

"If ever take any money from Joe."

"And did you?"

"No, but. . . ."

"But what?"

"The truth is, Joe, Pete, and I sometimes play a little poker. Ernesto quickly covered his mouth. "*Por favor,* forget I say that.""

"Do the deputies know about the poker games?"

"I don't think so; I hope not."

"How much money did you gamble?"

Ernesto looked sheepish. "Only a few dollars."

"I'm on your side, but I can't help if you're not straight with me. Is there anything I need to know?"

"No, no, *es todo.*"

Margot gave up quizzing Ernesto and went to find Pete hoping he could shed light on the poker games. She checked the solarium, his usual hangout, and sure enough, there he stood leaning on his crutches and acting as kibitzer-in-chief for a bridge game. Ignoring the dirty looks directed toward him, he whispered loudly to Max, a new patient, "Open three diamonds—you hold a seven card suit and an outside ace."

Max slammed his cards face down on the table. "For Pete's sake Pete, leave me alone; I know all about pre-empt bidding."

Margot tiptoed up behind Pete and tapped him on the shoulder. "Wouldn't you rather talk to me than pester these guys?"

"The heck with them; they're a bunch of amateurs. Imagine anyone disdaining the advice of a renowned bridge expert." He maneuvered his crutches over to a nearby sofa. "Besides, I can never pass up an invitation from Miss Margot."

Margot joined Pete, and he drew her close. "How's life treating you these days?"

"Not good, but I'm here to discuss other card games with you."

"Speak away, fair maiden."

Knowing how much he enjoyed turning anything into a joke, she ventured, "With your permission, kind sir, I have great curiosity about the poker games you once hath played with our dear, departed Joe and one Ernesto. Forsooth did these take place?"

Pete cupped his chin as though thinking. "Forsooth I believe they did."

"Pray tell me, how hath Ernesto afforded to gamble with big time knight-errants such as you?"

"Forsooth it only involved penny ante poker. No one ever hath won or lost more than a few dollars per game."

Having now enticed Pete into cooperating, Margot switched away from the Elizabethan vernacular. "Ernesto acted alarmed about the poker games, and I'm wondering why?"

"Maybe he fears the wrath of Helga the Hun; for such activities she would undoubtedly stomp all over him."

"It's not Helga who worries him; it's the sheriff's office."

Pete's brows narrowed. "Why the Sheriff?"

"Two deputies took him to headquarters for questioning yesterday."

"I hadn't heard. The poor guy."

"According to Ernesto, the detectives asked if he'd ever borrowed money from Joe? Did Joe ever mention it?"

Pete tapped his temple. "Hmm, let me see. Yes, I do remember Joe saying he would occasionally lend Ernesto a few shekels—whenever the guy fell behind playing the numbers game. Apparently, he had to pay up or . . . ."

"Do you know how much money Joe loaned him?

"No idea."

"Do you think anyone else knew about your poker games?"

Pete hesitated a minute. "I do remember an aide appearing during one game. She chuckled and said, 'naughty, naughty,' then smiled and left."

"So, it's possible Helga may have found out as well."

"I doubt it; she'd have axed Ernesto post haste."

"You're probably right, but I heard she's trying to pin Joe's death on Ernesto."

"That's our Helga for you."

"If you remember anything important, will you please let me know?"

Pete grinned. "I will inform you immediately and maybe even a little sooner. Are you taking up sleuthing now?"

"It varies the routine around here. Besides, I really liked Joe and I care what happens to Ernesto."

"Good luck, Miss Marple. Or is it Jessica Fletcher?" Pete saluted her. "You'd make the prettiest lady detective ever, hands down."

⚔⚔

During the course of rounds that morning, as Margot passed the director's office, she was surprised to hear loud arguing; Norwood generally did not raise his voice.

Margot ducked into the small reception area across the hall where she positioned herself to watch and eavesdrop.

A red-faced Helga sat across from Norwood's desk, shouting, "We have to fire that lazy Mexican orderly. Ernesto's been nothing but trouble since the day he arrived; now the authorities suspect he's involved in Joe's death."

Norwood shouted back. "Quiet down, will you. Racist talk has no place in this facility." Lowering his own voice, he said, "I can't fire him without cause, and I can't have you calling him names. These days the EEOC could be down on us in a flash for discrimination, especially if he's legal. He is, isn't he?"

"He's legal all right. We scour the records of those barrio people."

Norwood motioned his hands up and down for quiet. "Take it easy on him; let's wait and see how the investigation goes."

Helga pounded the table and thundered, "Don't tell me to take it easy. I want him gone. Today."

Norwood grabbed her hands. "Stop this lunatic behavior before the whole facility hears you."

"But Ernesto's . . . ."

Clenching his teeth and thrusting out his jaw, Norwood came from behind his desk and grabbed Helga's arm, "I said right now, and I mean it."

So Norwood does have a backbone, Margot thought.

As Helga shrugged off Norwood's arm and stood to leave, Margot almost laughed out loud at the picture of Helga towering over him by more than six inches and wagging her finger in his face. "I'll go, but you haven't heard the last of this. Any more bad things that happen because of Ernesto will be on your head."

Helga stormed out the door and spying Margot thumbing through a magazine, she spat, "Are you following me around? You're on duty; get your butt moving."

"Sorry. A patient asked me if we had any current issues of *People Magazine*. I couldn't find any, so I'm . . . ."

"Take the whole pile and let the patient choose; you're wasting time."

On leaving the reception area, Margot glimpsed Norwood, staring into space, shell-shocked from his encounter with Helga's evil twin.

⟞⟝ ⟝⟞

With no plans for the evening, Margot searched the paper, looking for something to do. *The Times* calendar section featured an ad for Laguna's first Thursday Art Walk, during which the galleries hosted open houses.

Sounds like fun, she thought. Maybe I'll bump into someone interesting; Hans might even show up. He loves gallery hopping.

Deciding what to wear, always cheered her up. But in choosing a pair of pants, she found that many no longer fit. Despite efforts to diet and exercise, a two-inch gap existed between the button and the hole on nearly every pair. At last, tucked in the back, she found white linen elasticized pants that were the right size and made a sharp contrast with a black silk shell and a shiny black poplin jacket bought on sale at *Escada.*

Her next choice, a wide metallic silver belt, also no longer went around her middle. Fingering her expensive belt collection, she complained aloud, "I'm losing Hans and now my waist is gone. What next?

Laying the pieces on the sofa, she chose silver accessories: a large medallion necklace, a chunky bracelet and long earrings.

At least I'm not too fat for my jewelry, she thought.

She dressed and carefully applied fresh makeup, then drove to Laguna where she spent a half hour at *Peter Blake* studying a new artist whose abstract works in shades of black and grey she found edgy and exciting. Outside the gallery, she boarded the free shuttle and descended at *The Whitney*, which featured figurative art, landscapes, interiors, and still-life.

Charmed by a figurative abstraction showing two little girls playing on the beach, she considered asking the price when she felt a tap on her shoulder. She turned, anticipating a friendly face and found her nemesis, Alice Marks, smirking gleefully.

"Margot, darling, how have you been? I see you're alone. Did that handsome fellow from the hotel fly the coop?"

"You mean Jim. He was here on vacation for a few days."

"I guess he's not the only one who flew the coop. I'm assuming you and Hans aren't a couple anymore since I've seen him with Diana Kennedy several times. They're becoming quite the twosome."

Waves of anger washed over Margot. In an icy voice, she enunciated slowly and clearly, "Whom I choose to hang out with is none of your damn business. Stop poking into my affairs, you gossiping old hag."

Having said her piece, Margot strode out to the street, now crowded with wine-toting art *aficionados*. She ducked into the next gallery and made her way towards the back, hoping to find a secluded niche where she could pull herself together. A young couple occupied one narrow space admiring a plein air landscape and discussing the palette and the brush strokes. Toward the rear she located an empty spot where she leaned against the wall and closed her eyes. Abruptly, she felt a pair of hands on her shoulders. Thinking Alice Marks had followed her, she spun around staring daggers.

A familiar voice said, "*Bella, Bambina*, don't be angry. It's me, Luigi. And by the way you need a haircut *prontissimo*."

Relieved, she fell into his arms, "Oh, Luigi, thank goodness it's you and not that dreadful woman."

"I've been called many names, but never dreadful."

"Please take me somewhere, anywhere."

"Of course. I'll go tell Cedric we're headed for *Las Brisas*."

Luigi soon reappeared and took her by the arm. "Come, *Bella*. Let Luigi rescue you." He guided her across the street to the restaurant bar where he found them a small table and cradled her head on his shoulder while she told him the whole sad story.

Luigi kissed her soundly on one cheek then pushed her away, studying her face intently. "*Bellissima*, you're not the woman I've always known. Call this man and say you must see him *pronto*. He handed her his cell. "Use mine; I promise not to listen."

Margot waved the phone aside and dived back into Luigi's arms. "I'm afraid."

"So give yourself a day to recover from that nasty woman; then call him." Luigi hesitated. "I have so much faith in you; if he doesn't come running back, I'll cut your hair free for the next six months."

"Six months?"

Luigi hit his head, "What am I saying; make it the next two months?"

Feeling encouraged, she extended her hand. "It's a deal."

⟢ ⟣

The following day at skilled nursing, Margot did a double take when Helga appeared, smiling broadly and distributing muffins and cupcakes from a large straw basket covered in a red and white checked cloth.

Even more startling, she offered Margot a muffin. "Here, sweetie. Try my favorite combo of chocolate and raspberries." Then, acting the happy homemaker, she continued on down the hall spreading cheer.

After her recent unpleasant counter with Helga, Margot didn't know what astonished her more, the "sweetie" or seeing the woman passing out homemade pastries. She rushed off and told Ginger, "I must be hallucinating; I saw Helga behaving human."

"I know it's a shock," Ginger said. "Sometimes she goes on a baking kick and brings the sweets to share—cookies, brownies, cakes, pies—the whole *schmear*. Then she gets over it and reverts to her mean, disagreeable self."

"Either they're poison muffins or she wants us to be fat like her."

"The woman has different sides to her personality. Mean as she can be, if a staff member has a personal problem, she often jumps in to help. A few years ago, when a former nurse had a child suffering from a brain tumor, Helga researched the best surgeon and the best place for after-care. But Helga kept calling non-stop with advice, and the nurse had to drop her."

Margot said, "Makes sense; she loves controlling people and giving advice."

"Helga's a lonely person; I also think she's trying to make friends."

"I'm glad she can be kindly, but here at work, we see her dark side, and personally, I'd rather deal with mean Helga than with phony-nice Helga shoving cookies in my face."

She hugged Ginger and raced off for a date with her golf pro, Rick, hoping she could pump him for more information on Joe's death.

CHAPTER THIRTY-ONE

A ware that Hans had a standing table at *Splashes* every Friday, Margot had deliberately suggested meeting Rick there that evening.

Maybe he'll see me here with a handsome hunk as my escort?

Exiting the elevator, she nearly collided with Rick and stopped short. "Hey, aren't you going the wrong way?"

"Lady, you're a half hour late."

Margot flashed him a coquettish smile. "I know and I'm really, really sorry, but I took my time dressing for you tonight."

Reversing course, Rick took her arm. "If you're fishing for a compliment, you'll have to earn it by being extra nice to me."

"Scout's honor, never happen again. And aren't I always nice?" Once seated at an outside table, she gestured towards the sun setting over the ocean, "At least you had this gorgeous view to admire."

"That gorgeous view is disappearing fast, like I almost did."

"Let's forget that. I'm here now, and I'm all yours. We can stay for dinner, if you'd like, or go somewhere nearby."

Enjoying the banter with Rick, she relaxed and found her good spirits returning.

"Dinner here is fine." Rick studied the cocktail menu. "Green apple Martinis all right with you?"

"Yum, just don't let me have more than one. I've been exceeding my quota."

"That's no fun."

"I cannot tell a lie. I'm in training for the LPGA championship."

Rick raised his head skyward. "I bet Joe loved your sense of humor."

"I certainly miss his. Speaking of Joe, one more tiny question."

"Not again."

"Do you remember my mentioning that Joe died from a combination of Valium and alcohol?"

A low growl emanated from Rick's throat. "I remember."

"I'm trying to figure out how Joe got hold of a hip flask?"

Rick frowned, answering in a loud, deliberate voice, "I told you I have no idea. Why do you persist in bringing up the hip flask?"

"I'm a curious person."

Rick paused and hung his head. When he looked up, his eyes brimmed with tears. "I hope I didn't kill the guy."

"So you were the . . .?"

He interrupted, "Let me explain?"

"Margot squeezed his hand. "Sorry."

"At first Joe asked me to sneak him *Snickers* bars, and I refused because of his diabetes. But he argued, 'What could it hurt? They regulate my sugar with the Glucophage.'"

"So I started small by sneaking him a few Snickers bars and progressed to high crimes and misdemeanors supplying the gin and a hip flask."

Rick paused until Margot squeezed his hand again and urged him to continue.

"We kept refilling the flask from the bottle Joe kept hidden, so no one would see us." Rick's voice broke up. "I'm so sorry."

"I know you didn't mean Joe any harm, but where did the Valium come from?"

"I swear; I know nothing about any Valium."

"I believe you."

Rick held up his empty glass, signaling for a second martini. "Do you think I should confess about the alcohol?"

"An orderly from skilled nursing is under suspicion for Joe's death; your information could help clear him."

Rick shook his head. "One day I might man up, but not right now."

"Maybe we should table this discussion for after dinner."

Rick fished out his wallet and set it on the table. "I've lost my appetite."

"I'm sorry I spoiled the evening; next time we get together I won't even mention Joe." Margot pulled out her date book. "Don't forget I'm scheduled for another lesson."

Rick consulted his *Smartphone.* "You're down."

They walked to the elevator and rode upstairs in awkward silence. As they stood at the hotel entrance waiting for their cars, she spotted Hans drive up in his Chevy convertible. The parking attendant opened the passenger door for Diana, then Hans took her arm to lead her up the steps. They were laughing and joking until Hans glanced up and saw Margot standing beside Rick.

The happiness faded from his face. "Margot?"

She took Rick's arm and snuggled close. "Hello Hans. Nice seeing you. This is my friend Rick."

CHAPTER THIRTY-TWO

Margot awoke the next morning feeling exhilarated. Appearing at Hans's favorite restaurant had paid off. Hans had blanched at the sight of her with another man, and a gorgeous man to boot.

More importantly, Rick had admitted bringing the alcohol involved in Joe's death.

She would keep him on the hook, not only because his testimony could clear Ernesto, but because he might have other crucial evidence.

Now to find where the Valium had originated.

At skilled nursing, she found the staff in the hall buzzing about something.

"What's wrong?" She asked.

Ginger took Margot aside. "It's Pete the Punster."

"Pete?"

"He fell out of bed last night and injured his hip."

"The hip they replaced?"

"Yes, and it's serious; they took him to Hoag immediately."

"Do you know how he's doing?"

"His surgery's tomorrow, a new total hip replacement. First Joe, now Pete. . . ."

Margot gasped, "That's awful. How did it happen?"

"We heard that Ernesto found Pete on the floor. Ask him; here he comes now."

Margot greeted Ernesto and said, "I just learned the bad news about Pete."

"Oh, Señora, is terrible—my poor amigo."

"And you were the one who found him?"

Taking her arm, he said, "Let's talk in the lounge; I need strong coffee today."

Once there, Ernesto brought two mugs and handed one to Margot. "I am coming down the hall last night when I hear loud voices and a crash. I run to the noise and find Pete on the floor of his room, screaming in pain, so I pull the chord for help, and I put a pillow under his head."

"Did Pete say anything?"

"He is calming *un poquito*; then he is moaning and asking, 'My piccolo, where's my piccolo?'"

"That's odd."

Ernesto took out a handkerchief to wipe his brow. "No big *sorpresa*; he play piccolo every night."

"Did you find the piccolo?"

"Is on the floor; I think he drop it when he falls."

"Did he say anything else?"

"*Nada*; he is only moaning."

"When you ran down the hall, did you see anyone leaving his room?"

"I swear I see Helga, moving muy *rapido*; I know her fat ass anywhere."

Margot took out a notebook and began writing. "You said you heard loud voices before the crash. Could you make out what they were saying?"

"Is too far away, but sound like arguing."

"You're sure you saw Helga?"

"I already tell you."

"If you remember anything else, let me know; I'm trying to help you stay out of trouble with the authorities."

"*La policia?* No, *Por favor.* "

⇁⊱ ⊰⇀

After Ernesto left, Margot thought about the pattern of death and injuries in the facility. She had discovered the source of the hip flask and the gin, but who had administered the Valium to Joe? And how did Pete injure his hip?

Knowing the poor woman must be distraught, she headed for Polly's room, and found her crying and twisting the tails of her shirt. She hugged Polly. "I heard the news and I'm deeply sorry. Pete adores you, and you seem to care for him as well."

"Pete is a dear, dear man; he's always laughing and joking—just the medicine I need to help me through my illness. I don't know what I'll do until he gets back."

"He'll be here soon enough. They'll operate and give him a new hip."

"I hope so, but I'm worried." Polly wrung her hands. "Why did this have to happen?"

"Ernesto told me he discovered Pete on the floor with his piccolo lying beside him. He wasn't surprised; he said that Pete played every night."

"He did until Helga told him to stop."

"Did he stop?"

"Pete can be stubborn when it comes to his beloved piccolo. He tried closing the door and playing quietly, but that didn't appease Helga; she threatened to take it away."

"Do you know if she ever did?"

"Once for several days—Pete went ballistic until they returned it. He even considered changing nursing homes. He only stayed to be with me."

Another mystery, Margot thought. But with no witnesses to Pete's accident, I'll have to wait until I can speak to him. I'll check his progress and visit as soon as the hospital lets me.

⇒⊹ ⊹⇐

A few days later, en route to visit Pete at Hoag, Margot stopped at *Laguna Beach Books* to find a present for him. While thumbing through various selections, she found a book, entitled, *Get Thee to a Punnery: An Anthology of Intentional Assaults Upon the English Language*, by Richard Lederer.

Perfect for Pete, she thought.

A day earlier, when Margot told Ginger she planned to visit Pete at Hoag, Ginger suggested, "My friend, Sonia's a nurse there. Look her up; she might be of help."

Luckily, Sonia was on duty. A curvaceous dark-haired Latina, she gathered Margot in a hug when she heard that Margot knew Ginger. "What brings you today?"

"I'm here to see Pete Peterson. Do you know anything about him?"

"He's on my floor."

"Pete and I became friends at the facility where Ginger works and where I volunteer. Can you tell me how he's doing?"

"Pete's surgery went well, but there are signs of an infection. At times, he's delirious, and his fever spikes at night."

"Can I see him?"

"Only for a few minutes. I'll walk you there."

As they proceeded to Pete's room, Margot noted that every man they passed followed Sonia's swaying walk with their eyes.

Once there, Margot could see the glorious Newport Coast with Catalina in the distance. Two flower bouquets stood on a table—slender yellow rose buds from Polly and the fat pink peonies Margot had sent.

She bent and took Pete's hand. "Pete, it's Margot. I brought you a book of puns; we can read them together."

He opened his eyes, struggling to focus, then mumbled, "Who?"

"It's Margot—from the nursing center. Remember me?"

"Where's my piccolo. Want my piccolo."

"I'll bring it next time."

Pete grew agitated. "Want my piccolo; let go."

Sonia said, "He keeps asking for his piccolo over and over again."

"Do you know if he has any relatives close by?"

"According to his earlier admission records, Pete has a son who lives in Detroit; he should be here in a few days."

"What a rotten deal for Pete. He's such a fun-loving man, always joking and making puns. Is there anything I can do?"

"Nothing right now; I'll keep an eye on him for you."

"I brought him a book on puns. Hopefully, he can read it when he's more alert. May I leave it on the bed table?"

"Sure, I'll tell him it's from you."

"I'd like to bring Polly Parker next time I come. She's a patient from skilled nursing that Pete's wild about."

"Great; she'll cheer him up."

Margot patted Pete's cheek. "Bye, handsome. I'll be back with Polly. You remember her, don't you?"

No response.

Sonia hugged Margot goodbye. "See you soon."

Remembering what Ernesto had told her and hearing Pete repeatedly ask for his piccolo, she felt sure that Pete's accident had involved a struggle over his piccolo.

CHAPTER THIRTY-THREE

The next morning, Margot stood checking off those Shady Palms residents signed up for the sewing clinic. So far, two women were no-shows.

"Why do I volunteer for this aggravation," she vented to Jane, who, along with Nancy and Barbara, had volunteered to help.

"You know you love it," Jane said. "These trips give everyone a lift, and the women adore you; they count on you to break up the monotony of their lives."

Margot tapped her pen impatiently and consulted her watch. "I'm not doing this from pure altruism; I have a stake in showing the conservator court that I'm a fully functional and capable person."

Jane laughed. "Can't accept a compliment, can you?"

The two stragglers appeared, one mumbling she couldn't find her teeth; the other complaining she had misplaced her glasses.

On the bus, the women juggled themselves and their belongings to find a seat with friends or beside a window. They pulled the shades up; they pulled the shades down. Once everyone settled in, Margot reminded them about the bathroom at the back—a major priority on a bus trip for the elderly. She certainly didn't consider herself elderly even though she increasingly found herself rushing off to find the "ladies."

Up front, she reviewed the day's agenda. "On arrival, you'll be served beverages and given an introductory talk and a tour of the facility. Next, with help from the staff, you can select fabrics and begin projects in classes of six with an instructor/designer."

A voice called out, "What about lunch?"

"After the morning classes, salads and sandwiches will be served. During the next round of classes you'll complete your project. Before leaving for home, we'll reassemble so you can dazzle us with your creations. Are there any questions?"

Every hand on the bus shot up.

"Can we use the potty when we arrive?"

"Of course, but there's a nice clean bathroom right on the bus."

"Ugh; I never use those."

"Then you'll need to wait. Next?"

"Can I have a private lesson? I think I'll need more help."

"Stitch assures me the group lessons provide excellent instruction. Next question?"

"How will I decide what to make?"

"That's where the instructors come in."

"I'm worried there won't be enough time to finish."

"It's figured out in advance. Because this is our first visit, the projects are simple."

"Are there ready-made clothes for sale?"

"Yes, and we've allotted time at the end for shopping. You can try on clothes or buy more fabric." She held up her hand, "Enough questions. You'll find the process easy to follow, and all your questions will be answered."

Ignoring the additional raised hands, Margot sat down beside Polly who had joined them. "I had hoped my friend Rachel would come too, so you could meet her, but she begged off. Rachel claims that she almost flunked sewing class in junior high and her mother had to send a note to get her excused."

Polly laughed. "I'm sorry she didn't come; she sounds like a character."

"Despite her abysmal failure at sewing, she has an eye for fashion; she's always impeccably dressed."

"I've been watching how you handle these women," Polly said. "And I don't know how you do it."

"Being a docent those many years afforded me the perfect training; I'm accustomed to giving information and answering questions."

"Still. . . ."

"I keep reminding myself that these women are constantly told what to do, where to do it and when. Getting sprung can be an adjustment."

"I'm happy I've maintained my independence until now. I'm not ready for senior residence living," Polly said.

"I chose this field trip because it brings out personal creativity; I'm working on an idea to channel their energies into a business venture that would make them feel useful."

"Whatever you're planning, let me know if I can help."

"That would be great; I'd love having your input."

Polly fiddled with the scarf hiding the shingles spots on her neck. "I thought you'd come by after your trip to the hospital yesterday. Did you see Pete?"

Margot sighed. She had deliberately avoided telling her the news. "I only saw him for a few short minutes. Sonia, a nurse friend of Ginger's sneaked me in."

Polly frowned. "But how is he doing? Are you holding out on me?"

"His surgery went well, but, apparently, he developed an infection, and he's been delirious most of the time."

"That's horrible. What do his doctors say?"

"I didn't meet his doctors; Sonia said that they need to get the infection under control, so he can heal."

"Did you talk to him?"

"Not really; he spent the entire time mumbling that he wanted his piccolo."

"The piccolo again."

"I told Pete I might bring you the next time I visit, but I'm not sure he understood. Are you up to it?"

"Of course. And in the future, please let me in on what's happening. Don't try to spare my feelings."

Once inside 'Stitch', they were greeted by the two owners, Nicole and Lisa, who showed them a room lined with shelves of fabrics: solids in a multitude of rich shades and an assortment of prints and textures. Margot and Polly rubbed the cloths between their fingers, proclaiming them to be of excellent quality.

Other shelves contained sewing guides, stitch guides, fabric guides, and patterns from *Vogue, McCall's, Butterick* and *Simplicity*. A vintage Vogue pattern book caught Margot's eye. She hugged it to her chest. "These clothes bring back so many memories. My whole past is in this book."

Nicole interrupted. "Sorry for spoiling your fun, but I'm sure you're eager to see where we do the actual work." She escorted them to a brightly-lit room housing pattern-cutting tables and sewing machines. Shelves displayed various sewing tools: shears and cutters, tapes and gauges, needles and pins.

Margot told Nicole, "I gave up sewing because of my tired old eyes, but your lighting is a pleasure, and you have everything right at our finger-tips."

The young and vibrant instructors possessed the know-how, patience and humor to put everyone at ease. After the women chose a design and the fabric, the instructors demonstrated how to cut the cloth to fit simple patterns involving no buttons or zippers and then sew them together. They would accomplish either a one-piece dress or a two-piece outfit. On future field trips, they could progress to more advanced projects.

As experienced sewers, Margot and Polly worked quickly and added extra flourishes to their garments. Margot completed a deep raspberry linen pants suit; elastic waist pants and a boat-neck shirt, decorated by pearls below the neckline. She designed both garments to be slipped on easily.

Polly fashioned a red, white, and black paisley cotton tunic, with buttons and frog closures; she paired the tunic with wide-legged black pants.

Following the sewing session, the women happily modeled their clothes until Margot clapped her hands and announced, "Chop, chop, let's all change. We only have forty-five minutes for shopping."

Toting their hand-sewn outfits in 'Stitch' garment bags, they attacked the boutique browsing among the ready-made designer clothes; money and credit cards rapidly changed hands.

Delighted with their sewing experiences and their new outfits, the women called out thanks and congratulations. Several said they wished the boutique clothes were available locally. Margot addressed the cheering group, "Glad you enjoyed yourselves. Want a repeat visit?"

The answer was a chorus of "yeses".

She continued, "I'm working on an idea for manufacturing clothing in similar styles and fabrics. I find most store merchandise depressing; they carry either boring fuddy-duddy clothing or teeny-bopper low-slung jeans. What do you think?" More cheers erupted.

Collapsing beside Polly on the bus, Margot said, "Wouldn't it be great if I could straighten out my own life this easily?"

A call from Hans capped off the successful sewing clinic. He said, "Hi, remember me?"

"I dimly recognize your voice, but I'm too tired to guess who you are."

"Tired, why?"

"I had a long, but amazingly successful day escorting the inmates on a trip."

"Sounds like it went better than your museum field trip to L.A."

"Happened like clock-work; no heavy traffic and no one got lost."

"What do you say to dinner at my place? My cuisine, my culinary expertise."

"Tempting—when?"

"Tomorrow would give me time to shop and prepare my Danish specialties."

"Wait while I check my calendar." Balancing the phone between her ear and shoulder, Margot scrolled through her date book. "Tomorrow works."

"Pick you up sevenish?"

Margot hesitated. The way things stood between them, she preferred her own transportation. "Make it seven-thirty; I'll come on my own."

Eyeing her new pantsuit from 'Stitch,' Margot knew exactly what to wear.

The next evening, Margot rapped lightly on Hans's door. He appeared wearing a long white apron and grinned at her from under his tall chef's toque. Bowing, he made a sweeping gesture. "Would Madame do me the pleasure of visiting my kitchen?"

She tapped his hat. "Very professional, Emeril or is it Mario?

Hans bowed again. "Tonight, I'm offering special Scandinavian cuisine."

"And what might that be?

"It's a surprise."

"You're full of surprises lately, and I can't say I've enjoyed them all.

Hans bumped her nose with his finger. "Play nice; we're here to make-up."

"Dinner and making up too?"

Ignoring the remark, he brought her hand to his lips. "Quite glamorous tonight; new outfit?"

Margot did a little twirl and said, "Ta-da. You're not the only one who's been cooking up a surprise. I designed and made this with my own little hands."

He bent and nuzzled her cheek. "That's amazing."

"I possess hidden talents you know nothing of."

"I'm beginning to realize. I hope my dinner compares favorably with the sewing expertise of my dining companion." He gestured to the living room. "Make yourself comfortable; I'll fix you a drink."

While she waited, Margot studied the geometric three-dimensional work by Laddie John Dill on the opposite wall. The rusty-oranges, yellows, greens, and grays reminded her of Yellowstone's geyser springs.

Soon, Hans reappeared, carrying glasses of Aquavit. He handed one to Margot and raised the other. "*Skaol*, a toast to my lady."

They sipped their drinks while she described the field trip to 'Stitch,' adding, "It worked out great. Everyone was so jazzed."

"Well done; sounds like you're back to your confident self again."

"I'm getting there." Margot put her glass on the tray and sniffed. "I smell eggs, smoked salmon, dill, and onion. I'm guessing egg salad, bagels, cream cheese and lox?"

"Good nose, wrong ethnicity."

Hans excused himself, and Margot used the moment to alert Shady Palms that she would be away overnight. How silly, she thought.

Hans returned bearing a proud display of hors d'oeuvres, arranged diagonally on a tray in the shape of a wheel: gravlax on black bread with mustard; crab and cucumber canapés; shrimp, garnished with dill and Danish Caviar on fried bread, topped by a sunny-side egg inside an onion ring.

Margot clapped her hands. "Magnifique. All this for us?"

"There's pickled herring coming. No respectable Danish cook would leave out herring, and for the *pièce de resistance*, my famous Scandinavian meatballs."

Margot tried each appetizer, savoring every bite. "What a feast. I didn't know you were capable of such gastronomic excellence."

"I thought it would be fun to dine on hors d'oeuvres and dessert instead of having a huge meal."

"Good idea; I love small plates and a variety of tastes. What are these breads?"

"Rye and pumpernickel—typical for smorrebrod."

"Smorrebrod?"

"It's bread smeared generously with butter. That's what the word smorgasbord comes from."

"Never knew that."

After they made a large dent in the smorrebrod, Hans disappeared into the kitchen and returned with a carafe of strong coffee and Norwegian hazelnut cake.

Margot patted her stomach. "Just a tiny sliver. That looks rich. And a taste of coffee; otherwise, I'll never fall asleep."

Hans smiled. "That's the idea. I want you awake, so we can make love all night."

"Hey slow down, we haven't reached the making-up part yet."

Hans took the cup from her hand and pulled her into his arms, murmuring softly, "This *is* the making-up part."

As he kissed her, the chef's hat bopped Margot on the head. Saying "Sorry," he yanked it off. Then while trying to remove Margot's tunic, her head stuck midway.

From underneath, Margot said, "Take it easy; you'll ruin my delicate handiwork."

"Then let's have some help."

After getting disentangled, Margot joined in by undoing his shirt buttons—until her long nails caught in the fabric. She tried pulling the shirt over his head, but he ended up stuck inside his shirt as well.

With Hans finally free, they headed towards the bedroom, tripping over each other and leaving a trail of clothes behind; they collapsed on the bed, laughing. Hans said, "These scenes work so well in the movies; we're a couple of clowns."

Much later, Hans kissed her and declared, "That was probably the best sex I've ever had."

"What do you mean probably?"

Hans squeezed her tight. "All I know is the earth *finally* moved."

Margot shook her head. "I can't believe I had hot steamy sex at my age."

"Which is what?"

Margot bolted upright. "What do you mean?"

"I'm referring to your age."

"You know the subject of age is taboo with me."

"Of course I could sneak your purse and check your driver's license."

Margot hit him with a pillow. "Not if you know what's good for you."

"You're what's good for me. Why do we fight and spend time apart?"

"That's because you keep hanging out with Diana."

"She's nice, smart, and yes, attractive, but compared to you she's. . . . ."

"Compared to me she's what?"

"On a similar subject, who's that guy I saw you with outside the Surf and Sand?"

"My dating Rick is all in the line of duty; he's a golf pro and a former friend of Joe, the patient who died. I'm taking golf lessons from Rick to pick his brain."

Hans planted a kiss on her shoulder. "And all this time I thought you were sitting home, pining away for me."

She tapped his cheek. "You know me better than that."

"Careful of all this sleuthing."

"I'm careful."

They spent the night talking and holding each other, dozing off from time to time, waking to make love again.

Hans sat up and rubbed his eyes, "Now I'm the one who's shocked. I haven't been this lucky since my youth."

"Is it me or are there little blue pills in your life?"

"Let's say a bit of each," he said sheepishly.

In the morning, Margot lay half-asleep, listening while Hans showered. Soon he appeared, shaved and dressed, and leaned down to tuck the covers around her neck. "I'm going out for bagels; stay there and catch some more sleep."

Margot gazed lovingly at Hans. "What a great night; I'm glad we're back."

"I'm happy too. Please, let's not fight anymore."

After daydreaming a while, Margot padded out of bed and slipped on a shirt Hans had left for her. In the bathroom, she noted her streaked make-up.

On the whole, not bad, she told herself. That's what happiness does—it even makes you think you look all right.

Removing cleansing cream from her purse, she wiped her face clean and showered, letting her curly hair dry naturally.

While applying fresh make-up, she smeared mascara on her upper lid and searched the medicine cabinet for a Q-tip, with no luck.

She opened the bathroom door and called out, "Hans where do you keep your Q-tips?" Remembering he had gone out, she rummaged through the drawers. One had jammed shut, and when she pried it open, she discovered a blue and white checked cosmetic bag.

Eyeing the bag suspiciously, she rifled through the bag and found salmon pink lipstick—definitely not her shade—a comb, a brush with blonde hairs—definitely not her hair color—a small mirror and a tiny pillbox, bearing the initials DK.

Furious, she stormed from the bathroom, dressed hurriedly and reached the entry just as Hans came through the door cheerful and juggling the groceries.

Margot hurtled past him, pausing to aim the cosmetic bag at his face.

Bewildered, Hans stammered, "What the. . . ." Before he could finish his sentence, Margot slammed the door.

A half hour later, when Margot stumbled back to her apartment, shrill ringing assailed her aching head. Noting the answering machine had accumulated seven calls—all from Hans—she pounded the off button.

Take that you lying philanderer.

She closed her eyes. What a humiliating end to our reunion. He's cheating on me and having us *both*. I hadn't thought of practicing safe sex, but now . . . .

CHAPTER THIRTY-FOUR

With time off from volunteering, Margot stayed home, wallowing in her misery. By late afternoon, when the phone rang, she refused to answer until she recognized Rick's voice, leaving a message. "You didn't show today, and you owe for the lesson. I'm canceling all future appointments unless you pay up."

She grabbed the receiver. "Sorry; I slept through the appointment."

"That's flattering."

"Sleep is how I handle stress, if I'm lucky. Otherwise, I'm awake all night obsessing."

"Stressed, why?"

"It's a long story." Thinking a date with Rick might take her mind off her problems, Margot suggested, "Can I atone with dinner and drinks tonight, my treat?"

"Twist my arm a little."

"I see a hill-top restaurant, an ocean-view, and plush surroundings in your future."

"Champagne and caviar?"

"The works."

"Sold."

Feeling heartened, Margot studied her wardrobe; she rarely stepped outside without doing her hair, applying make-up, and wearing stylish clothes—a way of living that helped her survive the terrors of aging. She now took extra care, selecting a long, double-strand of amber bead nuggets with matching earrings to accessorize a black cashmere sweater dress; she draped a black suede jacket over her shoulders.

On exiting the elevator, a voice called out, "There you are; I buzzed upstairs and searched everywhere I could think."

Margot continued walking.

"Hey, hold on a minute." Hans grabbed her arm roughly.

She shrugged him off. "Let go; I'm already late."

Hans eyed her up and down. "Where are you off to dressed like that?"

"Dressed like what?"

"Never mind. Gesturing to an empty sofa, he said. "Let's settle this right now."

"Settle what?"

"Stop playing games; you know very well I'm referring to your throwing Diana's cosmetic bag at me this morning and running off without a word."

"You mean the one she left behind when she spent the night?"

"Will you calm down and listen?"

Overhearing the argument, the permanently-planted lobby denizens quieted to enjoy the spectacle. Family squabbles often erupted during a Sunday visit; a lover's quarrel offered a rare treat.

Hans said, "Let's go upstairs where we can talk privately."

"Sorry, I'm already late."

"At least let me walk you to the parking lot."

"Walk anywhere you please; I can't stop you."

All the way to the garage, Margot ignored him. Once at her car, Hans took the keys, opened the door, and pulled her in beside him. "It's not what you think," he pleaded. "Diana came by for a drink and asked if she could use the bathroom before her next appointment; she probably brought the cosmetic bag to freshen up and forgot to take it with her."

Margot shook her head in disbelief. "Good story."

Hans enunciated through clenched teeth, "Let me finish. I didn't notice the bag right away; I don't go into the guest bathroom for weeks at a time. After I found the bag, I called Diana immediately, but she's out of town; that's the reason it's still there."

"Story's getting better and better. Why were you hiding it?"

"I wasn't hiding it. I put it in the drawer, to keep you from jumping to the wrong conclusions—which, of course, you did."

"You mean right conclusions. I'm fed up."

Hans grabbed her arm. "So where *are* you headed? Off to see your golf buddy?

"Why should my activities concern you?

"Talk about me. The first sign of problems, you run off with some guy. Well, I'm fed up too."

Hans slid out of the car, slamming the door, and stalked away, leaving Margot weeping—again.

As she entered the seaside restaurant, Margot spied Rick, drink in hand, happily chatting away with three men. Seeing that she looked distraught, he stopped mid-sentence and enveloped her in a bear hug. "Hey babe, what's wrong?"

"Everything."

Putting a protective hand on her back, Rick steered her towards a quiet corner. "Let's sit here away from those barflies; being that cheerful isn't normal."

Margot fought back a smile.

Rick took out a handkerchief and dabbed her tear-filled eyes. "Tell me your problems; I'm a good listener."

"I can't talk about it; the hug and being here makes me feel a lot better, though."

"I'm sure a drink would help."

"Just one; I have to drive home."

"You can bunk with me. I promise to kiss you only once on the forehead unless you beg on bended knee for me to crawl in with you."

She laughed, surprising herself. "You're a nice guy, but I don't need to complicate my life anymore than it already is."

"Got it. But any time you want someone to snuggle up with, I'm your man."

After the drinks came, they chatted a while and enjoyed the lights from the beachside homes, reflected on the slow-moving waters. By the time the Ahi Tuna and asparagus arrived, and Margot had accepted a second glass of La Crema chardonnay, she felt brave enough to say, "One teeny-tiny detail keeps bothering me about Joe's death."

Rick grimaced. "Not Joe again—you promised."

"Humor me, please; I've had a rough day. Just answer one question. Did anyone ever come into Joe's room while you two were sampling the gin you brought?"

"Now I'm the one who doesn't feel like talking."

"Sorry, this is important."

"Why does this concern you, anyway?"

"To use a tired cliché: 'The plot has thickened.'"

"Enlighten me."

"Another patient, Joe's friend Pete, is in the hospital after a suspicious accident."

"Did you say Pete—Joe's friend Pete?"

"Yes, the accident damaged his new hip. Now he's seriously ill after undergoing a second hip replacement."

"Not Pete too? What hospital is he in?'"

"He's at Hoag Hospital in Newport, but . . . you know Pete as well?"

"The three of us grew up together in Southie."

"In Boston? That's where I'm from."

Rick nodded. "Imagine that—another ex-pat from bean town."

"You, Joe, and Pete being friends is a huge surprise."

"I already told you, Joe and I worked together at Playboy; Pete, the third member of our triumvirate, turned high-brow on us; he graduated from The New England Conservatory of Music then played piccolo with the Boston Symphony, under Maestro Arthur Fiedler."

Margot scratched her head. "I don't get it; how did you all meet up out here?"

"We stayed in touch over the years; in fact Pete chose the skilled nursing facility because Joe told him about it. Whenever I came, I visited both men."

"I had no idea, but this is good information; it's lucky I asked. Back to my original question: did anyone see you and Joe drinking at the facility?"

Rick interrupted, "What difference would that make?"

"There may be a connection between Joe's death and Pete's accident; I'm trying to put the pieces together."

"I remember that Ernesto, an orderly, came in while we were drinking—made me plenty nervous—but Joe didn't act at all worried; he introduced me to the guy, and asked him to join us."

Margot turned pale. "Ernesto? You said Ernesto?"

"I'm positive and—oh, yes, someone else came in too."

Margot leaned forward eagerly. "Who?"

"A nurse named Betty."

"Betty? How did she react to your partying?"

"She acted pretty nasty. She told Joe, 'I can't believe you'd be stupid enough to drink alcohol, given your diabetes—serves you right if it kills you.'"

"Wow. What did Joe say?"

"He started kidding around, as always, but she didn't cotton to it. I wanted to stash the alcohol and leave. Suddenly, Joe cut the shenanigans and stared at her. He said, 'Hey, wait a sec, you look familiar. Haven't I seen you somewhere before?'"

"Betty shook her head, 'no,' and turned to leave. That gave me the same funny feeling—may have been the way she swung her hips when she walked."

"So you recognized her too?"

"I'm not sure. Anyway, she said something strange before she left."

"What?"

"She shot us a piercing stare and said, 'You'll find out.'"

"You'll find out? I don't understand what that means."

Rick said, "I didn't get it either."

Margot cupped her chin with her hand. "You're sure Ernesto and Betty are the only ones who saw you and Joe drinking gin?"

"Two people too many."

Margot signaled the waiter. "I need to get going."

Rick said, "I'll take care of this and drive you home. I can bring you back tomorrow to retrieve your car."

On impulse, Margot reached over and kissed him smack on the mouth. "You are a dear, dear man, but I'll be fine." When the check arrived, she scooped it up and handed the waiter her credit card.

Rick thanked her for dinner and repeated his offer to drive her home, but Margot refused. She needed time alone to digest the new information about Rick knowing both Joe and Pete and Betty and Ernesto witnessing the drinking.

CHAPTER THIRTY-FIVE

The following day, Margot took Polly with her to visit Pete, hoping that she would cheer him up and break through his mental fog.

At the nurse's station outside Pete's room, Sonia greeted them and said, "If you two lovelies can't wake up Pete, nothing will."

To their surprise, they found Pete sitting up, alert and practicing his usual verbal gymnastics. "Breathtaking beauties, bouncing into my bedroom—what a beneficent bestowal for my betterment."

Margot leaned over and hugged Pete. "Your alliterative prowess must mean you're on the mend."

Pete extended his arms to Polly. "Don't I get a hug from you, my love?"

"Coming right up." She sat on the bed and wrapped her arms around Pete; he squeezed her tight until she pleaded, "Whoa, I need to come up for air."

"No, you don't. I'm keeping you right here."

"We can take a hint." Margot took Sonia's arm. "Let's leave these two love birds alone."

They headed for the nurse's lunchroom where Margot poured coffee and broke off a piece of cake from the *Entenmann's* box on the counter. "I like the way they label their products, 'diet'; a hundred calories turns out to be one skinny slice."

"I know what you mean; sometimes I end up eating the whole cake to satisfy my cravings. I'm surprised Pete's so alert today. This is his best day since he arrived."

Margot brushed cake crumbs from her hands. "What a difference from my last visit."

"Pete's been drifting in and out of consciousness, but now he seems back to normal. I'm warning you though; patients often relapse before continuing to improve or they . . . ."

"Don't finish that sentence; let's take it as a sign that Pete's getting well." Margot checked her watch, "Do you think we've given them enough time?"

"I'm the one who needs to watch the clock. Come on, I'll walk you back."

As they strolled down the hall, screams rang out from Pete's room, shattering the tranquil mood; the two women rushed in and found Polly fumbling with the equipment to summon help.

Margot threw up her hands. "What's wrong?"

"I don't know. Please get help, quick."

After pressing the emergency button, Sonia listened to Pete's heart and felt his pulse. Within minutes, they were surrounded by emergency personnel.

Frantic with fear, Polly tugged at Sonia's sleeve. "What's going on?"

"I'm not sure; you'll need to wait outside while we work on him"

The color drained from her face. "But he's alive, isn't he? He'll be okay, won't he?"

"It's too soon to tell." Sonia pointed at the door. "Please go; I'll find you when I have more information."

Once at the solarium, Polly stared out the window; Margot brought coffee, but neither woman could bring themselves to take even one sip.

"I'm stunned," Margot said. "In less than a half hour, Pete went from his witty, jovial self to being comatose and unresponsive."

Polly sniffled. "It's my fault. I know it's my fault."

"Don't be ridiculous."

"We were so happy kissing and joking around until I mentioned the accident. Then Pete's face clouded over, and he looked confused. If I had only kept my mouth shut."

"Why do you say that?"

"I'm sure my mentioning the accident set him off; immediately he began repeating, 'My piccolo—I lost my piccolo. I held on tight, but I lost it.'"

"Ernesto told me he said those exact words when he found Pete after his accident. Did Pete say anything else?"

"When I asked how he lost it, he said, 'They pulled it away.'"

"Did he say who pulled it away?"

"He just kept repeating, 'You know, you know.' His face twisted with frustration and his eyes welled up; he began moaning and gasping for breath. I screamed and tried to ring for help."

At this point, she sobbed so hard, Margot gave up questioning her further; she rubbed Polly's back, until Sonia appeared, saying "Pete's still with us, but he's very, weak, and the prognosis isn't good. We may not know anything for hours; you two should go home. We'll call if there's a change in his condition."

"I want to stay," Polly pleaded. "It might help if I sit with him."

"I wish you could, but that's not possible. The emergency crew may be working on him for the next several hours. You get some rest, honey; you need to be fresh when he wakes up."

Margot took Polly's arm. "Sonia's right—we should go. She has my cell number; she'll call as soon as she has news."

Like someone in a trance, Polly followed Margot to the car where she slumped over and began crying softly.

Margot handed her a box of tissues. "This is a minor setback; Pete will be fine."

"He has to get better; it's taken me years to find someone. What will I do if he doesn't recover?"

"He'll rally; you'll see."

At Margot's apartment, they skipped dinner and munched on cheese and crackers. Margot selected a Pepe Romero Guitar CD, and both women stretched out on the sofas. Exhausted by the day's events and lulled by the soft melodies, they fell into a deep sleep.

Margot woke a few minutes before the phone rang; she ran to answer and her face darkened when she heard the news on the other end.

Under driving rain and gale winds, rare for a Southern California spring, a small group of mourners stood at Pete's graveside listening to a sermon delivered by Pastor Wright, the stand-in minister, included in Parkview Cemetery's deluxe burial package.

Shivering in the cold, Margot struggled to steady the large umbrella she shared with Polly, whose tears mingled freely with the falling rain. Luckily, Polly's daughter, Susan, had come for support and was holding her mother by the arm.

Members of the skilled nursing staff were there to pay their respects. Betty had declined, saying she had to work. Pete's son, Bill, had flown out from the mid-west.

Margot said quietly, "What a miserable day and what a sad, scraggly bunch of strangers."

Polly whispered back, "And a minister who doesn't even know him."

The service droned on while the minister delivered the usual boilerplate platitudes chosen to describe the departed.

Margot said under her breath, "Pastor Wright, is Pastor Wrong; Pete's personality is completely missing. I'm going to say a few words."

At the end of the service, she extracted a fisherman's rain hat from her pocket. Yanking it down over her ears, she pulled up her coat collar and stood, unprotected from the elements, before the assembled mourners.

"I thank you all for coming to say 'goodbye' to our warm and witty friend, Pete Peterson. Pete lit up the room and brought laughter to everyone who knew him. He performed perfect prose and puns, and his prowess will be appreciated in perpetuity."

All, except one unsmiling mourner, laughed and clapped. Helga, wearing a voluminous black cape that made her resemble a monster bat, stood under a tree, apart from the rest.

Polly approached Helga and glommed onto her cape. Inches from Helga's face, she shouted, "You're nervy showing up for Pete's funeral."

Helga pulled away. "Pete was my patient; I have every right to be here."

"I think you're happy he's dead and buried before he could recover and name you as the person who caused his accident."

"You have no proof; Ernesto was the one who found Pete on the floor. Why don't you ask him?"

Hearing his name, Ernesto glared at Helga and started toward her. Margot restrained him, and making him promise to stay put, she and Susan rushed over and dragged Polly away from Helga. "Leave it alone," Margot said. "Helga will get hers."

"How embarrassing," Susan told her mother. "How could you do that?"

Margot wanted to slap Susan.

Before leaving, they paid their condolences to Pete's son, Bill, and he invited the three women for dinner at his hotel. Susan begged off saying she had a prior engagement. Initially, Polly claimed she wasn't up to it, but Bill held her close and said, "I know my dad would want you, above all, to be there for a celebration of his life. Every time I spoke with him, he told me how much he loved you; he planned on bringing you to Detroit to meet the family once he recovered."

Hearing those words, Polly broke down. Bill hugged her again and Margot urged, "Come on, let's join Bill; we can't let him spend the evening of his dad's funeral alone." To Margot's relief, she agreed. It would be an appropriate homage for Pete, and she hoped Bill might shed further information on Pete's accident.

Susan made her goodbyes and drove off leaving her mother to ride home with Margot. All the way home, Polly cried so hard, Margot regretted persuading her to have dinner. But at six-thirty, she appeared, looking calm and nicely dressed in a grey silk pantsuit with a cream colored silk blouse.

At the appointed time, they found Bill in the St. Regis lobby admiring the blown glass sculptures whose vibrantly colored organic forms lit up the space.

Without even saying hello, Bill pointed. "Will you get a load of these gorgeous vessels."

Margot said, "They're by Dale Chihuly, a famous blown glass artist."

"If he's so famous, how come I've never heard of him?"

Margot shrugged. "He does installations all over the world, in gardens and parks; in snow, even floating. . . ."

"I just might buy one; if I 'Google' his name, will I find his website?"

"You can reach him at the Pilchuck Glass School in Stanwood, Washington or check out one of the galleries that carries his work. He's pricey, I warn you."

"No problem; it'll be a remembrance of my dad and the day I met his two lovely friends, also a good investment and a fat tax deduction for my office."

Polly shook her head. "You're Pete's son all right. You look exactly like him, and you're the same shameless flatterer."

Bill had made reservations at *The Stonehill Tavern* which featured a twist on classic American tavern fare. They were seated on the patio with its glorious ocean view; the downpour had stopped and a shimmering rainbow radiated over the pool.

Polly put down her menu and pushed aside her plate. "I love spending time with you both, but I'm not hungry. I shouldn't have come."

Bill said, "Please, I consider our gathering a wake to celebrate Dad's life."

"Put that way, how can I resist?"

"Tell you what, since Martinis are a house specialty, why don't I order you one and a jumbo shrimp cocktail to nibble on while you decide whether you want an entree?"

"I never refuse a martini."

When the drinks came, Bill proposed a toast to Pete. Studying the menu, he said, "In Dad's honor, I would like to order a Viking feast. Are you game, Polly?"

She rolled a shrimp in the cocktail sauce. "This is all I want."

Bill turned to Margot. "I guess that leaves us to forge on alone. I'd like to begin with the Chef's signature appetizer trios; its three different preparations of one ingredient, tuna, lobster, or duck. If I order the duck, would you like to try either tuna or the lobster. That way we could share."

"Sure, make mine the lobster."

"That's a deal. I'm ordering the red-wine-braised beef short ribs for an entrée."

Margot said, "And I'll have the shellfish stew. Want to share that too?'

Bill gave Margot's back a resounding slap. "You're my kind of dining partner."

Polly finished her shrimp and asked for another martini, while Margot and Bill relished every bite of their food, along with a bottle of Napa Valley Sauvignon Blanc. They topped off the meal by ordering two typical American desserts: a root beer float with chocolate chip cookies and the peanut butter cake, followed by lattes.

Bill said, "Margot, I'm impressed; I like a lady who can eat."

"There's a tread mill with my name on it waiting for me tomorrow; when I'm unhappy, I either I hardly touch a thing, or I pig out. Unfortunately, your check will reflect the latter."

"I'm not worried; this is my pleasure."

During dinner, Bill told them about his wife and his three children who were grown and attending college. He added, "You may be happy to know that my son, Pete Peterson, Jr., is carrying on his grandfather's tradition; he plays the piccolo and is a master punster."

Polly smiled for the first time that evening. "It's wonderful that Pete's spirit will live on in Pete, Jr."

Margot lifted her glass, "I propose another toast—to Bill's hospitality and his presence at Pete's funeral; it would have been even drearier without any family."

She kissed Bill's cheek. "While you're trapped and at my mercy, do you mind answering a few questions?"

"Ask away."

"Have you seen much of your dad in the last few years?"

"I haven't, and I'm feeling plenty guilty. I wish I had flown out as soon as I heard he had been injured. Optimistically, I thought he would recover soon."

"You're here now; that's what counts."

"Before his accident, I would call every few days and we'd jabber away for an hour or so. Taking Polly's hand, Bill said, "My dad told me he had fallen in love with you, and it surprised the heck out of him."

She dabbed at her eyes with a handkerchief.

Margot continued. "Did your dad ever mention having problems at the facility?"

"I know he didn't object to being there until the head nurse put a damper on his piccolo playing. Which reminds me—was she the big scary mama at the service wearing a black cape? She sure fits Dad's description of her."

"Helga—in the flesh. What did he say?"

"Apparently, she would bawl him out for playing his piccolo at night; she complained that he disturbed the other patients. Dad said that he always closed his door and tried playing quietly, but that didn't satisfy her."

Margot sipped her latte. "Do you know if she ever got physical with him?"

"Oh boy did she ever; they once had a tug-of-war with his piccolo and, naturally, she won. Now that I've seen her, I know why."

Margot looked puzzled, "Pete must have gotten it back because they found the piccolo beside the bed after his accident."

"The director made Helga return it when Dad protested."

"Hallelujah. Norwood finally showing some spine."

"I guess the guy panicked after Dad threatened a law suit for abuse."

"Abuse?"

"Apparently, Helga squeezed so tight one time, he had the finger marks on his wrist. Norwood called Helga into his office, and right in front of Dad, he lambasted her, told her to leave Dad alone, not dare touch him again."

"I never heard this, did you Polly?"

"News to me."

Margot scratched her head, "I wonder why he stayed on, taking that abuse?"

Bill said, "That's what I asked. Dad thought he would be well enough to leave soon; meanwhile, he could hang with Polly."

Margot said, "Your story corroborates other things we've heard. There are no eye-witnesses, but I suspect Helga had some involvement in Pete's accident and also in the death of his friend, Joe."

"Joe's death too? I remember Uncle Joe; he came to visit us a couple of times."

As Margot described the circumstances of Joe's death, Bill's eyes widened. "Do the police have this information?"

"The cities here contract with the Sheriff's department; I gave them a statement, but I'm worried that they're concentrating on Ernesto, one of the orderlies who played poker with Joe and your dad; I'm sure he's not involved."

Bill said, "Will you keep me posted about what they find out?"

"Definitely."

It seemed a shame to end the evening on a sour note, but the time had come to say, goodbye. In parting, they hugged and promised to keep in touch.

Before dropping Polly off at skilled nursing, Margot said, "With two suspicious deaths and now Bill's story about Helga's abuse, the situation is getting more and more serious. I need to take action."

"What kind of action?"

"I'll think of something."

CHAPTER THIRTY-SIX

When Margot arrived for work the next morning expressly to quiz Ernesto, she learned that two homicide detectives had again taken him off for questioning. She imagined various scenarios, all ending with Ernesto being accused of both deaths.

The following day, she hovered near reception and nabbed Ernesto as he arrived, looking pale and distraught. Almost immediately, Helga appeared and barked at him, "After your vanishing act yesterday, we're way behind schedule. Get a move on." Under her breath, she muttered, "You lazy Mexican."

Ernesto whispered to Margot, "I'm off at five; meet me out front."

A few minutes before five, Margot settled on a bench outside the building and pretended to read a book. Within minutes, Helga stuck her head out the door and called out, "You there. What are you hanging around for?"

"I'm meeting a friend. Is that against your rules?"

Helga walked to the bench and hovered over Margot. "I saw Ernesto signing out; you must be waiting for him."

Margot nodded.

"You're dying to ask him about his visit to the station, aren't you?"

"This is none of your business."

Helga pounded the bench. "My advice, Lady, is to stay away from Ernesto. He's in big trouble, and you don't want trouble of your own."

"Meaning what?"

"Meaning that you'd better stop nosing around, or you'll find yourself out of here; it would take only one word from me."

Ernesto emerged from the building and after spotting Helga, he ducked back inside. Helga smiled gleefully. "He's too chicken to come out while I'm here, but it makes no difference; I'm onto your little conspiracy."

Helga's lips curled in a mean smile. "Bye for now, dearie; remember I'll be watching."

A few minutes later, Ernesto reappeared and sat beside Margot on the bench. "*Que desastre*; let's get away from here *pronto*.

They walked without speaking until they reached Starbucks at the nearby mall, and brought lattes to a patio table where they could talk without being overheard.

"*Dios Mio*, what a terrible time I have yesterday." Ernesto began.

Margot flashed him a sympathetic smile. "Tell me; I'm anxious."

"Around eight this morning, two detectives they take me to the station. All the way, I keep asking why, but they don't never tell me. They put me in a small room with bare walls and no windows and leave me two hours; I have nothing to do, nothing to look at. I know they do that on purpose to make me worry, and it works; I am plenty worried by the time they come back."

"The same two detectives who interviewed you before?"

"Same two—Mulroney, the bad cop, and Mendoza, the good cop. I figure it out right away. Mulroney, the tall, skinny hombre, he work on me first. *Que miserable*—with his tight mouth and little beady eyes that bore into a person. He have this thin white scar on his left cheekbone, and his head is shaved.

"Sounds attractive."

"This Mulroney, he pace back and forth all the time asking me questions."

"What kinds of questions?"

"Do I play poker with Joe Farelli and Pete Peterson? How often I play? Do I win or lose and how much?"

"What did you tell him?"

"I say we play if I'm off-duty; I say sometimes I win, sometimes I lose, never more than fifty dollars either way."

Margot nervously twisted her curls. "Did Mulroney seem satisfied?"

"No way; he ask me how much money I make an hour. I tell him twelve dollars, and he say, 'So fifty dollars is half a day's pay—win or lose?'"

"I say I no play for the money; both men are my *amigos*. I play to be sociable."

"I'm guessing Mulroney didn't buy that."

"He ignore my answer, and he ask do I owe Joe and Pete money?"

"I say I owe them *nada*."

Margot shook her head. "What else did Mulroney ask you?"

"He ask if I ever see Joe Farelli drinking from a hip flask? I say, 'yes,'"

"You never told me that."

"Once I catch him drinking with a guy who visits, but I don't never tell anyone."

"Alcohol is dangerous for a diabetic; weren't you worried?"

"Is true, but I am more afraid of Helga. Anyway, Joe, he die two or three days later. I feel terrible, but I don't say nothing."

Ernesto squirmed. "I tell Joe to stop because alcohol can kill him. But I as soon as I say that to detectives, I know, 'kill' is wrong word to use."

"Why?"

"Mulroney, he get right in my face and say, 'So Mr. Valdez, as an orderly you knew the alcohol could kill him. Did it cross your mind that giving Joe Valium along with alcohol would be an easy way to get rid of him and the money you owed him?"'

"I tell Mulroney, I would never do that."

"Mulroney didn't pull any punches, did he? You must have been scared?"

"Scared? I am sweating."

"Then what?"

"They give me bathroom break and bring coffee. After that Mendoza, the other detective, he take over.

"How did that go?"

"He's like other *hombres* in my neighborhood; you know, a short guy, dark skin, brown eyes, black hair, so I think he'll be friendly. First thing, he hand me a cigarette, and he say, 'A smoke, *Amigo*?'"

"I say, I don't smoke."

"He ask where I live, am I single, do I have a girlfriend?"

"I say, I am single, but I have a *novia,* and I live in Santa Ana with my family.

"This Mendoza, he pat me on the shoulder, all friendly, and say 'I grew up in the barrio. Ever play the numbers there?'"

"I ask why, but he don't answer; he just keep repeating the question."

Margot began feeling uneasy. "And?"

"Mendoza, he say, 'How much are you into the numbers people for?'"

"I don't answer nothing."

"But he ask, 'Did you ever borrow money from your friends, Joe Farelli or Pete Peterson, to cover your gambling debts? Friends help each other out, right?'"

Margot raised her eyebrows.

"That's when I tell them I want a lawyer, and they let me go."

Margot said in a soft, cajoling voice, "Ernesto, you can confide in me; I'm your friend. Did you owe money to either Joe or Pete?"

Ernesto remained silent.

She persevered, "Did they ever lend you money for your gambling debts?"

Ernesto began fidgeting. "I swear I pay them back."

"You do need a lawyer."

"I ain't got no money to pay a lawyer."

"As you would say, that is one big *problema*. I'll see if I can find you some help." She patted Ernesto's shoulder and left him at the mall, looking depressed.

That evening Margot reviewed her evidence. She listed the possible suspects, their motives and their opportunities to commit the crime.

ERNESTO: He had gambled with the two victims, and, at least on one occasion, had borrowed money from Joe and possibly Pete.

MOTIVE: To rid himself of gambling debts.

OPPORTUNITY: As a staff member, he could have administered Valium to Joe after witnessing him drinking alcohol. He admitted being near Pete's room at the time of the man's accident; he could have yanked Pete out of bed in a dispute over money.

BETTY: She had witnessed Joe drinking with Rick, and, according to Rick she had told Joe, "I can't believe you'd be stupid enough to drink alcohol, given your diabetes; serves you right if it kills you."

After Joe said she looked familiar, she had replied, cryptically, "You'll find out."

Neither she nor Ernesto had reported the drinking.

OPPORTUNITY: As a nurse, Betty could have given Joe the Valium.

MOTIVE UNKNOWN: She had no apparent reason for harming Joe, or Pete for that matter. She had made negative comments about them, and she had not attended Pete's funeral. Did Betty know Joe and Pete previously, and did she hold some kind of grudge against them?

HELGA: MOTIVE: She had fought with Joe over his pinching women; she had fought with Pete over his piccolo playing; but murder?

OPPORTUNITY: not knowing about Joe's drinking, she could have administered the Valium to calm him down, accidentally killing him.

Ernesto told Margot that he saw someone who fit Helga's description disappear around the corner before he found Pete lying on the floor, writhing in pain. Helga could have caused the accident after they argued about his playing the piccolo. They may have struggled when she tried to take the piccolo away.

Margot planned to lay the information before Homicide after doing more detective work; she also needed to obtain legal counsel for Ernesto.

CHAPTER THIRTY-SEVEN

Margot phoned Gordon the next morning to tell him about the two suspicious deaths at the facility and Ernesto's questioning by homicide detectives.

"And this involves your conservator case in what way?"

"It doesn't, but Ernesto desperately needs help; I thought you might be able to give him some legal advice."

After a long silence, Margot asked, "Gordon, are you there?"

"I'm not pleased by your intruding yourself into a situation that doesn't concern you in the least."

"But, Gordon, the men who died were my friends, and Ernesto is my friend too."

"Friends or not, you're meddling; I've cautioned you to stay under the radar."

Margot felt a migraine coming on. "All I've done is ask a few questions."

"A few questions? You had the cheek to involve the Coroner; now you're advocating for a man already under suspicion."

"How did you know I visited the Coroner?"

"My investigators have friends everywhere; apparently the other side is keeping tabs on you."

"That can't be."

"Trust me."

"So about helping Ernesto . . . ? "

"Bloody hell; let it go."

"Please, Gordon, I won't bother you anymore if you just tell me where Ernesto can get obtain legal advice without paying a fortune?"

Gordon sighed deeply. "Oh bother. I do know a criminal defense firm that evaluates cases gratis and helps insure their legal rights. They may require a $200 deposit, but they charge a low fee."

"Sounds reasonable."

"I shouldn't encourage you, but if he is arrested, I also know several top law firms who offer pro bono work."

"Thank you, Gordon; you're a dear."

"All right. I'll connect you with my secretary. She'll provide you with the information.

Margot jotted down the phone numbers and scratched her head trying to imagine who could be spying on her. Undoubtedly, it had to be someone who knew about her activities and was also willing to work against her. The only people in on everything were her fellow-residents: Nancy, Jane, and Barbara.

Others, like Joe's daughter—Doris, Joe's friend—Rick, Pete's son—Bill, and Polly had some knowledge of her detective work, but none of them would have reason to squeal on her.

She had confided many details to Hans, and he had also warned her to stop meddling, but reporting her activities? She felt disloyal even imagining such a thing. Margot would have to think long and hard as to the identity of the mole.

⟨⟩

The next day after volunteering, Margot stopped by the restroom to refresh her make-up. She heard a door slam behind her, but not sensing anything unusual, she continued outlining her lips with a dark red pencil. She jumped as a hand grabbed her roughly by the shoulder, and she saw Helga's scowling countenance reflected in the mirror.

Helga spun her around until they were face to face. "I'm glad I ran into you," she said in a chilling voice. "I hoped to catch you before you left the building; we need to continue our discussion from the other day."

Margot braced her body against the sink.

"What are you up to lately?" Helga asked.

"Up to lately? I've been visiting patients, trying to make them comfortable—my normal routine."

"Don't play dumb with me"

Margot gave Helga a blank stare. "I'm confused."

"Besides getting involved in Ernesto's problems, I've noticed you're quite the busy lady poking around, asking questions."

Margot struggled to get free until Helga released her and jabbed her finger close to Margot's eye.

Helga's voice took on a mocking tone, "I know all about your recent activities, first investigating Joe's death, now Pete's. Those men died of complications from their illnesses. There's nothing more to it."

Unable to stop herself, Margot blurted out, "If that's the case, why are you trying to implicate Ernesto?"

From the fierce expression on Helga's face, Margot knew she had made a mistake.

As Helga clamped one hand on Margot's arm and tightened the grip, she said, "Now see here Missy, you're interfering way too much for your own good."

With her free hand, she reached into her pocket and pulled out a vial, which she held up for Margot to see, "This is lye. Ever use lye soap?"

Margot shook her head.

"Even lye soap can ruin your hands, and what I have here is much, much stronger—very caustic—eats away at the skin. Margot's arm ached from the increasing pressure as the woman slowly waved the vial in front of Margot's face.

Helga gestured to the counter where Margot's open cosmetic bag lay. "You know I could easily borrow that bag and put the lye in one of the jars. If you accidentally rubbed it on your face, you wouldn't look beautiful anymore, would you?"

Sick with fear, Margot summoned the strength to fight back and scraped Helga's arm with her long fingernails then twisted in an attempt to loosen Helga's iron grip. She yelled, "You let go or I'll scream bloody murder."

Helga squeezed harder, her voice soft and menacing. "Oh no, Missy, you're wrong there. I guarantee no one would hear you—not in these walls. Anyway, I'm not going to hurt you right now. I'm saving that for another time. There are many, many ways I can get to you; I could quietly add a few drops of lye to your coffee one day when you're not paying attention. It would be an easy thing to do. You might find it a wee bit hard to swallow after that."

Margot answered coldly, "You don't frighten me; you're the one who should worry. I bet the authorities would like to know about these threats."

"They don't worry me one bit. I hear they're getting ready to nail your Latino friend, Ernesto—try him, lock him up for good. Those Mexicans belong behind bars."

They stared each other down until Helga let go and said, "Remember, I'm on to you. Do your job and stop snooping around, or you'll be sorry."

After Helga left, Margot waited a full minute then rushed into the corridor. She slumped against the wall, her heart pounding; on the verge of fainting, she could hardly breathe. Worrying she might collapse and end up a patient at Helga's mercy, she inhaled deeply and opened her eyes to find Ginger standing over her.

"Margot, what's wrong? Are you sick or something?"

"No, but. . . give me a second; I'm really fine."

Taking her by the arm, Ginger said, "You don't seem fine to me. Come on sweetie, let's grab some coffee while you tell me what's wrong."

Coffee? Not coffee. I may never drink coffee here again.

Once in the lunchroom, Ginger placed a wet paper towel on Margot's forehead and felt her wrist. "Your pulse is racing. Sit down while I start a fresh pot."

Unable to speak, Margot motioned away the coffee Ginger set before her.

Ginger watched Margot with concern. "I saw Helga coming out of the bathroom right before you. Did she say or do something to you?"

"I'll tell you; give me a minute to calm down."

Margot used the wet towel to mop her face. "From the get-go, I found the deaths of Joe and Pete suspicious; I've been asking around to find out who may be responsible."

"You don't mean actual murder?"

"It is possible both men were murdered, either accidentally or deliberately; I'm not sure which."

"And Helga? Where does she come in?"

"She confronted me the other day while I waited outside for Ernesto and threatened to dismiss me from skilled nursing if I didn't stop snooping."

"But what happened just now that frightened you so much?"

Margot extended her arm which bore Helga's finger marks. "You can see where she glommed on to me; she also threatened to put lye in my cosmetics or in my coffee unless I stopped asking questions."

"Your coffee. Now I know why you were so upset when I brought you a cup."

Margot nodded.

"I can't believe she threatened you. She could be just acting territorial; skilled nursing is her personal bailiwick. Anything that goes wrong reflects on her."

"I'm not sure I buy that explanation, but I can't figure out what motive Helga would have to harm either Joe or Pete. And if she's not involved in their deaths, her behavior is more than strange; it's downright terrifying.

"Are you going to tell Norwood, call the cops, or what?"

"There were no witnesses. It's my word against hers; I'm going to lay it all out for Homicide."

"In the meantime, I'd avoid Helga. But in case she corners you again, maybe you should start wearing a wire to get her on tape."

"Good idea; online tonight, I'll check out what's available."

Ginger hugged Margot. "I'm glad you confided in me. I'll tell Betty, and we'll both watch out for you while you're on duty."

"Betty? Not Betty."

Ginger seemed surprised. "Why?"

"It's complicated."

"Tell me if you change your mind about Betty; I'm worried about what Helga may do next."

CHAPTER THIRTY-EIGHT

Hoping that Clarissa, might know important information about the upcoming conservator hearing, Margot phoned her niece. "Hi, it's me, your *former* favorite Aunt."

"You're still my favorite Aunt." Clarissa hesitated. "Wait, I need to make sure that Rudy's gone."

A minute later, Margot heard Clarissa say, "It's okay;the coast is clear."

"Aren't you afraid that Rudy has put a tap on your phone?"

"Stop joking. Even Rudy wouldn't do that. I'm his sister, for pity sakes."

"You're right. Rudy would never do such a thing unless . . . ."

"Unless what?"

"Forget I said that."

"Anyway, I'm excited you called. I can't tell you how this conservator business has upset me. I miss hanging out with you."

"We could still do that; call me anytime."

"I'm embarrassed."

"No need; you're family."

"I've tried discouraging him, but you know Rudy never listens to me once he's made up his mind."

"Unfortunately, I do know. The only thing I ask is that you warn me if he tries to pull any dirty tricks."

"Rudy keeps a lot to himself; I don't know half of what he's doing." Clarissa paused. "But, since you ask, while I was rummaging through his desk for a missing receipt, I found some jottings that involve you."

"Jottings?"

"It's hard to read his writing; I just remember, 'M snooping around—bears watching.'"

"Anything else?"

"The words were written on the last sheet of a writing pad. Rudy probably tore the other sheets off and missed that one sentence.

Alarm bells sounded in Margot's head. "As a favor, will you poke around and try to find out more."

"I'll try, but I'm not promising anything; Rudy would kill me if he knew I went through his things."

"Poor you, always caught in the middle; I wouldn't ask if this wasn't important."

Margot hung up the phone and mulled over the disconcerting news. For a second time, she ran down the list of people who had been in on her activities and possibly willing to sell her out. Of her friends at Shady Palms, only Barbara came to mind. At times she bombarded Margot with questions, and she seemed to have trouble looking Margot straight in the eye.

She scratched her head. How can I be sure it *is* Barbara? Perhaps I should try feeding her false information to see if it gets back to The Relatives. I wonder what could sound plausible and force Rudy to give himself away?

Until recently, Margot's detective work had put a spark in her life and had given her a sense of purpose. Now her activities not only might be used against her, but she could be in real danger. Perhaps she *should* consider giving up the investigations.

At dinner time, she encountered Barbara Turner, limping toward the elevator.

This must be a sign, she told herself. Just when I decide to spread false information, Barbara appears on the scene. Could she be the spy, and if so, why?

She called out, "Hi Barbara. How are you? Haven't seen much of you lately."

"I've been better; my hip's healing slower than I expected."

"What a shame. Let's eat together; we haven't had a heart-to-heart for ages."

Barbara perked up. "I'd love it."

They entered the crowded dining room and found a small corner table where they scoured the menu for a tempting dish among the usual bland, boring choices, and Margot took the opportunity to study Barbara.

What a sad, homely little thing she is—so different from Nancy and Jane.

She gave herself a mental slap on the wrist for being negative and smiled warmly.

"You look great, as always," Barbara said. "You're the most put-together person I know. I can't pull off the style thing the way you do."

"We should go shopping one day. I can show you my favorite haunts and introduce you to the sales mavens who call me every time something special comes in."

"Wouldn't help me any; you're tall and have a great figure. I'm short and dumpy and ever since my hip injury, I've had to give up exercising. Nothing fits me anymore."

"Maybe the instructor here can give you some isometric exercises—nothing too strenuous."

"That's a good suggestion, but my problems go far beyond my hip; I'm worried sick about my finances; they've taken such a dive during this crazy market, I could deplete my entire savings."

"That's awful. I didn't know you were having a rough time.

"I might even have to find a cheaper place to live." She threw up her hands. "Enough of my problems. What have you been doing lately? Still chasing down leads on the deaths of those two patients?"

"I'm giving it a rest." Margot picked at the filet of sole, covered with a watery sauce; it tasted worse than it looked. "Anyway, I won't be here much longer. My lawyer is working on an action to have my relatives removed from my house."

"That's not good news for us; you liven up this place. But I guess it's important to do what makes you happy."

Margot drummed her fingers on the table. "It's time I reclaimed my rightful home. I miss my place, my own cooking—real food—not this cardboard facsimile."

"You're lucky you have a house. I had to sell mine to move here." She shrugged. "Even then, I'm having trouble covering expenses."

"Cheer up. Maybe the economy will improve and your problems will be solved."

"Doesn't look like it."

"For starters, the hell with dieting; how about skipping the chef's world famous Jell-O pudding and splurging on hot fudge sundaes?"

They ordered the desserts and dove into them, licking the spoons, savoring every bite, and giggling like two little girls putting one over on the grown-ups.

Margot stood and held out her hand. "Good seeing you Barbara. We should dine together more often, anywhere except here."

So Barbara's having financial problems; that's interesting. I sympathize, but if she's spying on me for money, maybe the news about reclaiming my home will get back to The Relatives.

Should I telephone my niece, or wait and see if Clarissa calls me first?

That done, Margot returned upstairs and surfed the net for spying paraphernalia. She found sunglasses that allowed a person to look straight ahead and view what was happening behind. There were pens for writing secret messages or marking valuables; the writings invisible to the naked eye could be seen under ultraviolet light.

A miniature voice-changing device gave women the option of using a masculine voice on their answering machines. And practical jokers could set the device at a volume that sounded hilarious; it was so small, it fit on a keychain.

Margot chuckled at the idea of diversion safes resembling various grocery products, in which to hide valuables. Knowing how forgetful she was, she worried she would throw out a Doritos can concealing her diamond ring or another such valuable.

As for actual listening devices, most were too big, too bulky, and too obvious. But the 'Pi Pen' sounded perfect. A discreet digital recorder that wrote like a pen, it contained a hidden listening device, which clipped to a breast pocket. It would begin recording when the user slid the clip down. The recorder even worked in the dark—a little steep at $249, but probably worth the money.

Before ordering the product, she read a warning that certain states outlawed using an audio recorder without the consent of all parties. After more searching, she located the magazine *California Lawyer* which contained an article on the perils of using recording devices in California. It warned that any civilian caught violating the Federal Wiretapping Codes could not only suffer monetary penalties but even face incarceration.

Whoa, she thought. Wouldn't The Relatives love having me accused of wiretapping. They'd take everything I own and throw me in the loony bin forever.

⋙⋘

Still feeling skittish from her confrontation with Helga, she maintained a low profile at work the next morning and constantly peered over her shoulder. Later the receptionist informed her that Helga had taken a rare day off.

Back at her apartment, she found two messages, one from her niece, Clarissa, the other from her attorney, Gordon Jacobs.

Margot kicked off her shoes and examined her ankles; they puffed up no matter what she ate. Her rings refused to budge without first being drowned in cold water. She removed her bra, flung it on a chair, and breathed a sigh of relief.

Comfortable at last, she dialed Clarissa, who immediately began whispering, "I can't talk. Rudy is watching to make sure I don't run off and call you."

"Run off and call me? Why"

"I'd better phone you tomorrow morning, around ten; Rudy has a meeting then."

Margot smiled to herself. "I'll be waiting for your call."

True to her word, Clarissa called promptly at ten, saying, "I'm not supposed to tell you this, but Rudy heard you were getting a court order to have us evicted."

"What in heaven's name gave him that idea?"

"I saw him answer his cell and leave the room, so he could talk privately."

"And?"

"He came storming back. 'Your crazy Aunt says she's filing a court order to evict us. Just let her try it.'"

"How did Rudy get that idea?"

"Don't know; he just said, 'Margot will have a battle on her hands if she tries it. My attorney will stop her before she can make a move.'"

"How absurd, I'm staying right where I am."

"I'm sorry we ever started this mess; you've always been so good to me."

"Don't worry, sweetie, we're pals. I appreciate the heads up, but as another huge favor, please call if you hear anything else. And remember, not a word to Rudy."

"Of course; he'd throw a fit if he knew I even talked to you."

Margot hung up and clapped her hands. It worked; it worked; Barbara Turner's the one. I wonder what else she's told on me. At least now that I've caught her out, I can use her to spread false information. I think I'll call Gordon and play the innocent.

The next morning, when she placed a call to Gordon, his secretary said that she had just been dialing Margot.

Gordon picked up and said. "To what do I owe this call?"

"Your secretary said you wanted to speak to me."

"Come to think of it, I do, and it is rather important."

"Important?"

"I've been informed that you are planning to evict your relatives, so that you can move back home."

"Not true; I'm just my quiet old self, minding my own business."

"You quiet? You must be joshing."

"Where did that story come from anyway?"

"Your nephew's attorney rang me up yesterday and kept banging on about it."

"Why shouldn't I move back to my own house?"

"It's not prudent to stir up matters before we settle the conservator issue."

"Rudy and Clarissa must be conjuring up ways to get me in trouble."

"All I know is what I heard. And my advice hasn't changed; stay where you are until this case is resolved. Don't rock the boat."

"I told you Gordon, I haven't done a thing."

"I hope so. Have you stopped this amateur detective business as well?"

"Of course, I'm a little lamb, following orders, volunteering and helping people."

"I can picture that."

Grinning broadly, she put down the phone.

Undaunted by her lawyer's admonition, Margot re-checked her notes on the two deaths and called to make an appointment with Homicide. A few days later, she found herself mired in heavy traffic and choking exhaust fumes on her way to Santa Ana. Stopped for a traffic light, she began imitating a fish by sucking her cheeks in and out—a series of facial exercises designed to help eliminate wrinkles. In the next lane, she noticed a male driver staring; she smiled and waved. He lifted his shoulders, as if to say, "What's with you?" When the light turned green, she blew him a kiss then gunned her motor, leaving him far behind.

Once at Homicide, she crossed and uncrossed her legs, admiring her new black suede ankle boots. That morning, as she tucked a ruffled blouse into a grey pinstriped suit, she wondered aloud, "Whom am I hoping to impress?" The answer, of course, was *herself.*

She studied the outline she had composed and read a magazine; a half-hour passed before the door opened, and she was shown into the offices of detectives Mulroney and Mendoza, the two investigators that had interrogated Ernesto. Margot found herself nervous remembering his description of the detectives as "the good cop" and "the bad cop." But both men treated her with cordiality.

This day, Mulroney did all the questioning. First offering her a choice of coffee or water, he asked her to tell him what she knew about the case.

Margot began with her own stay at the facility where a patient had mysteriously disappeared. She described the death of Joe the Jokester, the hip flask found among his things, reports of arguments with the head nurse, and autopsy findings linking his death to a combination of alcohol and Valium.

When Margot mentioned Pete the Punster, Mulroney stared in disbelief. "Joe the Jokester, Pete the Punster; these men sound like made up characters."

"They were real people. It's all true, she replied."

"Please continue."

She recounted the details of Pete's accident, his own arguments with the head nurse over his piccolo playing, his falling and re-injuring his hip, his hospitalization for new surgery, and ultimately, his death.

Margot added, "Ernesto Valdez, an orderly at skilled nursing, told me he had been taken in for questioning. He couldn't possibly have hurt either man."

"We're not ruling out any possibilities. Is there anything else we need to know?"

"Yes, and it's important. Recently, the head nurse, Mrs. Hasse, cornered me and threatened me with lye, unless I started minding my own business."

Regarding her with new interest. Mulroney said, "Were there any witnesses?"

"No witnesses. She's too clever to threaten me with other people around. I had planned to wear a wire in case she threatened me again or even attacked me. But I discovered it's illegal in California to tape anyone without their consent."

"It's lucky you didn't try it. Otherwise, you could have been prosecuted."

"I know that now."

"We'll check into your information, but from hereon you must *not* involve yourself; if there's a murderer on the loose, you could be putting yourself in danger."

"I know you're right, but I care what happens to Ernesto."

"Miss Manning, let *us* handle this."

Both men stood to shake hands and thanked her for coming.

"Thank *you* for seeing me. If I hear anything, I'll let you know."

Mulroney's face clouded. "You're not listening;I repeat; stay out of this."

Margot offered an unconvincing "I will."

On the drive back, she reasoned maybe it was time she stopped playing detective. Hans and Gordon, and now Homicide, had all warned her.

Still. . . .

CHAPTER THIRTY-NINE

On Margot's return to Shady Palms, she found a short cryptic note from Hans. "I stopped off to say goodbye. Please call as soon as possible."

Alarmed she dialed his number and waited anxiously until he picked up. "Margot, I'm glad we connected before I leave town."

Her heart sank. "You're leaving? Where to?"

"I'm going to Denmark; my mother had a stroke."

Guilty relief washed over Margot. "Is it serious?"

"My sister, Ingrid, doesn't know yet; my mother's a strong woman, but she's almost ninety-five; a stroke at that age can be devastating."

"That's terrible. Is there a decent hospital on a small island like Aero?"

"Aero's not equipped to handle a stroke; they flew her to Copenhagen by air ambulance."

"Excellent; Copenhagen must have top hospitals."

"Ingrid says my mother's at *Rigshospitalet*, Denmark's national hospital. It's the leading hospital for patients needing highly specialized treatment; members of The Royal family have given birth to their children there."

"Those are good credentials. I guess you're in for a long flight."

"*Ja*, Ja, it's a schlep, but I'm flying business class, so I'll probably sleep a little."

"I'm proud of you for being there for your mother."

"My sister and I are her only relatives besides my Aunt Dagmar in Copenhagen, and she's in her late eighties."

"I understand."

"The thing is I'll be gone at least a couple of weeks, and I hate leaving with all these misunderstandings between us."

"Don't worry; I'm not going anywhere, except back home—I hope, with this conservator nightmare behind me. Lets' visit your mother in Aero once she's well. Rick Steves did a segment on it the other night. He calls it the 'Fairytale Island.'"

"Believe me it is, with its cobblestones and seventeenth century houses."

"I'm holding positive thoughts for your mother. Let me know what happens."

"I will, definitely. Pray *Gott* my cell works there. Otherwise, my sister has a cell and a regular landline."

"You're dealing with a lot."

"I'll be fine. Take care of yourself. I love you, and I hope you're still my lady."

"I am your lady, and I love you too."

A day later, Hans called and woke her from a deep sleep; hearing her garbled voice, he apologized for forgetting the time difference."

Margot rubbed her eyes; the clock read, five a.m. "Is your mother okay?"

"Thank *Gott*, she had a mild stroke, no serious damage; she's doing much better.

"How long will she be in the hospital?"

"I'm not sure—maybe three or four weeks."

"That long?" Margot quickly added, "Ignore that; I'm being selfish. Where are you staying?"

"I'm at my Aunt Dagmar's. She lives near the hospital. Just call my cell."

"Good; I hate dialing all those numbers to reach Europe."

"What's new with you? Still investigating the death you told me about?"

"There's another mystery; Pete the Punster died, after a supposed accident."

"A *supposed* accident?"

"I'm suspicious that his fall resulted from an argument with Helga."

"What makes you say that?"

"Several of the staff told me Pete had been fighting with her during the last few weeks over his piccolo playing at night; they found the instrument beside him when he fell. I've told Homicide what I discovered."

Hans's voice rose. "You did what? You're getting in way too deep."

"To be honest, I'm reconsidering. You're not the first person who's warned me; Gordon, my Attorney, has been saying the same thing."

"So you're sticking with Gordon; I won't bug you anymore about that. This detective business, though. . . . Drop it, please."

"I *already* said I'm considering the idea."

"Just do it."

"I know you're right, but they're trying to blame the two deaths on Ernesto."

Hans raised his voice again. "You are one incorrigible woman. You need to quit right now. Believe me; everything will get solved without you."

"I hear you."

As she clicked off the phone, she thought, if Hans only knew about Helga's threats, he would pitch a fit and insist I stop snooping around. Maybe he's right; maybe I am too old to be playing sleuth.

Margot resolved to end her detective work once Ernesto got squared away. She had passed on Gordon's legal references to Ernesto, but she wanted to make sure he followed through and found himself a good lawyer.

CHAPTER FORTY

The next day, Margot was alarmed to find Polly pacing her room and clenching her fists. "What's wrong?" She asked.

"That woman is what's wrong. I told Helga I planned to move out,and you know what she had the nerve to say?"

"In my experience Helga is liable to say anything."

"She put her hands on her hips and began mocking me, "Oh, how terrible; we're going to miss you. Be sure you take your troublemaking friends along.'"

"I vowed to keep quiet, but the way she carried on, I couldn't help myself."

"What did you answer?"

"I said, 'It's strange that every time you have a problem with a patient, something bad happens; I bet the cops would like to hear everything I know.'"

Margot covered her face.

"As I started to walk away, she grabbed the back of my neck and pressed down hard. Then she jerked me around and glared. "I've done nothing wrong. You're the one who's asking for trouble; you'll be sorry if you mess with me."

"I've heard that tune before."

"She scared me bad; I can't wait to move out."

"Helga threatened me the same way a few weeks ago. She told me to stop snooping around and mind my own business—scared me plenty too. Ginger spent almost an hour calming me down."

Polly shuddered. "All the more reason I should move. Do you know a broker who can find me a condo near the beach? I'm not familiar with real estate around here."

"I do know a sharp and reliable broker; she won't push you into something just to make a sale. She found my house, which is now occupied by squatters."

Polly looked puzzled. "Squatters?"

"Haven't I ever mentioned my problems with my greedy relatives? I've been battling them in court."

"You never told me that."

"Got an hour to spare?"

"All I have here is time."

As Margot related the details of her conservator case, Polly's face registered mild surprise then bewilderment. "You mean they can push around a savvy woman like you?"

"As my friend Jane would say, 'you betcha.' My nephew, Rudy, and his sister, Clarissa, are powerful people in these parts. What makes matters worse, the sitting judge on my conservator case is rumored to be accepting bribes from them."

"Goodness, what are your chances of winning?"

"I read in the newspaper that the courts are finally paying attention to the conservator scams being perpetrated against the elderly. My lawyer says that times are changing, and he thinks I have a decent shot at winning. But enough about me; I'll tell my broker to call and discuss the areas you might be interested in and your price range."

"You're a real pal; I can always count on you."

Margot stood to leave. "How does lunch at noon tomorrow sound?"

"I'd love to get out of this place."

At lunchtime the following day, Margot stopped by for Polly and found her on the verge of tears, "What's wrong? Are you still upset over Helga's threats?"

"It's not only Helga; it's Betty too."

"Betty? What did she do?"

"She walked in and found me crying, but instead of being sympathetic she turned on me and said, "If you're crying over your boyfriend, Pete, don't waste your tears; he and Joe were no-good cowards; they got what they deserved."

"Cowards? I can't believe Betty said that."

"I asked what she meant, but she wouldn't answer. I felt as if I'd been slapped. First Helga, now Betty; every day is worse around here."

"I'm shocked." Margot rummaged through her purse for a card, "This is my broker's information; I've already spoken to her; she should be calling soon."

"Can't be too soon for me."

Margot took Polly's arm. "Ready to leave?"

"I'm not hungry anymore."

"Come on. It's two-for-one Tuesdays at *Hennessey's Tavern*; they serve big, juicy hamburgers with all kinds of yummy toppings—mushrooms, onions, cheeses . . . . "

Polly patted her stomach. "A hamburger would be way too much food."

"No problem, we'll order two and split one; I'll bring back the other for tomorrow's lunch. Afterwards, we can browse the shops around the harbor."

Less than twenty minutes later, they entered the saloon-style restaurant in Dana Point and lunched on the patio to enjoy the sunny and clear day. Polly developed an appetite and appeared more relaxed. Then they drove to the nearby Marina and took a long walk across the bridge to the island and back to where the boats left for Catalina.

Polly pulled Margot onto a bench. "I'm pooped. Let's enjoy the ambience; being by the water has a calming effect on me. That's why I want a place at the beach."

On the way to the car, when they passed a shop selling brightly printed Hawaiian clothing, Polly said, "Poor Pete, he told me he had dozens of these shirts, but I only knew him at the nursing facility; I never had a chance to see him wearing them."

"I know it's hard for you; my house is the same one Ted and I lived in. The entire neighborhood reminds me of our life together." She sighed. "Let's not dwell on the past; let's binge on two-scoop ice cream cones? Besides shopping, eating always cheers me up; of course, until I get on the scale the next day."

Polly laughed. "Let's do it."

Later, back at the entrance of skilled nursing, Polly hugged Margot. "Thanks for rescuing me again."

"My pleasure, sweetie; I'll call you soon."

A feeling of dread came over Margot as she waved goodbye and watched her small figure disappear into the facility.

CHAPTER FORTY-ONE

At nine-thirty that evening, Margot lay curled on her sofa studying the growing piles of books and DVDs scattered around the room and clamoring for her attention.

When the phone rang, she smiled, expecting Hans on the other end.

Instead, a woman's high-pitched voice screamed, "Margot, it's Ginger; Polly's been injured."

Margot jolted upright. "That can't be."

"I checked on Polly an hour ago and found her lying in bed asleep—or so I thought. But something made me take a closer look, and I noticed her arm limp and dangling. Then I tried rousing her, with no response."

Margot gasped. "My God."

"Ernesto and Betty came after I pressed the call button, and we checked her over; she has a nasty bump on her head. Her arm may be broken as well; it's hard to tell without x-rays.

"We didn't want to handle her too much, so we waited for the paramedics."

"What did they say?"

"They never say much; they just stabilize the patients and transport them to Emergency."

"Where is Polly now?"

"At Saddleback Hospital, here in Laguna Hills."

Margot edged off the sofa and stood. "That's close by; maybe I'll walk over."

The phone rang a second time, and thinking it was Ginger again, she said, "Did you find out anything else?"

"I don't get it."

"Hans, it's you." Margot's voice quavered. "I'm so upset; Polly's been injured." She told Hans what she knew and added, "I wish you could be here."

"I wish I could too, but my mother needs me."

"I understand; I don't mean to pressure you, but Polly's like my family."

Margot slapped her forehead. "Speaking of family, I hope someone at the hospital contacts her daughter, Susan. She'll be frantic when she finds out her mother is hurt and unconscious."

"Susan's an emotional woman; she doesn't handle stress well, and she's very flakey. I suppose that's why I feel responsible for Polly. After the nurses call back, I'm heading to the hospital."

"You should hold off until morning; they probably won't know a whole lot yet."

"I'm going over there anyway."

"Miss impetuous."

"Hans, she's my friend."

"I'm not there to stop you, and I probably couldn't anyway, but you should start protecting yourself. There have been far too many suspicious fatalities in the nursing facility, and you could be the next accident."

"My news should make you happy; I'm giving up the investigations. Polly had been planning to leave skilled nursing and move to the beach; this very day I told her that I'm through volunteering on the day she leaves. I've just been hanging around for her sake. Anyway, my conservator hearing comes up in a few weeks, and if I win, I get my life back."

"Amen to that."

"Listen, Ginger may be phoning with more news. I'll call tomorrow, okay?"

"Please; I'm anxious to hear."

With sleep no longer possible, she leafed through a book describing life in *Lake Wobegon*. But not even Garrison Keillor's wit could shake her somber mood. Instead, she reviewed her journal on the mysterious deaths of Joe the Jokester and Pete the Punster. To what she had already written, she added the little she knew about Polly's injuries and Polly's recent confrontations with Helga and Betty. Then closing the journal, Margot stared out the window until first light. With no news from Ginger, she decided to eat breakfast and head for the hospital.

At six a.m., the corridors of Shady Palms remained quiet; the only people in the dining room were two old men at a corner table having a heated argument. Jack, her next-door neighbor, snapped open a newspaper and slammed his hand down hard. "Those tax and spend democrats are at it again."

The other man's face reddened as he shook his fist. "You Orange County people are all the same. Every time I open my mouth, some right wing jerk says, 'What are you, a liberal?' What gets me is the way they say 'liberal' in a voice dripping with sarcasm."

The men began shouting so vehemently, Margot worried they might come to blows; she moved to a table further away. On edge from lack of sleep and with her head already pounding, the fight between the two men made her feel worse. She sipped her juice, ate a bite of toast, then hurried away.

The cool morning air helped clear the cobwebs from her head, and she resolved to begin a fitness regimen.

Once at the hospital, she unexpectedly ran into Ginger. "Aren't you scheduled to be at work today?"

"I had the night shift; remember? I came to find out about Polly's condition."

"And?"

"As we suspected, the x-rays show her arm's broken; they've scheduled a cat-scan to determine her head injuries; she may have a concussion."

"A concussion; is she conscious?"

"She's in a coma."

"How do you know when someone's in a coma? Is there a special test?"

"We use the Glasgow coma scale. It has a rating system of 3-15 points. Those who score in the 3-8 point range are said to be a coma."

"What's the scale based on?"

"I'll make this as uncomplicated as possible. The scale is based on eye response, verbal response, and motor response: patients who open their eyes spontaneously, score 4 points; eyes opened in response to a command, score 3 points; eyes opened only in response to pain, score 2 points. I'll print you out a copy.

"Bottom line, what's her status?"

"Don't know yet, but it could be serious."

Margot's stomach tightened. "What are the odds she'll come out of this?"

Ginger shrugged.

"Just when she's on the verge of leaving, this happens. Can we see her?"

"For now, we should only poke our heads in the door. Apparently, they gave strict orders she be left alone."

"Orders from whom?"

"No idea. They probably want her to settle in."

The two women proceeded to Polly's room, eerily quiet except for the humming and blips of the various monitors at work. There, they found Polly with her right arm in a cast and her head swathed in bandages.

Margot patted Polly's healthy arm gingerly, then bent to kiss her cheek. "Darling, it's Margot."

Seeing no movement or sign of recognition, Margot began crying; Ginger put her arm around Margot's shoulders. "Come on Babe, let's go. There's nothing we can do for her right now."

"I feel so helpless."

As they walked toward the exit, Margot met Polly's daughter, Susan, and her husband. Red-eyed from crying, Susan released her husband's arm and grabbed Margot in a tight hug. "Oh, Margot, why did this happen to my Mom? I can't imagine what caused her broken arm."

Margot shook her head.

"They say she has a concussion, and she's in a coma."

Margot nodded. "Let's go to the cafeteria where we can talk."

"I should stay close by; they may need me."

"Of course; I understand."

⸺⸱⸱⸺

Late that morning, Margot returned to Shady Palms where she found Nancy and Jane in the lobby and called out, "There you are, the very two the ladies I want to see." Guiding them to an empty sofa, she told them the bad news about Polly.

Both women expressed shock and wondered aloud what could have happened.

"This is my line of thinking," Margot said. "Joe and Helga argue; Joe dies. Pete and Helga argue; Pete dies. Polly accuses Helga of being involved in the deaths of Pete and Joe; Polly ends up with a broken arm and a possible concussion. Those deaths and the accident are more than a coincidence."

Nancy patted Margot's knee. "Girlfriend, we need to talk. For a mighty long time, we've both been fixing to leave this place. We figure now Polly's gone, there's nothing to hang around for. You just say the word."

Margot stretched her long legs and stared at the carpet. "I can't make any rash decisions; I'm staying put for now."

"We won't desert you," Nancy said. "But maybe we should quit volunteering in that creepy care facility?"

"I don't know," Jane said. "If Polly gets sent back to skilled nursing and we're not around to watch her. . . ."

Margot said, "There's no way I would let her come back here. I'll make sure she goes to another nursing home to recuperate. But with two deaths to be solved, I can't leave. And there's Ernesto to consider. He had duty the night of Polly's accident. Besides being a suspect in the deaths of Joe and Pete, he could be implicated in her accident as well; I can't abandon him."

Nancy took Margot's hand. "Ernesto can take care of himself. How about you, though? With bodies and broken bones popping up all over the place, you don't fancy waking up dead one day, do you?"

"I can take care of myself."

"Well if you're sticking, we're sticking. We're gonna keep a sharp eye out, especially after this filly fessed up that Helga threatened her purty face with lye; right Jane?"

Jane nodded. "You betcha."

A few days later, Margot spied detectives Mulroney and Mendoza asking for Ernesto. Soon they were ushered into the conference room with Ernesto in tow; he wore an expression of "not this again." Margot tip-toed into the alcove across the hall and sat down to eavesdrop. At first, the only words she could make out were, "Polly," "accident," and "on duty."

Then she distinctly heard one detective say, "Can you explain why you're always on the scene when a patient dies or has a serious accident?"

Ernesto piped up, "I work many hours every week. Is reason I am around when Pete and Polly have accidents. Don't forget, I am off-duty when they find Joe's body."

An angry voice replied, "That proves nothing; you could have already given him the alcohol on top of the Valium you administered."

Ernesto burst out, "You guys don't have no rights to all the time ask me questions. Here's my attorney's card. From now on, you call him, not me."

The questioning continued another ten minutes, but the voices grew too faint for Margot to hear. Soon, both detectives walked past the alcove and left the facility. A few minutes later, Ernesto followed. Margot found him leaning against the stucco building and smoking a cigarette. She reached for the cigarette. "Cut that out; you know smoking is unhealthy."

Ernesto waved her away. "Leave me alone. I need my smokes real bad right now; those guys are railroading me."

"Listen Ernesto, Joe's friend Rick admits bringing Joe the gin. Maybe I can convince him to tell the detectives."

"When I mention this Rick guy, everything get worse."

"How come?"

Ernesto stamped out the cigarette. "They say finding them drinking make me think to finish Joe off with the Valium."

"I hoped Rick could help; now I don't know. It's your lawyer's call."

Having left a disheartened Ernesto lighting up another cigarette, Margot returned inside. While sorting through the patient mail, she couldn't shake the feeling that she had missed something or someone. She walked from room to room delivering mail, smiling and chatting with the patients, then stopped by the lunchroom for the bottled water she stored in the frig. Helga's threat had ended her coffee drinking at the facility for good.

There she found Betty resting her head against the back of a chair. Margot said, "You seem beat this morning. Is something wrong?"

Betty closed her eyes, "I'm already tired and it's only eleven a.m."

Margot hesitated. "This may be a bad time to ask, but I'm curious."

Betty remained silent.

Margot said, "I've been talking to Rick; he was friends with Joe and Pete, the two men who died recently. . . ."

Before Margot could finish, Betty straightened up and gave her a piercing look. "Why were you talking to Rick?"

"Uh, I visited Joe's daughter, Doris, to express my condolences and . . . ."

Betty interrupted again. "I remember your asking me for the address. You went to a lot of trouble finding Doris. Why all this interest?"

With Pete no longer around to contradict her, Margot ventured, "It wasn't a lot of trouble; Pete gave me her phone number."

Betty stood to leave. "Your sudden concern for Joe, Pete, and Rick is very puzzling. Believe me; they're not worth the effort."

CHAPTER FORTY-TWO

With Hans away, Polly comatose, and her conservator case unresolved, Margot's life took a dreary turn. She daydreamed about her old neighborhood: its diverse residents, children shouting to each other and skate boarding up and down the street, gardeners and handy men working, delivery trucks coming and going, and sweet tea at Mirabelle's house.

She continued volunteering, though simply going through the motions. The facility's narrow corridors made it impossible to avoid crossing paths with Helga. Every time they met, Margot could feel her breathing fire like the ferocious Minotaur guarding the labyrinth at the Palace of King Minos in Knossos.

One day, as she signed out, Loretta, the facility's receptionist, called out, "Margot, got a minute?"

"Sure, what's up?"

"Thought you might be interested; your friend Polly's due here on Wednesday."

"There must be a mistake."

Loretta held up the intake book and pointed. "Her name's right here on the list."

Under incoming patients, Margot read, Polly Parker, 121. Not able to believe her eyes, she reread the posting three times then dropped the book, and without a word, rushed off to call Polly's daughter.

Susan sounded none too pleased when Margot asked why her mother was being sent back to the nursing facility. Margot could picture Susan's petulant face as she said, "My mom will only be there temporarily. Anyway, Bob and I are leaving tomorrow for a conference in Barbados."

"Is it important that you go with him?"

"You don't seriously expect me to miss a Caribbean trip; I've never been there."

"Can't the hospital keep her until you return?"

"I begged them to let her stay," Susan said. After all, she's no trouble; she's still in a coma."

"No trouble? You must be joking. Patients need their vitals checked; they need nutrition; their bodies need to be cleaned and cared for; the mechanisms that sustain them need sterilization to prevent infection; they. . . ."

"Spare me the details; since the hospital's refusal, I called all over heck and back to find another facility, but the best ones are full. Luckily, Rest View Terrace promised me a room within a week."

"A week? You're putting your mother in danger for a whole week? No one ever determined the cause of her injuries; what makes you think this couldn't happen again."

"That nice Helga Hasse, explained . . . ."

"Helga, nice? You're not serious. Don't you remember your mother having it out with Helga at Pete's funeral? I had to stop Ernesto from confronting her as well."

"I thought they both behaved very badly at a solemn event like a funeral. But, as I said before you interrupted me, Helga had a perfectly reasonable explanation for my mother's injuries."

Margot groaned.

"She said a maintenance man had been under suspicion for mistreating the patients, and they had to let him go. The authorities are investigating."

"I never heard that story."

"Well that's what she said, and now that the man is gone, my mom will be safe. How could she not be with all you mother hens watching over her?"

Margot exploded, "Mother hens—you beat everything. Should I order up a cot and sleep in her room?"

"Oh would you?"

"You must be kidding."

"I'm sure you can arrange it."

"Yah, right, Helga would bend over backwards to let me sleep there. She'd happily supply a coffin for me to bunk in."

"Enough, I don't have time for this. I have to take my dog to the vet, decide what to bring, and then pack." Susan hung up the phone leaving Margot dumbfounded and desperately worried.

Early on the day of Polly's scheduled arrival, Margot rushed over to skilled nursing and found Ginger hovering near the reception desk.

"I've been waiting for you. Polly's in 121; it's a big corner room. I'll take you there."

"Thanks. You're an angel."

They walked down the hall arm in arm until Ginger spied Helga coming towards them and quickly disengaged herself.

"Look at you two girlfriends out for a stroll," Helga barked. "This is a care facility; act professionally."

Ginger studied her shoes and mumbled, "Oh, go stuff it."

Once in the room, they found Betty smoothing out the bed to make Polly comfortable.

"How's she doing?" Margot asked.

Betty answered in crisp, polite tones, "There are no signs she's waking up, but all her readings are normal."

Seeing Polly's lifeless body connected to the tubes controlling her functions, Margot said, "I'd appreciate it if you and the other staff members would look out for her. I'm worried about her lying there helpless, at the mercy of . . . ."

"I look out for all my patients without being told," Betty said. "In fact, I need to check on another woman right now."

After Betty left, Ginger said, "I'm worried about Polly too; when I came earlier, I found Helga standing over the bed with satisfaction written all over her face. She had the gall to say, 'Polly's my kind of patient—quiet, no back talk, no disobeying the rules. I hope she stays that way a long, long time."

Margot shivered.

Ginger put her hands on her hips, "That's not all. She said, 'Be sure to find me right away if Polly shows signs of waking up.'"

"*Au contraire.*" Margot shook her head. "You tell me or Ernesto first; once she's awake and able to explain how the injury occurred, she could be vulnerable to another attack. We'll have our hands full keeping her safe until they find room for her at Rest View Terrace."

As Margot exited Polly's room, she noticed Betty hovering outside. On a hunch, she waited nearby to watch. Sure enough, she spied her standing near the bed, reading Polly's chart. Something about her demeanor made Margot remember the angry words Betty had said about Joe, Pete, and Rick. The time had arrived to question Betty further.

Margot moved closer to the room and busied herself reading a notebook. When she saw Betty leave, she called out, "Got a minute?"

"I have patient rounds."

"Maybe I can help out."

"Another time."

"Just a quick question?"

Betty frowned. "What's so important?"

"I'm not sure how to say this, but I've been wondering what you have against Joe, Pete, and Rick?"

In a flash, Betty erupted, "Who told you that?"

"You once said I shouldn't be concerned about them, that they weren't worth the effort."

"I don't remember that."

"But do you have something against them?"

Betty twisted her hands and started to the door until Margot stopped her. "Come on Betty, out with it."

Betty opened her mouth to speak and shut it.

"Please," Margot said.

Betty dropped into a chair and hung her head. "My poor mother is what I have against those men."

"Your mother?"

"Every time I visit her, I don't know what to expect; one day she's happy and lucid, the next day she's almost catatonic."

Margot reached over and patted Betty's hand. "I'm so sorry, but I don't understand what your mother has to do with those three men."

Tearing up, Betty said, "Ask Rick. He's the one who's left."

⟞⟢ ⟣⟝

Betty rushed away, leaving Margot dumbfounded. Now she definitely needed answers from Rick, but every time she mentioned Joe's death he threw a fit. In the past, she had scheduled a late day golf lesson then suggested drinks afterwards. Perhaps she could use the same ruse again.

Luckily, she had arranged a four-o'clock appointment for the next day. He sounded friendly and, remembering she had been upset when they last met, he asked if everything had turned out well for her.

"Yes, at least I hope so."

At the lesson, Rick concentrated on her putting game, which he said had improved over the last time; he readily agreed to drinks next door. Margot waited until they had two rounds of Margaritas before broaching her subject. "I'm glad we have a chance to talk today because I've been curious ever since you told me that you, Joe, and Pete grew up together in Boston."

Rick drew his chair close. "You want all my secrets, don't you?"

"It's not a big deal." She kissed him lightly on the lips. But I ran into Betty today; you know, the nurse who came into Joe's room, when you two were drinking."

Rick jerked his arm away. "Not that drinking stuff again."

"Don't move away," Margot leaned in towards Rick. I like sitting close to you. But I can't help being puzzled."

"Puzzled?"

"It's Betty's behavior. She said the strangest thing yesterday; I had the impression her mother knew the three of you."

Rick bolted upright and gripped the sides of his chair. "Betty's mother knew us? How could that be? Unless..."

"Unless what?"

Rick hesitated, seeming to wrestle with a thought. At last he said, "After Betty came in and found us, Joe said she looked familiar, and, as I told you before, something rang a bell, something about the way she walked?"

"I remember that."

Rick hit his head and stood abruptly. "Could Betty's mother be . . .?"

Margot grabbed his arm. "You're not going to leave me wondering?"

Rick picked up the golf sweater draped over his chair. "I need time to think this through."

CHAPTER FORTY-THREE

With Betty studiously avoiding her and reluctant to press Rick further, Margot put her energies into monitoring Polly as best she could. Several days following her arrival, Margot dropped by the receptionist's desk. "I guess Polly will be moving to a different facility soon, right?"

Loretta glanced up from the patient log. "Why do you say that?"

"Her daughter promised me that her mother would be transferred as soon as a room becomes vacant at another facility."

"Far as I know, she's here until she recovers or . . . ."

"That can't be true."

Loretta shrugged. "I take reservations; I don't get involved in the fine points."

A few days earlier, Susan had phoned Margot raving about Barbados: the villa accommodations, the pool, the view, the food, the weather. She added, "In fact, we're extending our stay another week."

The news had hit Margot hard, and she reminded Susan that her mother would be in danger if left at the Shady Palms facility.

Undaunted, Susan said, "Stop worrying. They found my mother another room at Park View Terrace; it's all set."

Now, finding Loretta unaware of any plans for transferring Polly, it became imperative to reach Susan. Margot consulted her watch; it was six o'clock in Barbados, seemingly a good time to catch Susan in her room.

Hearing Margot's voice, Susan wailed, "Not you again; you're ruining my vacation."

"I'm calling because your mother's been here a week, and no one knows anything about her being transferred to another facility."

"Oh, that. You worry too much. I had another long talk with that nice nurse, Helga something, or other."

"Helga's something, all right. When did you talk?"

"After you got me all upset, I called, and she gave me a glowing report of my mother."

"A glowing report? Her condition hasn't altered a bit. What did she say?"

"She said they loved having my mother there, and that she's well cared for. Helga's confident she'll make a full recovery."

"You know nothing about what goes on."

"Please Margot, you misunderstand the woman. She's a very sweet person."

"Sweets can be lethal."

"Don't be melodramatic. Bob and I feel strongly that my mother should stay right where she is. I asked Helga to cancel the other nursing home."

Margot felt as though she had been kicked in the stomach. "Cancel? You're not serious?"

"Darn right."

"You don't get it, do you? Your mother might be safe if she remains comatose, but if she regains consciousness something bad could happen again."

Silence.

"You could hire a private caregiver for the night shift, when things quiet down. That's when she would be in the most danger."

"Aren't caregivers expensive?"

"It's only until you come home; we can make other arrangements then."

"That's something Bob and I need to discuss. I'll let you know what we decide. I've got to hang up now; we have dinner plans with this darling couple next door. Linda and I have a ball shopping together while the guys play golf. Anyway, kisses to my mom and toodle loo."

The phone went dead.

Margot heaved a great sigh. I can't fix anything. I can't help Polly; I can't help Ernesto; my relationship with Hans is shaky; I'm stuck at Shady Palms.

She grabbed a jacket and headed for a walk to calm her anxiety and think things through. By the time she returned, she had resolved to keep Polly from becoming the next victim. With or without Susan's permission, she would foot the bill for a caregiver until Susan returned.

⚊⚌ ⚌⚊

Initially, Margot searched the internet until she realized that the office must keep a list of recommended care givers. Congratulating herself on the return of the dauntless, resourceful woman she had always been, she headed downstairs for the information.

Though Margot spent the entire next day interviewing various caregivers, none had proved satisfactory.

The first applicant impressed Margot as a sweet and caring woman, but at four-foot nine, Margot feared she would be no match for Helga.

She immediately rejected Fernando, a muscular émigré; with his poor English skills, he might frighten Polly once she wakened from her coma, and Helga would hate any Mexican on sight.

A retired Indonesian sea captain with excellent references stood out as a strong candidate, but he was tied up on his current assignment. Margot berated the agency for wasting her time, and they hurriedly sent over two promising "ready to go" contenders.

Margot blinked as she opened the door to admit a pair of tall identical women, with hefty builds and large bosoms; they had short, tight-curled white hair and boasted flawless creamy skin, apparently never touched by a single ray of sunlight. Their flower printed dresses, one blue and white, the other green and white, with V-necklines, were carefully pinned at the top, ensuring that no cleavage could possibly offend.

The slightly taller woman extended her hand. "Top o'the day to you. We're the O'Donnell twins; I'm Patty, and this is me sister, Matty."

"Uh, uh, come in," Margot stammered. She gestured to the chairs flanking the coffee table. "Please make yourselves comfortable. Would you like tea?"

"Lovely," they said in unison.

On her way to the kitchenette, Margot heard a whisper, "I bet she won't be fixing us *brewed* tea."

While the kettle heated, Margot rummaged through her stash of sweets and found a tin of Irish Shortbread she had snagged during her latest shopping expedition.

Returning to the living room, she set the tray on the coffee table and handed a cup to each woman. The two ladies sipped the tea, exchanging glances that proclaimed, "Teabags—as expected."

"Please tell me about yourselves." Margot passed the cookies.

Patty put down her cup. "We're newly-arrived from Dublin where we did our nursing at St. Vincent's Hospital."

"How long were you at the job?"

"For over thirty years," Patty said proudly.

"Why did you decide to leave?"

"The hospital is closing down, and we needed new jobs; she gestured toward Matty. We came here because me sister's married daughter lives in Irvine."

"Do you have any references in this area?"

Patty answered sheepishly. "Not exactly; the truth be known, this would be our first case here."

Margot wrinkled her brow. "The problem is I need someone to start almost immediately, and I'm not comfortable hiring applicants without local recommendations."

Patty jumped in quickly. "Oh, but we have references in Dublin."

Margot thought a minute. The women radiated a no-nonsense, we-will-take-no-guff attitude. "Tell you what," she said. "If you jot down the names and phone numbers, I can make a few calls early tomorrow. You wouldn't be starting until the evening anyway; the job is for the night shift. I hope that's all right?"

"That would be grand, as long as we can work together, of course not both at the same time, but on the same case. We could alternate nights. Is it a lady or a gentleman we would be caring for?"

Margot described the injuries and the coma, for the time being not mentioning possible dangers to Polly.

Again it was Patty who spoke up, "The poor little darling."

"I forgot to mention—the pay is fifteen dollars an hour. If that's agreeable and your references check out, we could meet tomorrow before your shift, so I can introduce you around."

Margot handed each woman a card. "This is my information. Please leave me your phone numbers and the Ireland contacts; I'll get back by late tomorrow."

They both nodded and said in unison, "That would be lovely."

As she saw them out, she appraised the two carefully. They appeared to be strong women who could stand up for themselves and handle any problems that arose.

⊷ ⊶

Anticipating the alarm, Margot sat up at six a.m. sharp. The eight-hour time difference put Dublin at two p.m., well within normal business hours at St. Vincent's.

The evening before, she had researched the international dialing codes and had studied the names provided by the twins, deciding that the hospital administrator would be the proper person to contact.

After going through channels and struggling to make herself understood, a cheerful voice said, "Sharon Murphy here; delighted to help, if I can."

Margot explained she was calling from California regarding the O'Donnell twins as potential caregivers; she added that they had listed Ms. Murphy as a reference.

"So that's where the girls have gone to. How's the weather out there and how are the darlings?"

"The weather's fine, and they're fine. I recently interviewed them to work as caregivers for an ailing friend."

"Oh, they'll do a grand job."

"That's wonderful. Can you tell me how long they worked at St. Vincent's?"

"An interesting question; it's sure, I am, they started here way before my time. Word is those two practically opened the place; now the powers that be are closing down the old wreck."

Margot listened patiently, while Ms. Murphy warmed to the subject. "There are grand plans afoot to build a huge facility, all modern and fancied up with the latest technology. It might take years, but soon we'll all be trotting on out of here."

Margot interrupted, "Can you tell me a little about the two women? They have no local references."

"Oh, let me think. I suppose what comes to mind first is they're both hard working and caring ladies."

"Those are the traits I'm looking for."

"You could also say they're what you call a wee bit stubborn."

"Stubborn good or stubborn bad?"

"Oh, definitely not bad. What I mean is that they stick to things; they don't give up easily."

"I like what I'm hearing. Is there anything else I should know?"

"No, love, that's it. Can you be telling me your number, in case I forgot anything?"

Margot gave Sharon Murphy her cell and thanked the woman for her time.

Sharon replied, "My pleasure, it was. Be sure and send the girls my best."

The talk with the administrator had been reassuring. Helga would test them at every opportunity and do her upmost to drive them away. But with two strong and stubborn women on her side, Polly might be safe until Margot could convince Susan to make other arrangements. She called and hired them.

⟞⟝

Later that day, Margot found the O'Donnell twins at skilled nursing, happily chatting away to Loretta, who would be visiting family in Dublin during that summer.

"It's sure my relatives will give you a warm welcome, if you'll be good enough to call," Patty said. "Of course they'll be having you to tea, maybe even do a nice supper."

Loretta rolled her eyes silently signaling for help.

Taking each twin by the arm, Margot propelled them away, saying, "Time's up, ladies; there's a lot to show you."

"Don't forget the application forms," Loretta called out. "You can fill them out at your leisure or while you're sitting with Polly. It'll give you something to do. Heavens knows, you won't be having any conversations with her."

Margot eyed Loretta coldly. "She could wake up anytime."

After pointing out the restrooms, the lunchroom, and the lounge, they visited Polly's room.

"Isn't she the comely lass?" Patty said.

Matty broke her usual silence. "Oh, the wee poor darling."

Just then, the light from the hallway disappeared, blocked by a hulking shadow in the doorway. "Who are these people, Mrs. Manning, and why are they disturbing a very sick patient?"

Margot gulped. "Helga, I thought you'd gone already. These are the O'Donnell twins; they'll be taking turns watching Polly during the night shift."

"On whose say so? Her daughter hasn't mentioned anything to me."

"Well, uh, you know since Susan's still away, I've been worried Polly might wake during the night and not know where she is, so I hired Patty and Matty to care for her. I'm certain Susan will be relieved when she gets back and finds out."

"You mean you did this without the permission of her own daughter?"

"We did discuss it on the phone, and Susan seemed agreeable."

Flashing Margot a look of pure hatred, Helga said, "We'll see."

CHAPTER FORTY-FOUR

Having obtained care for Polly, Margot's thoughts now turned to Betty as a suspect in the two deaths and the attack on Polly. She pondered her next steps in investigating Betty's hints at a connection between her mother, Pete, Joe, and Rick.

Then, without further prodding, Rick called Margot, saying, "I have news on two counts; I manned up and confessed to bringing Joe the gin."

"That bodes well for Ernesto, but what are the consequences for you?"

"Zilch, I hope. Two detectives grilled me all one afternoon, but I think I convinced them I had nothing to do with giving Joe the Valium."

"I'm proud of you; that must have been tough."

"They lectured me pretty hard about the gin."

"What made you change your mind?"

"As a dutiful former altar boy, I went to confession, and the priest convinced me."

"You mentioned other news."

"I want to meet the nurse whose mother may have known me and my friends."

"Why? Did you have a memory flash?"

"It's just a hunch; I'm hoping Betty can say if I'm right or wrong."

"Hang on while I check her schedule." Margot turned to examine the board behind the nurses' station. "She's down for Thursday—that's tomorrow—and again on Saturday, but I don't know whether she'll meet with you."

"Saturday afternoon works; if I can reschedule two lessons."

"Visiting is between two and four; that might be the perfect time. On Saturdays there are no tests, and the nurses have light duty."

"Should I just show up?"

Margot tapped a pencil against the counter. "Call first to confirm and make sure I'm around, so I can act as go-between."

"Will do."

Saturday afternoon, at promptly two-thirty, Rick called. "Betty working today?"

"She is. Are you headed over?"

"Be there in an hour."

"Come find me at the nurses' station. I'll try softening her up a little."

"Okay and thanks again."

Soon, she spied the nurse coming down the hall and called out, "Betty, long time *no see*; are you ignoring me?"

"Been busy."

Margot ventured, "Rick, the friend of Joe and Pete, called a few minutes ago. He wants to meet with you this afternoon."

"I have nothing to say to him."

"He has a few questions about your mother."

Betty folded her hands across her chest.

"Will you see him?"

Anger flared on Betty's face. "I'll see him all right."

Rick arrived, looking pale and nervous, and Margot paged Betty who met them at the conference room. Both refused Margot's offer to bring coffee.

Seated at opposite ends of the table, with Margot in between, they stared at each other. Rick began. "When Margot first said your mother knew me and my friends, I was incredulous. But the more I thought, the more it made sense; you remind me so much of my friend from the old days in Boston. Is your mother's name Roberta, by any chance?"

"My mother's name *is* Roberta, and you were no friend of hers."

Puzzled, Margot glanced from one to the other.

"Go ahead and tell her," Betty said.

Rick squirmed in his seat before answering, "I never did find out what became of Roberta. The last time I saw her must have been over fifty years ago in the hospital when she was still unconscious."

Margot was taken aback. "Unconscious?"

Betty stood and walked over to Rick; she yanked his chair around and eyed him without speaking. At last she said, "My mother spent weeks and weeks in the hospital recovering; after that the family moved away because of the shame."

Rick hung his head. "Where is Roberta now?"

A sardonic laugh escaped from her lips. "My mother's not far, at a clinic where she goes for treatment whenever she's so depressed, she can't function."

"Will one of you tell me what this is about?" Margot interrupted.

Betty turned toward Margot. "Rick and his friends ran off and abandoned my mother while a gang of thugs attacked her; they didn't lift a finger to help her."

"We did help her."

Betty sneered, "That's not the way I heard it."

"On weekends, we would ride our bikes to the dump and sit on the boulders to sneak smokes. Roberta was a pretty blonde like Betty; we all had crushes on her."

Betty's face turned crimson. "Crushes on her, and that's how you behaved?"

"Will you listen? We had to watch out, so we could high-tail it if a gang showed up. One day, we weren't paying attention and somehow they crept up on us from behind."

Margot asked. "What did you do?"

"We scrambled to get away, but they grabbed Roberta and pushed her to the ground. A huge guy, who acted like the leader, laughed and said, "We can have a little party with this one; you babies get moving." Roberta started screaming, and we didn't know what to do. Joe, Pete and I were three skinny teenagers, outnumbered by five big hoodlums, swinging tire irons."

Betty wiped her eyes. "So you ran off and left her."

"Not true; we rode a mile down the road until Joe stopped us and said, "I'll go to the police station. Pete, you find your brother, and Rick, you get Roberta's family. We were miles away from town, but luckily, half-way back, we flagged down a patrol car. The cop radioed for reinforcements and sped to the area where he scared off the gang. We pedaled back and found Roberta passed out on the ground."

"This is news to me; my mother recalls waking up in the hospital after being unconscious and wondering where you all had gone to; she never saw any of you again."

"She may not remember seeing us, but we visited her plenty. At first the Docs weren't sure she would make it because of her head injuries; it was pretty dicey for several weeks. When she began to recover, the staff said that our bringing help so quickly probably saved her life."

"Did they ever catch the gang?" Margot asked.

"The police did catch them, but since the guys were under eighteen, they were tried in juvenile court and sent to reform school."

Betty said bitterly, "Why is it I don't believe you?"

"I don't know what Roberta remembers and how much her parents told her."

Margot patted Betty's hand. "I'm confused. You mentioned your mother suffers from depression. She must have recovered enough to marry and have you."

Betty wrinkled her brow. "She did, but do you think a person gets over a brutal attack without suffering after-effects? My mother has been seriously depressed ever since I can remember."

"I understand, but how did you connect the three men with your mother?"

"It happened as a fluke. To cheer her up, I sometimes bring photos of me with my patients." Betty began crying. "One day I showed my mother a snapshot of Joe and Pete joking around in the solarium. She stared for a long time without saying anything. Then she asked me, 'Betty, who are those two men? They remind me of boys I once knew.'

"I said, oh, mother, those are two of my patients."

"But she insisted on knowing their names, and when I told her the patients were Pete Peterson and Joe Farelli, she gasped and turned pale; after that she withdrew into her own world for several weeks.

"Once she became more coherent, she explained that she had known Pete and Joe. In bits and pieces she relived what she recalled of the horrible attack. The image of Joe and Pete clowning around just tore me up; while they were having fun, my mother lay in a deep depression, just a short distance away."

Rick said, "I'd like to meet Roberta and explain that we tried to help her."

"If I don't believe you, what makes you think she would?"

"It's been over fifty years, but the police may have records to prove I'm telling the truth."

Betty pushed her chair back and stood. "All I know is Joe and Pete are gone; maybe fate intervened to make them pay the price for deserting her. You stay away from my mother before something gets you as well."

CHAPTER FORTY-FIVE

After the meeting, Margot and Rick puzzled over Betty's refusal to accept his explanations. In light of her veiled threat, Rick promised he would avoid any future contact with Betty or her mother.

An uneventful week passed without changes to Polly's condition; the O'Donnell twins seemed to be settling in, and Helga had not caused further problems. Each day, when Margot called, one of the twins would say, "We're happy as two clams here."

Susan sent a postcard saying they were adding yet another week of vacation; Margot had no idea when the card had been mailed, and she wondered how Bob could afford so much time away from work.

Not my problem, she thought.

Two days later, she heard Susan's angry voice on her cell. "I'm back. What the hell's going on?"

"If you're asking about your mother, her condition hasn't worsened, and she's being kept comfortable."

"Stop play acting. You know very well I mean those Irish twins you hired without my authorization. Why would my mother need extra help? There's an entire staff to care for her."

Margot wanted to scream, why can't I get through to you? Instead, she calmly said, "Susan, your mother's in grave danger here. Now that you're home, she should be moved to another nursing home."

"But Helga assures me she's perfectly safe at their facility."

Words from the fox guarding the chicken coop, she thought.

"As I already told you, I feel better having a caregiver during the night when it's quiet, in case your mother wakes up and is confused."

"I suppose that's all right, since you're the one paying."

Margot sighed. I sometimes regret not having children, but with a daughter like Susan. . . .

━┼ ┼━

Several days passed quietly. One night, Margot contemplated the mound of paperwork and bills on her desk, accumulated while she had been off playing sleuth. In the midst of attacking an envelope marked 'Urgent, Second Notice,' the phone rang. She let the machine pick up until she heard Patty say, "I don't know what to do."

Margot grabbed the phone. "What's wrong? Is Polly all right?"

"Saints be to God, she's fine. I mean there's no change for better or worse."

"You frightened me."

"It's that Helga person."

Margot steeled herself. "What now?"

"She marched in here and said she would speak to Polly's daughter about having us dismissed."

"What did you reply to that?"

"I told her that we take orders from you."

Margot closed her eyes. "How did Helga react?"

"She stomped off saying she would end this foolishness. I try to pay her no mind, but you don't like staying where you're not welcome."

"I'm so sorry, Patty; you and your sister are doing a great job. I hope you won't let her drive you away."

"Sure it will take more than Helga to scare us; we'll be sticking to this job. Don't you be worrying your pretty head."

A voice interrupted, and Margot heard Patty say, "Really and truly? I haven't noticed anything."

Margot's ears perked up. "What's happening?"

"Oh, it's Matty, me sister, come to relieve me; she says yesterday she saw the little lamb stirring around some."

"Stirring around?"

"I'll let her tell you herself. Here, Matty, talk to Margot."

"Evening, Margot. Yes, 'twas only a little bit of moving."

"That's fantastic. How long did it last?"

"Not long, just some wee restlessness and shifting around."

"Did she open her eyes? Margot asked. "Did she move her lips?"

"No, neither one. At least I don't think so."

"Did anyone else notice a change in her?"

Matty hesitated. "Maybe."

"What do you mean, 'maybe'?"

"Around eight last evening, Helga examined Polly; she looked her over—studied her a while. Then she muttered something and left. I couldn't make out what she said."

Margot thanked both caregivers and cautioned them to watch for further signs.

So that explains Helga's scene with Patty, she thought. Helga's worried Polly's waking up, and she's trying to drive away the twins.

I dread what she'll do next.

—✦ ✦—

Margot rose at six the next morning, skipped breakfast and hurried off to check Polly's condition for herself.

At seven a.m., the staff was busy distributing breakfast trays and medicine; Polly's room remained quiet, except for the usual monitor noises.

Margot sat beside the bed and said softly, "Hi, it's Margot; can you hear me?"

No response.

She tried again. "Darling, it's Margot; can you open your eyes?"

Nothing.

Margot took her hand and thought she detected a slight pressure.

"Did you just squeeze my hand?"

Nothing, not even a twitch.

After waiting a half hour for a sign, Margot bent to kiss her. "I'll come back soon; I know you're in there somewhere."

On one last try, she detected movement in Polly's hand. "You are conscious after all; do it again, please."

This time Margot felt two squeezes in a row.

"One more time, darling?"

When another half hour passed with no further movement, she gave up.

Margot found Ginger checking on another patient and pulled her down the corridor towards Polly's room, saying, "I have exciting news. I think Polly's waking up."

"Why? What did she do?"

"Last night, Polly's caregiver, Matty, reported she was moving around a little, and this morning, she squeezed my hand a few times. I need your opinion. Can you examine her for me?"

"I'm coming. You can stop dragging me along like I'm a pull-toy."

But on reaching Polly's room, Margot stopped short. "Oh no, Helga's in there. Matty said Helga examined Polly last night for a long while; now she's back. I think Helga's worried she'll wake up and identify her as the assailant."

They moved back down the hall, where they could talk without being overhead, and Ginger said, "You know it's possible Polly will wake up with no memory of what caused her injuries. That's often the case in comas brought on by trauma."

Margot said, "So if Polly has no memory of the incident, her attacker is safe; if she does remember, she's in danger of another attack."

"Exactly right."

"Is it possible to wake up with no memory and remember later on?"

"Happens."

"What do we do now?"

Ginger said, "I can't start examining her with Helga there; anyway, I have morning rounds. Why don't you keep an eye on Helga and see what she may be up to?"

"I'll try. Hope the witch doesn't chase me off."

Margot stood in the doorway, watching quietly as Helga stared down at Polly, and said, "Polly, can you hear me?"

No response.

Helga repeated, "Can you hear my voice?"

Again no response.

Helga picked up her hand and squeezed. "I swear I saw you move yesterday; can you move again for me?"

Nothing.

"Damn you, do something. I think you're playing possum. I need to know what's going on with you."

A few minutes passed with Helga trying to rouse Polly.

Margot remained quiet until Helga began poking and prodding Polly. She ran to the bed and grabbed Helga's arm. "You leave her alone."

Helga jumped and quickly released Polly. She swung around, glaring at Margot. "Where did you come from, and what are you doing here?"

"More importantly, what are you doing to Polly?"

"I'm examining my patient; or aren't you smart enough to figure that out?"

"Examining is one thing, poking is another. You may be frightening her."

"You're only a volunteer; you know nothing about treatments for coma patients."

Margot jabbed Helga's arm. "How would you like someone poking *you*?"

Her eyes blazing fire, Helga said, "That does it; your services are no longer needed; get out and take your useless volunteers with you."

"You can't keep me away; I'm Polly's friend."

A mean smile crossed Helga's face. "Oh, but I can."

Margot walked down the hall with slow, deliberate steps, pretending to be unconcerned. Inwardly, she panicked. What will happen to Polly, without us to watch over her?

As soon as she exited the building, Margot rushed to telephone Susan. "Please," she begged, "You must do something; I found Helga poking and prodding your mother; I had to scream at her to stop."

"Don't be so dramatic; I'm sure that Helga was just testing her reflexes."

"Testing her reflexes? No way. She kept jabbing your mother repeatedly."

"I'll talk to her."

"She needs more than a talk. That woman is a menace. She fired me and said to never come back. Now that Polly may be waking up, someone has to keep a close watch over her."

"My mother's waking up? I haven't seen any evidence."

"Yesterday, one of the caregivers thought she saw Polly making a few deliberate movements, so this morning, I went there to check."

"And?"

"I got your mother to squeeze my hand, more than once."

"That's amazing. Do me a favor and keep an eye on what's happening. Let me know if you see any more changes."

"I already told you. Helga dismissed me and my entire group of volunteers. The only way I can visit your mother now is if you take me with you."

Susan hesitated. "If I have time; we're busy fixing up the house to put it on the market."

"You're buying a new place?"

"We might relocate."

"Relocate? Is Bob's company moving him or did he find a new job?"

"Not exactly; Bob may work for his father back East. Anyway, I need to go; I'm expecting a call."

"But who will make sure your mother's receiving the proper care?"

"I'll see to it."

Now more worried than ever, Margot knew she had to brief the facility director on the history of Helga's behavior.

⇒⋅ ⋅⇐

Before she had a chance to call Mr. Norwood, her attorney phoned, saying, "Gordon here. How is it going?"

"Fine," she lied.

"Your hearing is popping up two Fridays from now, and I need to check a few details with you. We can discuss them over the phone; that will save you a trip here."

Margot had been so looking forward to finally settling the case, but now with Polly in jeopardy, even that seemed unimportant. Reluctantly, she said. "Go ahead."

"Let me see. As I recall you're still volunteering at the care facility and doing a smashing job."

Margot gulped. "Not exactly; I'm partially on leave."

"Meaning what?"

"There's been a slight misunderstanding. I'm just about to contact the facility director to straighten things out."

"Straighten out what, old girl?"

"I told you, it's a misunderstanding."

"You haven't gotten yourself in trouble again?"

"Don't worry; there's plenty of time to . . . ."

"To what?"

"Gordon, please, I need to make the call I mentioned."

"Just let me know if you foresee any problems."

Margot hung up and dialed Mr. Norwood; his secretary answered and informed her that the director had left for a two-week vacation.

"But, I need him now."

"Sorry. Would you like the head nurse, Helga Hasse, instead? I can put you right through."

CHAPTER FORTY-SIX

Despite being banished from the facility, Margot did her best to track Polly's recovery. Ginger alerted the staff to watch for improvements in her condition, and she called Margot every few days to report any progress. Besides moving around, Polly had fluttered her eyelids a few times. Tests proved she was now responsive to pain stimuli.

Once the doctor examined her and found her able to breathe on her own, he recommended taking Polly off the respirator.

The O'Donnell sisters continued their night shift caring for Polly until the day Patty called Margot, saying, "We've been discharged."

"Discharged? Impossible. I'm your employer. It's for me to decide."

"Not according to the head nurse; she came in, looking pleased as could be, and said our services were no longer required."

Margot's shoulders slumped. "What did you do?"

"I started to argue, but she had a note signed by Susan, our little lamb's daughter."

"A note?"

"It said, 'Effective immediately, our family is terminating your services.' We were given no notice, whatsoever; Helga handed me my purse and told me to evacuate the premises. Then she took me by the arm and escorted me out of the building. Never before in me life, have I been treated so rudely."

Margot shook her head. "So there's no one watching over Polly?"

"It's sorry, I am, but what could I do under the circumstances?"

"I understand." Margot took a deep breath. "Please come by at six tomorrow to pick up a check for what I owe you."

Margot looked at the clock and decided that midnight was too late to call Susan. She phoned early the next morning, and before she could say a word, Susan said, "Listen Margot, we sold our house; we're flying back East today to look for a new one."

"But Susan . . . ."

"Sorry, gotta go; the airport shuttle's waiting outside. I'll call when we get back." With that, Susan hung up leaving Margot aghast at the turn of events.

⊷ ⊶

News of Polly's steady improvement continued to filter down from Margot's sources in skilled nursing. She could now open her eyes and respond to some commands, but she had not yet spoken.

As Polly exhibited more and more signs of alertness, Margot became increasingly worried that an attempt would be made to silence her permanently.

All at once, an idea hit her; she would enlist her two friends, Nancy and Jane, to thwart an attack on Polly. Of the three, Margot had the lowest degree of physical strength, due to the after-effects of her accident, but she had recently begun exercising and lifting weights in her apartment. Nancy continued her regimen of running several miles a day; Jane, having fully recovered from her hip surgery, often accompanied Nancy part of the way. Margot felt confident the three women could handle all contingencies.

One night, she corralled Nancy and Jane, enticing them with the promise of take-out Mexican food and Margaritas at her place. Before the delivery arrived, Margot dipped the rim of the Margarita glasses in salt and poured a blend of *Tequila*, limeade and *Triple Sec*. Nancy sipped her drink and licked her lips. "Yum—this sure is an unexpected treat. If Barbara hadn't turned rat fink, she could be here, indulging with us."

"Doncha think it's creepy the way she keeps watching us? Jane said. "She must be feeling left out since we've pretty much dropped her."

Margot stirred her drink. "After I caught her feeding information to my lovely relatives, I can't trust the little traitor."

Nancy raised her glass in agreement. "Yeah, me neither. Helga may have the varmint spying for her too."

"Forget Barbara," Margot said. "Our job is to protect Polly. Any bright ideas?"

Jane scratched her head, "You got me; we can't even set foot inside the place."

"Here's what we can do," Margot said.

⟞⟜

During the graveyard shift, the most likely period for an attack, Margot, Nancy, and Jane sneaked into Polly's room for the second night in a row. This time, Margot brought along a video camera.

The night before, they had watched Betty approach Polly's bed and study her for a few minutes. The three women had waited uneasily wondering what would happen next, but Betty simply read through her chart before disappearing.

Next, Ernesto had entered the room. Margot shivered and prayed to the spirits. Please, don't let it be Ernesto. He had halted near the bed to check the monitors and left.

Now once again jammed together in the closet of Polly's room, complaints flew fast and furious. Nancy wailed, "It's brutal in here. The closet's way too short and way too shallow for women big as us. I can't stand up straight, I can't kneel, or nothing."

Jane chimed in, "I was so cramped and squashed last night I hurt all day today. I don't think I can take this again."

"Simmer down," Margot said. "At least this corner room has a nice long closet."

"Ouch, Nancy, cut that out. That's the fourth time you stepped on my foot with your cloddy cowboys boots," Jane said.

"I'm real sorry, sweet pea."

"Can't you Texans wear sneakers or flats like normal people?"

"I said I'm sorry."

"Cool it," Margot hissed. "Someone will hear us. It's bad enough being stuck in here without all this bickering. Did you both remember water?"

"You betcha. I thought I'd die of thirst last night." Problem is the more I drink, the more I need to go."

Margot poked Jane. "What are you, a five-year old? Can't you even hold it?"

"It's worse than that. I'm a senior citizen with a prolapsed bladder."

Margot whispered loudly, "Shush, you're making too much noise."

The women listened as footsteps stopped outside the room; with hearts pounding, they held their breaths. After what seemed an eternity, the footsteps moved off.

"Phew—that sure was close," Margot said.

Jane began squirming. "I'm trying to ignore it, but I keep seeing lakes and pools, even a river flowing by. Maybe I should have worn Depends."

Margot and Nancy laughed when Jane cried, "Now there's a waterfall; I need to use the bathroom right away."

"Okay, but be quick about it and don't flush," Margot said.

To save time, Jane unzipped her pants. She slid the door carefully, leaving it open a crack and hurried off.

Seconds later, Margot and Nancy heard footsteps in the hall. Again, they stopped outside for a minute but now continued into the room and slowly approached the bed.

As Margot peered through the crack, she saw a caped form, like a large bat, looming over Polly. No mistaking Helga.

Helga studied Polly, as though deciding on the next move, then reached down to remove the pillow from under her head. She stirred, moaning softly.

"Stay calm, lady; everything is all right. I'm just making sure you're comfortable," Helga said in a low voice. "I'll fix you up so you'll have a nice long sleep. Yes, a long, peaceful sleep."

Polly moved fitfully, her moaning growing louder.

Margot slid the door wider to point her video camera at the bed as Helga lifted the pillow, placing it over Polly's face and pressing down.

She kicked and fought.

Margot laid the camera on the floor and said, "Let's go." She and Nancy burst from the closet, almost tripping over each other and shouting for Helga to stop. Margot reached Helga first, grabbing the pillow, while Nancy pulled Helga away from the bed.

Helga released the pillow and turned, screaming, "Get away from me or I'll kill you." She wound up and socked Margot in the jaw with a sharp jab that sent her reeling. Nancy caught Helga from the rear, pinning her arms behind her back, but Helga spun around elbowing Nancy in the stomach and leaving her on the floor doubled up in pain.

By then Margot had recovered enough to begin raining blows on Helga's head. She called out, "Jane, get in here."

Jane yelled back, "I'm coming."

Helga seized Margot's hands and viciously swung her off to the side, banging her head against the bed railing. Both women, having been put out of commission, Helga sidled away and almost made it out the door when Nancy sprang up and lunged toward Helga grasping onto her cape to tug her back into the room.

With her grip slipping, Nancy shouted, "Jane, now."

"Damn zipper's stuck."

"Just get in here," Margot screamed as she dodged a blow from Helga.

Jane emerged from the bathroom, holding up her pants with one hand, dragging a walker with the other. She shoved the walker hard against Helga, who withstood the blow and pushed Jane to the floor. Helga turned and head-butted Margot in the stomach.

With her pants now around her ankles and still clutching the walker, Jane edged away from the action where she pulled up and zipped her pants. Steadying herself against the walker, she struggled to stand then used the walker to trip Helga, who fell with a thud.

Nancy peered down at Helga. "That should hold the varmint."

Instead, Helga glommed onto Nancy's ankle, dragging her to the floor. In the confusion, Helga scrambled to her feet and headed towards the door again. Margot followed, yanking Helga by the hair. To Margot's surprise, she found herself holding a fistful of wig.

Helga patted the top of her head and screeched, "My hair; give me back my hair."

"Well, I'll be danged, she's a baldy." Nancy marveled.

Infuriated, Helga rushed towards the two women flailing her arms.

Jane retrieved a folded wheel chair she found in the bathroom and came from behind Helga using enough force to throw Helga backwards into the chair. She spun it in dizzying circles until Helga fell forward in a heap. Helga struggled to stand, but Margot and Nancy used all their strength to hold her down.

At one point, Helga lifted her head and directed a globule of spit at Margot's face. "I'll get you for this," she crowed.

As Margot let go one hand to wipe her face, Helga bit Margot's other wrist. Margot retaliated, delivering a vicious karate chop to the neck.

"Hey there gal," Nancy asked, "where'd you learn that move?"

"Must be those Jackie Chan movies Hans drags me to."

The kicking and struggling continued unabated until Margot screamed, "Jane, we need tape to tie her up."

"Tape? Where ?"

"Try the bathroom cabinet."

Both women sat on Helga until Jane returned carrying a roll of tape and knelt to bind her ankles. Unable to stop Helga from thrashing around, she said, "I need help."

"I can do that like nothing," Nancy said. "Switch places, would yuh, honey bun?"

While Jane took over sitting on Helga, Nancy expertly twisted the tape across Helga's ankles. She continued binding Helga's hands, all the while looking pleased with herself and chortling, "You gals are witnessing the hogtieing champ down East Texas way. Aren't y'all impressed?"

"You betcha we are." Jane jumped up and went to the closet, returning with an empty bed pan. "Doncha think Helga deserves a crown and something to keep her bare head warm?" She adjusted it over Helga's head at different angles until she felt satisfied and looked around for approval.

"Good job, honey bun," Nancy said.

"The symbolism is perfect," Margot added. "Too bad the pan's empty."

CHAPTER FORTY-SEVEN

A loud moan from the bed broke their mood of elation. Margot ran to embrace Polly whose eyes were wide with fright. "It's over, darling; you're safe," she said.

Ernesto and Ginger came running and stopped short in the doorway to gawk at the four bruised and battered women, all smiling except for Helga.

Seeing Helga trussed up like a chicken and wearing a bedpan on her bald head, Ernesto shook with laughter; he tapped the bedpan. "I dig your sombrero."

Ginger could only ask, "Lordy, Lordy, what started all this? Seems we need some triage here."

"What kept you," Margot asked, "We needed your help!"

"No one could miss the ruckus. As soon as I finished an injection, I found Ernesto and dragged him along."

Margot explained they had caught Helga trying to smother Polly; her voice was drowned out by Helga's loud sobs and shouts for help.

After a brief conference with Ernesto, Ginger left to summon the sheriff. Fifteen minutes later, when two deputies from the Orange

County Sheriff's Department arrived, Nancy, Jane, and Margot began talking simultaneously, and Helga continued her yelling.

One deputy took charge. "Ladies, ladies, settle down; we'll get to the bottom of this." He ordered the other deputy to untie Helga and call for backup and the paramedics.

Once free, Helga pleaded, "Officer, arrest these women; they jumped me while I was quieting a sick patient. The poor woman was thrashing around so much, I worried she would re-injure her broken arm.

"Yeah, quiet her for good by holding a pillow over her face." Margot said.

Helga pointed to Margot. "She's hallucinating."

"Hallucinating? I have proof." Margot walked to the closet to retrieve her video camera which she held up. "Let's rewind the film, so we can take a look."

A deputy reached for the device. "That's evidence Ma'am."

"But I brought it with me in case of an attack; I'd like to see it."

The deputy shook his head.

Once two additional officers arrived, he conferred with Ginger as to what rooms were available to interview the four women separately. They took Helga to the conference room, Margot to the kitchen, Nancy to the reception lounge, and Jane to the game room.

A team of paramedics examined the women and administered first aid as needed. To everyone's amazement, despite all the kicking and punching, there did not appear to be any broken bones or internal injuries.

An hour later, Mulroney and Mendoza, the two detectives on the case, came to interview the women and record their statements.

Even though Margot had previously testified to Homicide, she repeated the whole story beginning with her experiences during her own confinement at the nursing facility: the suspicious sounds, the disappearance of patients, the rumors of patient injuries. She described the arguments between Helga and the three victims—arguments that, to her mind, resulted in two subsequent deaths plus an attempted murder.

"You must believe me," she pleaded. Helga has been involved in all these crimes, one way or another. We all saw her trying to smother Polly. If you'll just view the video, you'll see I'm telling the truth."

The detectives asked a few questions, then abruptly stood and said, "Wait here."

Exhausted, Margot rested her head on the table, but pain quickly jolted her upright; her face, her head, her back, her legs—every part of her body hurt.

Hoping to reach Hans, she searched her pocket for her cell and found a message from him. She quickly dialed the number. On hearing his voice, she broke into tears.

"Margot, what's wrong?"

"Oh, Hans, you won't believe what happened; I wish you were here."

"It's okay; I'm at John Wayne. The plane beat the 10:30 landing curfew."

"Can you come? I'm at skilled nursing with the detectives."

"Detectives?"

"I'll tell you when I see you. Just get here, please."

Mulroney returned about twenty minutes later and handed back her camera. "We're holding onto the memory card, but you're free to go."

"I am? Did you look at the video?"

He smiled and nodded. "Nice shooting."

"What about Helga?"

"She's in custody."

━┿ ┿━

Holding tightly to the arms of three deputies, Margot and her two friends slowly shuffled out of the facility to waiting cars. All at once,

Hans rushed over and said to the officers, "I'm here for Margot; is it all right if I take her?"

They agreed, and he helped her into his car where he ran his finger over her chin. "You did it again; your face is as bruised and swollen as after your accident."

She brushed his hand aside. "Careful, that hurts."

Remembering Hans had just returned from Europe, she studied him anxiously. "Is your mother feeling better now?"

"Thank *Gott*, she made a miraculous recovery; she's staying with my sister until I return to Denmark. We need to make new living arrangements for her." Hans held her close as they rode the elevator to her apartment at Shady Palms; once there he propped two large pillows on the sofa so she could stretch out comfortably. "Is there anything you need?"

"Besides you, all I want is some fruit juice. And ice, not for the drink, for my right leg. It got hammered." She blew him a kiss.

Hans rummaged around the kitchen, opening and shutting drawers until he found a giant zip-loc bag which he filled with ice. He handed it to Margot along with a glass of apple juice. "This is the best I could do; I hope the ice helps."

Margot blew him another kiss and adjusted the bag over her leg.

He sat down, pulling her feet onto his lap. "Tell me how you got so banged up."

"You can't imagine what I've been through. We caught Helga trying to suffocate Polly with a pillow; it took three of us to stop her. If we hadn't been standing guard, she'd be dead now."

Hans held her hand and nodded supportively during Margot's description of the long battle to subdue Helga.

"Are you proud of me?" She asked.

"Of course I'm proud of you; I'm thrilled you saved Polly. I just hope that now you're going to let the sheriff handle the case. I have enough problems with my mother being sick; I don't need to worry about you as well."

Margot frowned and slid her feet from his lap; the ice bag landed on the floor. Struggling to stand, she said, "I think you'd better go; you must be exhausted and jet-lagged, and we both could use some sleep."

⟚ ⟛

The next morning, Hans arrived, carrying groceries and *The Los Angeles Times*. He put the bag on the kitchen counter and kissed her. "I brought hot coffee and sweet rolls so we could have breakfast and read the write-up together."

"That bad, huh?"

He took two placemats from the drawer. "We'd better eat first."

While Margot set out the plates and spoons, she glanced at the headlines, "Senior Women Brawl with Head Nurse at a Skilled Nursing Facility." A lengthy article described the fight between Helga Hasse, the facility's Head Nurse, and the three women.

"Oh brother," she said, taking a seat and reaching for her glasses. She read aloud, "'According to sources, Margot Manning, Nancy Ewing, and Jane Driscoll, three residents of Shady Palms, had long suspected the Head Nurse of committing violent acts against patients and had banded together to stop her from further attacks.'"

"They got that right," Margot said.

Looking over Margot's shoulder, Hans read, "'Helga Hasse swore her innocence, insisting that the three women had dreamed up the fantastic scenario, after being dismissed as volunteers in the skilled nursing unit.'"

"Iniquitous, yes; innocent, never."

Hans read on, "'The Orange County Sheriff's Department is reviewing a video of the alleged attack. Helga Hasse is in custody while the investigation continues.'"

Her heart sank as Hans continued, "'Margot Manning, a former socialite, is currently involved in a court case with her nephew and her niece, Rudy and Clarissa Sampson, who are petitioning to become Manning's conservators. A hearing is scheduled for November.'"

Hans dropped the paper. "This is exactly what I've been dreading; they've gone and dug up the conservator business."

"Are you saying I told you so?"

"Don't get mad; I only said I'd been dreading this."

Margot buried her face in her hands, then stood, limped to the door, and opened it. "Thanks for breakfast and the paper, but I think you need some more sleep."

Hans put his arms around her. "Hey, you, I'm on your side; remember?"

"Maybe so, but, as always, your words have the ring of disapproval."

Hans threw up his hands. "I can never win."

CHAPTER FORTY-EIGHT

Learning that Polly had regained her voice, Margot's outlook brightened considerably. During their first visit, Polly reported that she had given the detectives details of Helga's earlier threats and the subsequent attack that left her comatose and with a broken arm.

Through friends in the Sheriff's department, Gordon provided Margot with further information on the case:

Margot's video had shown clear evidence of Helga's assault on Polly.

Helga had sworn her innocence for Joe's and Pete's deaths. Maintaining she had given Joe the Valium to lower his libido and stop him from pinching the women patients, Helga insisted, "I never would have administered the Valium if I knew Joe had been simultaneously sneaking gin. Alcohol and Valium can be a lethal combination for a diabetic like Joe."

Under lengthy questioning by investigators as to the legality of a nurse administering Valium without a doctor's order, Helga confessed that she had saved up unused Valium from various patient prescriptions.

Regarding Pete's accident, she admitted trying to take Pete's piccolo away to stop him from disturbing the other patients with his nightly playing. In resisting, Pete had fallen out of bed damaging his newly replaced hip. Helga added, "I'm not the guilty party; the hospital's to blame for the microbial infection that caused his death."

Helga denied responsibility for Polly's injuries and dismissed her attack on Polly as pure fiction, saying she had been arranging pillows to make Polly more comfortable; in no way had she attempted to smother her.

While the District Attorney weighed manslaughter and attempted murder against Helga, *The Orange County Edition of The Los Angeles Times* ran an exposé on lapses in the state's regulation of nurses licensed to practice in California, even though their licenses had been suspended elsewhere for serious misdeeds.

Entering Helga's name in the national database, investigators found out that she had been dismissed from an Arizona hospital after two patients died under suspicious circumstances. This new information bolstered the case against the head nurse.

The authorities undertook investigations of mysterious deaths and injuries, dating back to the time Helga first arrived at the skilled nursing facility. Margot and Nancy had told of two patients who had mysteriously disappeared from skilled nursing, but, in the end, records showed that they were transferred by their families to other facilities.

The District Attorney formally charged Helga with manslaughter in the deaths of Joe and Pete; he also charged her with attempting to murder Polly.

Reporters began calling to interview the three women they now dubbed, "The Heroines of Shady Palms."

One morning, Margot picked up *The Los Angeles Times*. Seeing a headline in the *California Section*, she threw on sweats and drove to Hans's home where she rapped loudly on his door.

Hans, dressed for his morning jog, answered. "To what do I owe this visit?"

Thrusting the newspaper at him, Margot said, "I'm returning the favor. This article should interest you."

Hans gawked at the photo of Margot, under the caption, Former Socialite Turns Detective to Solve Nursing Home Crimes.

When he opened his mouth to speak, Margot interrupted. "I'm sorry I didn't bring breakfast, but I couldn't find any crow for you to eat. The butcher doesn't carry bird meat and shooting crows in *The Laguna Niguel Regional Park* is a criminal offense."

With that, Margot left.

⋯

A week later, Margot's attorney phoned, reminding her of the upcoming conservator hearing. He had successfully lobbied for the removal of Judge Garrote; Judge Farley would be hearing the case instead.

For the first time, Gordon sounded optimistic. He grudgingly praised her recent accomplishments, mumbling a sheepish apology, "Good work, old scout; glad you didn't let me down."

At the conservator hearing, Detective Mulroney testified on Margot's behalf, crediting her for saving Polly's life. Gordon wordlessly laid before the judge the many newspaper clippings heralding Margot's detective work in solving the "skilled nursing crimes." The courtroom waited anxiously while the judge read through every article.

Judge Farley pushed the papers aside, and gesturing with his glasses, he said, "Dismissed—there is no case against this woman."

In a scathing lecture, he told The Relatives, "Your greedy attempts to control your elderly aunt's person and her estate are beyond belief. Ms. Manning is not only fully capable of caring for her properties and her person, she has also proved herself a valuable member of the community by apprehending a criminal at the center where she volunteered."

The judge further ordered Margot's relatives to vacate her home within a week, and said he would consider a motion to hold them liable for damages and all court costs.

Thrilled by the outcome, Margot refrained from jumping up and down in full view of the spectators; she quietly thanked the judge and her friends for their loyalty throughout the ordeal.

On the way out, she praised Gordon's work and added, "I'm delighted the judge gave Rudy and Clarissa their much-deserved comeuppance." She bristled. "But why would he refer to me as 'elderly'?"

Two months later, a special ceremony outside city hall honored the three women for their roles in capturing an assailant. Pinning medals on each and handing them individual plaques, the Mayor said, "You are a trio of feisty old ladies. Who would have thought women your age could act with such heroism?"

The audience laughed, but Margot glared at the Mayor until he stammered, "I mean you are truly feisty women, and I applaud you."

The papers had a field day poking fun at the Mayor's gaffe; they took every opportunity to cite his mistake in calling the three heroines, "Feisty Old Ladies."

Later, the women decided they liked the epithet, and it became their own private name. From then on they referred to themselves as Feisty Old Ladies.

———≺∔ ∔≻———

Fed up with life at Shady Palms, Nancy and Jane searched for a promising rental and found a house on the sand in *Capistrano Beach*; they invited Polly to join them. Led by Margot, the four women put their heads together and roughed out plans for fabricating stylish clothing geared toward seniors. The business would also be operated by seniors, and aptly named, *FOL* (Feisty Old Ladies) Enterprises.

Margot spent weeks refurbishing her home with new paint and new carpeting. The furniture had been scrubbed and polished; the mattresses had been replaced to remove all traces of the recent squatters. "Out, out, damn relatives," she repeated, as she oversaw the work.

During this period, she and Hans were constant companions. He had stood by her, time and again. Though his criticisms of her behavior still rankled, they returned to their amiable relationship, before her accident, before the conservator case, before their respective jealousies over Diana, Jim, and Rick, and before her detective work. They still had their usual squabbles, after which they always enjoyed making up.

Exhausted by the move and exhilarated at being home with the difficult past few months behind her, Margot sat on the back patio to view Saddleback Mountain with Hans. Rachel had sent flowers as a welcome home gift, and a giant basket of assorted herbs from FOL Enterprises waited to be planted in the garden.

Margot poured Hans a glass of Mirabelle's sweet tea. He took a sip and leaned over to fondle her neck then extracted a small wrapped package from his pocket. "This is a present from me to you with all my heart."

She undid the ribbon and opened the box, which held an exquisite emerald and diamond ring. Her eyes danced as she slipped it on her finger and twirled her hand in the sun to watch the jewels sparkle.

Flashing Hans a mischievous smile, she said, "This is the most magnificent friendship ring I've ever received."

"Friendship?" Hans scratched his head. "I'm asking you to marry me."

"Oh—*marriage.* Now there's a serious topic. We should talk about that after dinner."

ACKNOWLEGEMENTS

First and foremost I want to thank Laurie Thomas, an instructor in the Saddleback College Emeritus program, who taught me the basics of writing. Substantive editor, Ellen Larson provided me with many pages of in-depth critique and set my mystery on the right track. Noosha Ravaghi edited the copy.

Over the years, members of my critique group listened to and gave me advice on my many revisions. (Thank you, Patricia Day, Gwen Fannin, Lea Groves, Susan Matsumoto, Farie Momayez, Jeanette Rizzo, Theresa Schultz, Sharon Langdale, and Helene Wright). Libby Coleman, a friend and retired teacher did a "cold read" of the manuscript.

Gary Bale, of Blade Investigations, a reserve deputy sheriff with the Orange County Sheriff's Department offered much-needed assistance. A consultant to mystery and crime writers, he generously evaluated my manuscript and educated me on police procedure in Orange County,

Cardiologist and Edgar Award Winner DP Lyle, answered such delightful questions as: The best libido reducing drugs, how to smother a victim without leaving clues, and signs a patient is emerging from a coma.

Mary La Greek, a fellow-writer was one of my top boosters. She loved Margot Manning, my heroine and kept bringing me ideas for enhancing her glamour. She also made it her mission to find names of Agents who might be interested in *Feisty Old Ladies*. Mary wanted to be first in line to purchase the published book. Alas, Mary is no longer with us, but she remains vivid in my memory as special person who died much too young.

Many thanks go to my son Marc who switched roles with me. After years of editing his school papers and his writing, he turned out to be a maven on grammar; he's now in charge of correcting my work.

And I'm particularly grateful to the writer Barbara DeMarco-Barret who piqued my interest in creative writing when I heard her speak at an American Association of University Women luncheon. She not only inspired me to buy her book, *Pen on Fire,* but what she wrote convinced me to try my hand at creative writing.

READER THANK YOU

Thank you for reading *Feisty Old Ladies*. Composing the book over several years has been a worthy endeavor on many levels. Writing is therapeutic; it keeps me productive; it keeps my mind working; it also saves me from being "A lady who lunches and shops at the mall."

The mystery is mostly a fun caper, but I also included some serious commentary on the aged, who, as Rodney Dangerous used to say, "Don't always get no respect."

If you enjoyed the book, I'd appreciate your telling your friends, in person or through social media. And if you have time, please post a review on such sites as, Amazon, Goodreads, or wherever you made your purchase.

ABOUT THE AUTHOR

Cynthia Weitz is a writer whose work has appeared in the Orange Herring newsletter for Sisters in Crime Orange County, *Mused-The Bella* online literary review, *The Cynic Online,* and publications of Saddleback College: *The Wall Literary Journal* and *Reflections.* A veteran of the publishing industry, she worked in marketing research for a New York advertising agency, *McCall's* magazine, Condé Nast Publications, and *The Los Angeles Times.* Her writings have been enriched by her travels throughout the world.

A native New Englander, she attended The University of Vermont and graduated from Simmons College in Boston with a bachelor of science degree in psychology. She also earned a certificate in interior design from UCLA extension.

She is currently writing a collection of stories, as well as the second Feisty Old Ladies mystery. The author lives in South Orange County, California, not far from the ocean.

Contact her at www.FeistyOldLadies.com or e-mail Cynthia@FeistyOldLadies.com.

36227284R00186

Made in the USA
Charleston, SC
27 November 2014